Patricia Crossley was born and brought up London, England and has lived and traveled in many exciting places in the world. She now resides in Victoria, British Columbia, Canada where she and her husband enjoy the great outdoors, many friends and three children (not necessarily in that order.)

It could be that Charles Dickens, held by family tradition as a many-times-great-grandfather, spurred her interest in both reading and writing. Whatever the reason, she turned from studying French language and literature to her own writing and has a whole host of characters and stories in her head, just waiting to be born.

A SUITABLE FATHER

Kurt Rainer left his hometown with a bad reputation and bitterness in his heart. After twelve years he's back — and involved in a high profile murder ... Maggie has plans for herself and her young son that certainly do not have room for a former lover who abandoned her when she was pregnant. When Kurt turns up, Maggie faces hard choices. He never was a suitable father for a boy, even less so now as a suspected accomplice in a crime. She wants passion and integrity, strength and independence. Can she find these qualities in Kurt Rainer?

PATRICIA CROSSLEY

A SUITABLE FATHER

Complete and Unabridged

ULVERSCROFT
Leicester

First published in Canada in 2000

First Large Print Edition
published 2003

British Library CIP Data

Crossley, Patricia
    A suitable father.—Large print ed.—
    Ulverscroft large print series: romance
    1. Romantic suspense novels
    2. Large type books
    I. Title
    813.5'4 [F]

    ISBN 0–7089–4889–8

Published by
F. A. Thorpe (Publishing)
Anstey, Leicestershire
Set by Words & Graphics Ltd.
Anstey, Leicestershire
Printed and bound in Great Britain by
T. J. International Ltd., Padstow, Cornwall

This book is printed on acid-free paper

1

The headline leaped out: **'Star's death suspicious. Guide in hospital.'** In smaller letters a sub-heading flared: 'Guide outfitter being questioned.'

The harsh, black print seemed to shimmer, hurting Maggie's eyes. Under it was a picture of Johnny Gunn, the macho hero of four action movies, and next to him was a grainy photograph of her missing brother-in-law, Kurt. Kurt Rainer: her son's father, her betrayer, the fickle lover. There were many other words she could have used for him.

The camera had caught him full face, his head cocked in the old 'damn your eyes' stance. All Maggie's senses became sharply focused as the world seemed to hold a breath. She kept a tight grip on the folded newspaper and felt carefully for the high back of the nearest chair.

'It was the name,' Ellen said. 'I thought you should know.'

Maggie nodded and sank into a wicker chair. The article was a blur of print.

'Is he a relative?' Ellen's voice seemed to come from far away.

'My husband Steve's half brother,' she whispered through dry lips. 'He's been — gone for a long while.'

'Thought I'd never heard of him.' Ellen had only moved to Branscombe five years ago, so hadn't known Kurt. That was one reason why Maggie felt comfortable in her company. Most of her other friends from high-school studiously avoided all mention of the Rainer family, in case they touched on Steve's death and Kurt's disappearance. They did it from the best of intentions, but the ghosts of the brothers often seemed to hang in the air at any gathering of old friends.

'They seem to think he might be involved,' Ellen said. 'Would he have done something like that — killed someone?'

Maggie shook her head. 'It's hard to believe. He was wild, but . . . '

'Here,' Ellen was holding out a glass. 'Have a drink. You look as if you've had a shock.'

Maggie took the cold drink and sipped at the lemonade. The ice rattled in the glass.

'Do you want to tell me about it?'

Maggie put down the glass very carefully and hugged herself as if to keep warm. She heard her son Jeff yell something from the touch football game way down the yard.

'Kurt was older than Steve — Kurt's mother was his father's first wife. He — ' she

2

hesitated, ' — had a reputation. About twelve years ago, he left town. No one has heard from him since. Not even Frieda Haydon, his grandmother.'

'How sad for her.' Ellen was quick to empathize.

'I should go to her.' Maggie struggled to her feet. 'Can Jeff stay here for a while?'

Ellen nodded. 'Of course. Glad to help.' She touched Maggie's arm. 'Just do what you have to do.'

Maggie checked her watch as she drove. A few minutes after seven thirty. She hadn't even taken a shower to clean up after the long, hot day. The setting sun flamed in a blood-red sky, sending flamboyant tentacles of gold, orange, and pink across the horizon. One small black cloud hovered, pretending a threat to the summer heat wave. Overhead a plane heading south to California left a vapor trail in the remaining blue.

As she took the turn to the Glenhaven Retirement Manor, the blazing golden light flared directly into her eyes. She pulled down the visor against the glare and braked before the curve into the clinic grounds. Nursing the car gently through the gears, she coaxed the engine back to life before it died on her. The old clunker would surely give up one day soon.

The cooler evening air wafting around her face and arms through the open window was refreshing at last. She pushed her damp hair back from her forehead and blew an obstinate wisp from her cheek.

In front of Glenhaven, sprinklers were gently watering the beds of flowers and shrubs that lined the driveway. Maggie pulled into her reserved spot, marked 'Administrator,' noting at the same time that Dr. Roger Saint George's car was in the Director's space. He must be catching up on paperwork since he was taking the day off tomorrow to drive her and Jeff to camp. It jarred her to see his car with her thoughts so full of an old lover. Roger made no secret of his wish to take their relationship a step further during her vacation and while Jeff was gone. She needed time to sort out her emotions, time to pull herself together after the shock of seeing Kurt's picture.

No one knew Kurt was Jeff's father. Now was not the right time to start spreading the news if she wanted her life to stay on track. She'd chosen to be alone since her husband's death, but Roger was beginning to mean a lot to her and most likely would become even more important. Nonetheless, she couldn't help hoping she wouldn't have to face him until the turmoil in her

4

mind had died down.

Inside the building, the air was cool, smelling faintly of lemon polish. Maggie nipped a wilted head from the display of daisies on the coffee table and dropped it in the waste basket. Automatically, she reminded herself to leave a note for them to be replaced tomorrow.

The faint hum of a TV came from the residents' lounge. There was no one behind the desk. According to the roster posted over the counter, Dianna was on duty. Maggie had never warmed to the girl, but she knew there was no need to worry. Dianna seemed very reliable.

Maggie hurried through the deserted dining room and glanced out the window. The residence she managed occupied a prime piece of land near the harbor entrance with lawns sweeping down to the water. Clusters of tables and chairs dotted the grass, their colorful umbrellas furled for the night. There was someone in the gazebo down by the shore. Maggie could make out the outline of a head and shoulders against the backdrop of the shining water. The gazebo was Frieda's favorite spot. Surely she wasn't sitting out there so late?

Frowning, she pushed open the French doors and met once again the moist blanket of warm air after the welcome air conditioning. There was no point in calling out, Frieda's hearing wasn't that good anymore.

The gazebo was in shadow now, a slight breeze ruffling the vines on the trellis as the evening cooled down. Maggie strode rapidly across the lawn, her heart quickening. It was Frieda, sitting very still. She reached the wooden gazebo and crouched down by the old woman.

'Frieda?' she said gently. 'Frieda? It's Maggie.'

The old lady's eyes were closed, and her hands clutched a newspaper. Once a journalist, always a journalist. She read every paper available. She must already know about Kurt.

Hesitantly, Maggie put out a hand to touch the thin arm. 'No,' she thought. 'No, Frieda, not like this.' Had the news been too much for her?

If Frieda died, the last links with her childhood and youth would be severed. She needed more time. Tears pricked her throat as she stroked the mottled hand. Suddenly, Frieda drew a deep sigh and opened her eyes.

Maggie jumped. 'Oh Frieda,' she said. 'You frightened me.'

'Why? Did you think I was dead? Not going to go yet. What time is it?

Frieda sat up straighter on the wooden bench and shivered.

'You're cold. Come inside. Did you have supper?' Maggie asked. 'No, I didn't have supper, and I'm fine right here. Don't fuss, girl. I know what I'm doing.'

'Of course you do.'

Maggie rose from the crouching position and sat on the wooden bench next to her old friend. She reached for a hand, but the newspaper was still firmly in Frieda's grasp.

Frieda thrust the newspaper at her, folded to the same photograph of Kurt with a text in the same box. Maggie fought for control over the wave of apprehension that swept through her yet again at the sight of him.

It was very quiet by the water. The trees stood black against the purple sky. The red, orange, and green of Frieda's thin shawl blazed against the weathered wood of the gazebo. A seagull squawked raucously, and another bird swooped low over the lawns with a beating of wings. The scent of the grass and the flowering bushes was suddenly cloying in her throat.

She closed her eyes and took a deep, trembling breath. 'You know,' she whispered.

'It's Kurt,' Frieda said unnecessarily. 'He's in some kind of trouble. He's in the hospital. Hurt. I want you to go and see him.'

'It's Kurt, it's Kurt,' had not ceased to echo in Maggie's head, a persistent refrain since she'd first seen the newspaper. Her heart raced as if she had been confronted by the man himself and not just his photo in a newspaper. She swallowed hard and took a deep breath. She couldn't imagine what she would feel if she saw him again in the flesh.

Before she could find any words, a clear voice called from across the lawn. 'Mrs. Haydon, Mrs. Haydon, are you still out here?'

Maggie stood up. 'Yes, Dianna,' she called. 'It's ok, she's with me.'

Dianna came around the corner of the gazebo, slightly out of breath and clutching a blanket.

'Oh, Mrs. Haydon,' she said. 'You frightened me when I saw you weren't in your room.' She turned to Maggie. 'Mrs. Rainer, I'm sorry. Mr. Blacklock had a dizzy spell, and I was checking on him and didn't realize that Mrs. Haydon was still out here.' The girl looked flushed and uneasy. Maggie figured she was mortified at being caught out by her supervisor.

'It's all right, Dianna,' Maggie replied. 'No harm done.' She took the blanket from Dianna's arms and placed it gently round the old lady's shoulders. 'Mrs. Haydon seems to have given both of us a bit of a scare. Now,

Frieda, let's go inside.'

Frieda rose to her feet and leaned on her cane. She thrust the newspaper toward Maggie. 'Read it,' she commanded. 'Take it home with you. You taking Jeff to camp tomorrow?'

Maggie nodded.

'Good,' Frieda said. 'We'll talk about what to say to Kurt when you get back. Come along, Dianna, you can help me back inside since you're here.'

Maggie stood motionless, absorbing the news for a long while after the sounds of their footsteps faded. Kurt, who'd callously abandoned her when she needed him most, was insinuating himself back into her life, whether he knew it or not. He was involved in something criminal. What could be worse than murder? The man she'd loved so desperately had proved himself undeserving, untrustworthy, unfeeling, unlovable.

She tucked the newspaper under her arm and slowly retraced her steps into the building. Her breathing had slowed almost to normal, but she was chilled despite the muggy, summer air. Her knees felt wobbly. Her throat was dry. She made for her office. A few minutes to recover, and a glass of water were all she needed.

She slid behind her desk, taking comfort in

the familiar tools of her work. Everything was already in order for the start of her vacation, her files neatly stacked at the side, her project list and notes to hand for reference while she was away, her 'to-do' list ready for her first day back. The Manor ran smoothly, thanks to her. She was good at her job.

She poured some water from the insulated carafe and sipped it, thinking, remembering. It was twelve years since Kurt had disappeared. Those days were a blur, with the quality of a nightmare, the horror of her parents' car accident, Kurt wild with anger at his father, pleading with her to run away with him.

When she refused, he left town, not knowing she carried their child, and never gave a sign of life again. He didn't know of her desperate marriage to Steve, his half-brother, of Jeff's birth, her parents' deaths, and the plane crash six years ago that had claimed Steve. And no one knew anything about Kurt. What had he done, where had he been all these years? Did he still think about her, or had he put everything to do with his former life behind him? He probably didn't even know about his father's will. There were few people left from those days. Only Frieda, his grandmother, and Maggie, his abandoned lover, and Jeff, his unknown child.

Jeff was the most important thing in her life. She'd loved him desperately from the moment he was first placed in her arms, a red, squalling bundle. She'd been protected and loved as a child, and she longed to give Jeff the same security of two parents in a loving relationship. Every time she looked at her friend Ellen with her husband Cliff, she felt a familiar twinge of envy. It was a long time since she'd been part of a family where people played silly games and loved each other no matter what. Jeff had never known that bond with a caring father, but that could change. Roger St. George was a fine man, he said he loved her, and she'd thought herself on the brink of returning that love.

A knock at the door pulled her from her reverie. She looked up as Roger poked his head around the door. 'Hi there. Two workaholics on a beautiful Sunday evening,' he said with a grin. 'Shameful. What are you doing here?'

The glimpse of his car had reminded her earlier of the relationship developing between them. Now she was filled with memories of Kurt. At this instant, her mind balked at the prospect of a new love when tortured by recollection of the old. She stood up.

'I'm not working,' she said, 'I just had to see Frieda. It was personal.' She hoped he would think it was something to do with the house which Frieda still owned, but which Maggie and Jeff occupied. The arrangement, planned with Frieda's usual foresight and efficiency, worked well for them all.

'I'm glad you're here.' Roger's eyes were tender. 'Want to go for supper?' he asked. 'Or a drink?'

Maggie shook her head. 'No, thanks,' she replied. 'I have to pick up Jeff.'

He was right in the room now, and she took a step forward, towards the door. She didn't want to prolong this conversation.

His expression showed his disappointment. 'I wanted to congratulate you,' he said.

'What for?'

'Negotiating that deal with the linen suppliers. It's going to save us a lot of money. And Pete Moss, the owner, was talking to me. Said his people were most impressed. 'Professional, honest, but tough.' Those were his words.' He put out a hand to touch her arm. 'We make a great team.'

'Thanks,' she said. She was numb, unable to feel the usual sense of elation at a job well done and acknowledged. She had to leave. Her tongue moistened dry lips. It was bizarre to talk to the man she might marry while her mind was full of Kurt.

'Is anything wrong?' His hand was warm

and heavy on her arm.

She forced herself to smile at him. 'Just tired,' she said and swung her big leather purse onto her shoulder. 'I walked a long way this afternoon. Took some good shots. It was pretty hot.' She moved towards the door.

'Can't wait to see the prints. Walk you to your car?' Roger took her hand. She hadn't the heart to withdraw. It wasn't his fault she was feeling guilty, angry, and fearful as the ghosts from the past materialized in her head.

At the car, Roger grasped her arms lightly and placed a soft kiss on her forehead. 'Take care,' he said. 'See you and Jeff tomorrow, bright and early.'

★ ★ ★

Maggie tucked the newspaper article under her camera case and drove back to Ellen's to pick up Jeff. Her heart had slowed down from the adrenaline-produced racing caused by the sight of Kurt's face, but she still had the sick, hollow feeling in her middle. Could he possibly be involved in a murder?

'Was Frieda okay?' Ellen asked, rocking on the porch swing with Jennifer, her seven year old.

'It was a shock. But she already knew. I'll talk to her tomorrow.'

'Thought you were taking Jeff to camp and spending some time with Roger.' Ellen raised her eyebrows and grinned meaningfully.

'Yes, well, there may be a change of plan.'

Jennifer was draped on the swing like a rag doll, her straight black hair hanging in limp strands. She revived with a whoop of joy when Jeff appeared at the top of the steps from the direction of the back yard. Maggie turned to smile at him. He groaned and made a face at Jennifer, bouncing the ball on the wooden boards.

'I heard your car, mom,' he said, 'from three blocks away.'

'It got me here,' Maggie said and turned to Ellen. 'Got to run,' she said. 'Thanks for helping out, Ellie. A few things left to do before Jeff takes off.'

Ellen sighed and then grinned. 'Tell me about it. Jennifer goes next week. What we put ourselves through for a week of peace.' She hugged her daughter to her. 'Just kidding, kiddo,' she said.

'Three weeks for me. He's going to the survival course.'

'Hey, playing with the big guys, eh? Good luck Jeff. Be careful.'

Maggie and Jeff walked through the grassy yard to the car, watched by Ellen and Jennifer from the porch.

'Cliff wasn't here, you know, mom,' Jeff grumbled. 'He went to the hospital.' Cliff Yeung, Ellen's husband, was a pediatrician with a thriving practice. 'So we couldn't play anything good,' Jeff finished. Maggie understood 'good' to mean a game that involved running hard and shouting.

'I could've stayed home by myself for an hour,' Jeff insisted. 'I am nearly twelve, you know. I don't need to be 'minded'. Especially not with a *girl*!'

Maggie's fingers itched to ruffle his hair, but she refrained from adding insult to injury in front of a *girl*. 'Dr. Yeung, to you,' she said. 'You didn't have to play with Jennifer if you were too tired,' she continued briskly.

Jeff looked at her with scorn. 'Of course I had to play with her, mom. Chinese Checkers,' he said in disgust. 'Or she'd tell stuff about me at school.'

Maggie repressed a sigh at the politics of the school yard and opened the car door.

Jeff climbed in the car, waved at Ellen, and stuck out his tongue at Jennifer as they pulled away. He pushed aside the camera bag to click his seatbelt.

'Hey, watch my camera, kid.'

'Sorry, mom.' The newspaper fell to the floor, and he wriggled down to pick it up.

'Wow,' he said, 'this guy looks a bit like

15

dad. In that picture at home.' He frowned as he concentrated on the text. 'Guide to the stars,' he read. 'Kurt Rainer, guide and well-known outfitter . . . ' He looked up at Maggie. 'Hey, he's got the same name as us!'

'Has he?' Maggie felt her throat tighten. Her heart was pounding again in her ears.

'Wow,' he said again. 'This is awesome. Do they think he let Johnny Gunn fall from the cliff? Did you see the pictures?'

How could she stop him talking about this? Her hands were white on the wheel.

'Hey, look out, mom. You're drifting.'

Maggie pulled herself together. She wasn't going to ruin her life again and Jeff's because of Kurt Rainer. He'd done enough damage. He'd stayed away for all these years, and if she had anything to do with it, he would come no closer than the hospital bed fifty miles away where he was now being treated for his injuries.

'Do you know this guy, mom?'

'Yes, I do. He's a relative.' The small evasion of the whole truth stuck in her throat. It hadn't seemed so bad to let Jeff believe Steve was his father. After all, everyone else took it for granted. She had never actually had to say it out loud to her son. She had some vague notion of letting him know the truth when he was eighteen. If she had to.

16

Until then, she would let sleeping dogs lie. When all was said and done, Kurt Rainer was not the kind of man a boy could proudly claim for his father.

Thankfully, Maggie pulled into the driveway of the old clapboard house before Jeff could ask any more questions she couldn't answer. The scent of the flowers hung heavy on the air in the closing dusk. She swiped a mosquito from her arm. 'Come on,' she said, 'enemy aircraft sighted! Last one in's a goner!' Laughing, they ran for the protection of the screened porch, Kurt Rainer and his past misdeeds put out of mind for the moment.

★　★　★

An hour or so later, Jeff was in bed and his bags for camp had been checked for the last time and stacked around him. Maggie settled back in the porch with a glass of fresh, icy lemonade and the newspaper. She'd scanned the article before, but a closer reading gave a few more details than Jeff had read out. Kurt had been working in the bush for a film company, and someone had rigged the ropes when the star of the movie had to do an action shot hanging off a cliff. Johnny Gunn had fallen three hundred feet to his death.

Kurt had slid down, perhaps trying to save him. He'd suffered 'unidentified injuries.' She searched in vain for more information.

She looked again at the photo. He hadn't changed much. Older of course, but still lean and broad shouldered. A little gray around the temples, but that looked good against his dark, curly hair. He wore it shorter now. The eyes were mocking as usual and, because of the angle of the camera, followed her as she moved.

The article implied it might have been a trick gone wrong. Someone might have wanted to scare Johnny. He wasn't the most popular of actors amongst the film crews. There was an investigation going on, but it seemed no one had access to the ropes except Kurt. Did that mean he had deliberately murdered the movie star? The newspaper tiptoed carefully around that question but added detailed examples of Kurt and Johnny's hostility around each other. Whatever the truth, Kurt was assisting the police with their inquiries.

Maggie drained the last of her lemonade. Why did he have to come back into her life just when she was at peace and content? She led a quiet life with Jeff, she loved her job and the photography that had started as a hobby but was growing into something more. Jeff

18

was happy at school. He was wildly excited about the three-week camp in the wilderness. While he was gone, she would work on her book illustrated with her own photos. And then there was Roger. There was a good relationship developing there.

She stood and stretched. Halfway across the living room, she hesitated and took a book from the shelves. *Branscombe High School Year Book* was inscribed in gold on the spine. *Class of 1982.* She sat cross-legged on the floor and flipped through the pages. There he was: 'Kurt Rainer: Most likely to break hearts' was the caption. You could say that again! All the girls thrilled if he even looked their way. And *she* was the one he chose.

She read on. Ambition: 'To do my own thing without interference.' She smiled. She could understand that, knowing his father. She looked again at the small black and white photograph. No, he hadn't changed much. They had all figured he would end up badly. Despite everything that had followed, she wasn't pleased at their predictions coming true. She sighed in sadness for the 'might have been.' Gently, she pressed her finger to her lips and transferred the kiss to the mouth in the picture. She closed the book, smoothed the cover with the palm of her hand, stood up, and slid the album back onto the shelf. No way she would go to see him.

★ ★ ★

The next day, just before noon, Maggie watched Jeff lug his duffel across the open space in front of the cabins towards the group of camp counselors. She knew the clothes would come back untouched below the top layer, still neatly folded, their name labels pristine. He would wear the same underwear, socks and shirts every day until they would almost stand up on their own. That was the story of every year at camp, yet she still followed the lists the organizers sent, regardless.

One of the counselors bent his head down to Jeff, checking his name on a list and her son took his place in the line of adolescent boys. Was he too young for this challenging course? During the two hour ride up to the camp on Mount Vardon in Roger's car, she'd listened to Jeff's vivid description of the activities that awaited them, her heart sinking at the list of potentially neck-breaking undertakings that he could get into. Jeff thrived on challenge and adventure, loved the outdoors. She knew exactly where he got it from!

Jeff waved at her, his baseball cap turned backwards, his eyes bright with anticipation and her heart lurched. Suddenly, she saw Kurt at twenty something, waiting for her down the road because she begged him not to come to her door. When had Jeff grown so like his father? When had the childish curves of his face smoothed out to reveal the high cheekbones and firm jaw? When had his dark eyes taken on the daredevil look, the lock of black hair begun to fall just so over his forehead?

She forced herself with an effort back to the present moment, to the shouts of the boys, to the whistles of the leaders, to the chatter of the parents. Jeff leaned forward to speak to someone, and suddenly he was a boy once more, the manly planes and structures of his face dissolved into softer pads and dimples. A trick of the light, that was all.

The camp bus lumbered into the parking space, cutting off the view of the welcoming activities. Maggie swallowed hard and took a deep breath. The reminders of Kurt were no longer confined to her son's features and her own memories. There was news of him, he was close by. But even if he was in trouble, he'd maintained the same silence that had swallowed him up twelve years ago. He hadn't turned to the people who'd loved him in the past. And now Frieda wanted her to go and see him. Of course she couldn't do that. Her whole carefully constructed life would come tumbling around her ears if she saw him.

'Penny for them,' Roger said from behind her, putting his hands carefully on her shoulders.

She blinked, startled to find Roger so close. She'd almost forgotten he was with her, distracted as she was with memories of Kurt. She turned her head to glance at his handsome profile. His hands were strong, nails carefully manicured. He no longer practiced as a doctor. The many years of administration had given him a smooth, diplomatic finish. She suspected he no longer kept up his medical knowledge. She felt the increased pressure of his fingers.

'You seemed a bit preoccupied in the car,' he said. So he had noticed. 'You're far away still,' he continued. 'What's wrong? Not worried, are you?'

She seized on the excuse of the earlier conversation about the older boys, the longer hikes, rock climbing, and canoeing. 'Just an anxious mom,' she smiled. 'Camp's tougher this year.'

'He'll be fine,' Roger said. 'Don't worry.'

She took a small step forward, turning away to fiddle with the lens on her camera and held it up to her face, focusing on Jeff and the groups of excited boys in front of the log dining hall.

She'd been happy to accept Roger's offer to drive in his sleek new Land Cruiser because her own car would never have made it. Besides, she wasn't the world's best driver under any circumstances. She tended to lose herself in her thoughts, usually planning the layout of her photos for her book, and her concentration suffered. Jeff could've taken the camp bus, but going with Roger allowed her a bit more time with her son before the three-week separation. They'd never been apart that long before, not even when she was taking her business courses because the junior camps never lasted beyond ten days. Roger had jumped at the opportunity to drive them, and it'd seemed a good idea at the time. He'd even hinted at staying longer, overnighting at an inn he thought she'd like.

But some things weren't possible. There would be no leisurely dalliance with Roger today. She glanced at her watch. 'I should be back by four,' she said, avoiding his eye.

'Four?'

She felt him tense and turned to him. 'I'm sorry, Roger. I have to see Frieda Haydon. I told you, there's a problem . . . '

'Then we should get going if we're going to

have any time to ourselves.' Roger checked his watch. 'It's nearly noon now.'

He strode ahead of her to the car, annoyance plainly transmitted in the set of his shoulders, the impatient jab of the key into the ignition. She knew how years of negotiating sessions had taught him not to flare, not to lose his control. Kurt would have told her in no uncertain terms what he thought and would have driven off with her, kidnapped her if necessary, kept her prisoner until she fulfilled her promise. She sighed and told herself she was glad not to be with Kurt, driving off into the mountains with a few precious hours stretching before them to enjoy as they pleased.

She paused to replace her camera in the bag on her shoulder. A week ago, she'd thought maybe this would be the day, this would be the ideal moment to respond to all Roger's kindness, all his caring, all his help. Not to mention his patience at waiting for her to make up her mind to take their relationship that important step further. But that was a week ago. Now she felt an emptiness in her middle at the thought. Now Kurt Rainer had intruded himself back into her life after twelve long years.

Why did the idea of making love to Roger feel like a betrayal of Kurt? Why should Kurt

24

have anything to do with her life, her plans, her decisions about any man in her future? She was going to have to sort out this tangle of feelings. It wouldn't be fair to Roger to let him think she was at last going to make a commitment to him if it wasn't so. She would have to find a way to put him off, tell Frieda she couldn't help her contact her grandson and put the ghost of Kurt Rainer to rest. Then she could reassess her relationship and mend fences with Roger. She gave a last wave to Jeff and turned away.

She watched Roger settling himself into the leather seat. He was a good man, he liked Jeff, would be a good father to him. The boy needed a strong male influence in his life. So what if she didn't feel the rush of desire, the urgency to touch and hold that she'd felt with Kurt? She was older now, more in control. Love was different at thirty-three than at twenty. Roger could give her stability, a caring and united family. She was comfortable with him, would be able to love him.

2

Just before four o'clock, Maggie kicked open the front door and dumped her camera bag on the hall table. She was tense and irritable, but that was no fault of Roger or his comfortable air-conditioned Land Cruiser. She pulled her blouse free from her denim shorts and started along the hallway, shedding clothes as she went. Naked, she headed for the shower. She needed a few minutes to collect her thoughts before she went to see Frieda at Glenhaven.

She set the water jet to high and let it play on her tense shoulders. The day with Roger had raised more problems than it had solved.

Roger had prepared an elegant picnic, chose an idyllic spot to eat and smother her with attention. After lunch, they'd walked by the stream, and he'd taken her hand and kissed her very gently. He was kind and patient, and she hated herself for not responding to him. What more did she want? What more could Roger do or be? What perverse streak in her was holding her back, whispering that she would be wrong to agree to his suggestion of a long weekend away together while Jeff was at camp? She'd told him she would think about it.

She turned off the water, stepped out of the shower, and wrapped a towel around her head. She knew perfectly well what was holding her back. All the time she was comparing him to Kurt.

Slowly, she rubbed cream on her arms and face.

The last picnic she'd shared with Kurt had consisted of Kaiser rolls and baloney washed down with warm beer. She'd supplied it all, but he'd carried it most of the way. They'd hiked for hours, then scrambled up a rock face to sit at the top to admire a breathtaking view. She'd pulled well back from the edge, her head swimming at the height, but he'd been close behind her and settled her comfortably between his legs.

She replaced the top of the jar of cream and stood, looking at herself in the mirror, remembering.

He'd held her shoulder and run his hand down her arm as he pointed out stands of trees, birds and animal tracks around them. Her eyes in the mirror watched her hand lightly trace the line on her skin where he'd touched her. Her flesh seemed to quiver and burn under the gentle fingers.

She'd been weak with love for him. He'd

nuzzled the back of her neck and whispered, 'Come away with me, Maggie. Leave it all. We can do it.'

She shut her eyes again as she had years ago at his question and repeated her words in a whisper, shaking her head. 'You know I can't.'

She made herself move from the image in the glass and pulled on a skirt and ran a comb through her damp hair.

At the time, she'd truly believed what she said. Truly believed that running off with the town's bad boy would kill her dad. Her brother Phil had done enough, getting himself involved with that dreadful invest-ment scam. Phil never had been able to resist a get-rich-quick scheme. Dad had always been so good, so patient. He was a big bear of a man, considerate and slow moving, and thought the world of his kids. She couldn't add to the pain in her family.

She thrust her feet into leather sandals and grabbed her car keys. So history was repeating itself. Kurt was interfering in her life again. She was refusing to go away with Roger, a man who loved her, promised to care for her, all because of Kurt Rainer. And Kurt's grandmother wanted her to go and see him in hospital when the mere sight of his photograph raised this turmoil. How could she go and face him? On the one hand was her sense of obligation to her old benefactor and on the other her instinct to preserve her emotional security by refusing to meet Kurt Rainer.

She would have to screw up every ounce of courage she had to get behind the wheel of her car and point it towards that hospital where Kurt lay injured. So she was a coward, she was going to let Frieda down. For once, she would have to do that and hope Frieda respected her decision.

★   ★   ★

Kurt Rainer parked under the huge elm that overshadowed the roadway. He folded his arms on the steering wheel and rested his head on his hands. A couple of times on the highway he'd thought he wouldn't make it. 'Fade to black' as they say in the movies. And then when he took to the back roads, the rough surface had nearly jolted his insides through the hole in his gut. He sat up and pressed a hand to his abdomen. Bleeding again. The makeshift bandage wasn't much use.

He felt in his pocket and pulled out the bottle of pain killers and dry swallowed two. He needed a minute to rest before he went to find his grandmother. A few deep breaths, let the pills kick in, and he wouldn't frighten her. Then Oma would look after him, like she always had in the past. Hell, he wasn't in much worse shape than a couple of times after Dad had been at him when he was a kid. She'd looked after him then. But Dad had never taken a knife to him, although he'd used almost everything else.

He needed a couple of minutes to collect himself. The tumble down the damn mountain had been bad enough. The questions and the hospital had nearly driven him crazy. How did *he* know what had been going on in Johnny Gunn's life? As far as he was concerned, the star had been a self satisfied jerk, that's all he knew, and that's what he'd told the police.

He eased his shoulder in its strapping and couldn't stop the small grunt as the pain shot down his arm, despite the pills. Ten years as a top notch outfitter and guide, and a stupid accident had him in the hospital and under investigation. Except that the wound in his side was no accident. Someone had wanted him out of the way.

The arm would heal and so would the leg. He would make damn sure they were back in working order in less than the three months the idiot doctor had predicted. What did those guys know of the strength of Kurt Rainer's willpower? Besides, he needed to be up and about to keep his business running, keep it in good shape if he wanted a good price. Although he wasn't sure selling out was the right thing. He'd felt restless, unsettled for a while. Maybe he was at the threshold of a new stage in his life, needed to find new challenges, new peaks to scale. This damned business with Johnny Gunn had certainly provided a detour!

He wriggled his fingers and pulled the support away from his body with his right hand. God, it was uncomfortable. He peered up into the branches of the massive elm. Despite the protest of his cramped muscles, a small smile moved his mouth as he saw the remnants of the tree house way up there. Was it only fifteen feet up? Steve had thought they were at the top of the world at age ten. Even then it had never been high enough or dangerous enough for him.

The stab of pain with each breath was easing now, and he wiped the film of sweat from his forehead. He would make it to the door on his two legs without keeling over. He slid carefully out of the car, stretching the stiffness out of the wounded leg with a grimace, hung on to the roof for a moment while his head cleared after the movement, and took in his grandmother's house. It looked good. Someone had been taking care of the flower beds and the lawns. He remembered pushing the old hand mower for what seemed like hours over the tough grass. Sometimes he'd pretended it was his father he was manhandling after one of their spectacular flare-ups.

He'd not even kept in touch with Oma, cutting himself off thoroughly and effectively. No news about the family, or anyone else in the town. But she'd let him know often enough in the past that she loved him. He knew she thought about him, missed him. She was the only one who cared anything about him. If there was anything in his life about which he felt a stab of guilt — and he had to admit there were one or two — it was never trying to let her know about his success.

Bag in his good hand, he limped up to the front door and noted the shining brass knocker against the black paint. He was good with details like that. Equipment had to be well maintained and had to look in good shape. The silence was heavy in the late afternoon. He could hear a big truck change gears on the freeway. Somewhere, an ice-cream cart started to play Pop Goes the Weasel.

He put down the bag and used the knocker. Nothing. He bent down to the old-fashioned letter box, opened the flap, and peered in. The maple staircase was immediately opposite. When you go upstairs, he recalled, you have to walk on the outside of the second and third steps, otherwise they creak. Many was the night he had done just that after leaving Maggie, before Oma had given him the room at the back of the house. He grimaced, straightening his back. He had to get that woman out of his head.

Satisfied there was no one home, he turned and walked slowly round the side of the house. His old room was attached to the main kitchen by a short passage. Calling it an apartment was a stretch. One big room with a bed and a couch. He'd shared the kitchen and the downstairs bathroom with Oma. But what a refuge it had been from his father's wrath.

He peered in the windows. This part wasn't as well looked after. The windows were grimy and smeared. He put his bag down and rubbed a section of the glass clear with the back of his free hand to look in. The furniture was just as he had left it, his old football pennants and a couple of tattered posters still on the wall. There was even a sweater flung across the bed. A film of dust lay over everything, fading the colors and blurring the outlines.

He reached above his head with his good arm and felt in the low eaves' trough. Under a layer of dry leaves and debris, his fingers closed around a key. Gran would be pleased to see him back in his old place. A bit of a rest, and he would get it cleaned up in no time. He'd lived in a lot worse. And no one except his grandmother need know he was there.

★   ★   ★

Maggie found Frieda sitting in the shade on the brick patio in Glenhaven, a pile of untidy newspapers by her side. The old lady pushed aside a mess of clippings and placed her scissors and a notebook on top.

'Jeff OK?' she asked.

Maggie pulled a chair closer to the table. 'Ecstatic,' she said. 'I don't think he even saw us leave.'

'Us?' Frieda raised an eyebrow.

'Roger drove us.' Maggie gave an embarrassed smile.

'I see.' Frieda placed one hand on an envelope on the table.

Maggie cleared her throat and edged her

chair a little closer. She took Frieda's hand.

'I read the article,' she said.

Frieda remained silent, her bright eyes fixed on Maggie's face. Her knuckles were white on her cane.

'It brought back a lot of memories.' Maggie took a deep breath. 'I don't think I can go to the hospital,' she said in a rush.

'I see,' Frieda said again. She let out her breath and leaned back against the cushions. 'Don't worry about it. I've written.' She patted the letter under her hand.

'I'm sorry.'

'Don't keep saying you're sorry. If you can't go, you can't go. I'm the one who's sorry about yesterday. I panicked, but I've had time to think since then.'

Maggie felt miserable. Was this the way she repaid Frieda for all her kindnesses, for the house, for her encouragement to follow her heart and pursue her photography? She shifted uncomfortably on the slatted chair. Looking up, she saw Dianna approaching across the lawn.

'Maybe — ' she began.

'Don't say it. Stick to your decision, child. You've thought about it and so have I. I won't ask you to drive over to see him if you can't face him.'

Maggie let out her breath in relief.

'Though God knows why,' Frieda continued. 'You two were thick as thieves before.
Anyway, I have a better idea. I've asked him
to come to Branscombe to recuperate.'

Maggie stared at her. 'You've done what?'
she said, barely above a whisper.

'I've asked him here.' Frieda patted the
letter again.

Suddenly, Dianna stood at Frieda's shoulder. Maggie and Frieda looked at her in
silence. The girl seemed to have a knack of
appearing at a pivotal moment.

'Hallo Mrs. Haydon, Ms. Rainer,' she said
brightly. 'How are you?'

'I'm quite well, thank you.' Frieda waited,
obviously expecting the nurse to leave before
she resumed her conversation.

'Good. Shall I take your letter for you?'
Dianna stretched out her hand.

'Thank you, my dear. That won't be
necessary. Maggie will mail it for me.' She
passed the letter to Maggie, the address
turned away from Dianna.

'Of course,' Maggie replied. 'No problem.
I'll take it right now.' Frieda hooked her cane
over the arm of her chair and placed her
hands to push herself up.

'Don't just stand there,' she said to Dianna.
'Give me a hand to get on my feet.'

Dianna hurried to assist and handed

Frieda her cane. The old lady drew herself up and looked at Maggie.

'You're old enough to make your own decisions,' she said. 'I respect whatever you think is best. But the invitation is there, not for the first time. Please see that the letter leaves with today's mail.'

Maggie slid the letter into the pile waiting for collection without looking at the front of the envelope. She had no wish to see his name, nor to know exactly where he was. So all her agonizing had been for nothing. Like it or not, she was likely to see him again if he accepted Frieda's invitation. The thought filled her with a tingling apprehension, a fascination mixed with dread, like looking at a beautiful but deadly snake.

She continued through the foyer and opened the door to her office. While she was here, there were a couple of things to take care of, and she needed the reassurance of routine familiarity to calm her down. Frieda had certainly highjacked the agenda, she thought as she sorted some papers. She would have a few days before he received the letter and could act on it. A few days to decide what to do. If he answered, if he announced that he would return to Branscombe, she could always remove herself from danger.

Maggie swung into the driveway of her house and parked alongside the rhododendrons. The bushes were shedding their petals on the lawn, their pink and white beauty already over for another year. A clean-up job for sometime soon. She got out of the car and stretched, breathing in the warm air of mid summer. Idly, she glanced back towards the street and noted the strange car under the elm. Most of her neighbors and their guests parked on their own property. Then she remembered the Wilsons next door had talked about renovating. Probably someone over to give an estimate. She lingered, letting the peace of the setting settle around her like a soft, silk scarf, obscuring the worries and the frustrations of the day.

What a relief that Frieda hadn't been upset about her refusal to see Kurt, or at least had graciously hidden her disappointment. Maggie figured it would be at least a week before there was any likelihood at all of Kurt responding to the invitation in the letter. Depending on how badly he was hurt. She had a momentary vision of that muscular body immobile in a bed, subjected to nurses and routines and instructions. She could imagine how he was taking that. Maybe she would phone the hospital and ask, just to make sure that he was recovering. Frieda would like to know. And if he wasn't? She shut down the thought. He was an old acquaintance and, as such, she would check into how he was. No more, no less.

The warm scent of newly cut grass floated in the air. One of the neighbors was starting up a barbecue, and the aroma made her suddenly hungry. All was right with the world, or soon would be. She had time to figure out what to do, and one whole week of freedom. Maybe she would call Roger to talk about the plans for the weekend after all.

Dearly as she loved her son, these moments were precious to her. As a single mother she craved time on her own and someone to share the decisions and problems of a family, to take some of the weight. Roger was more than ready to do just that. He would be a good father to Jeff. Certainly better than a suspected murderer. And Roger had hinted at more children. She would like to be surrounded by a complete family, maybe a daughter, with blonde good looks from both her parents. Roger's children would be healthy, happy, loved and with both a father and a mother. But she would not think about such things for the next while. She would wallow in selfish, female pursuits and answer only to herself.

Jean Thompson, her next door neighbor, came alongside her with Muffy, the golden spaniel, on a leash. 'Hi, Maggie. Taking it easy?'

Maggie laughed. 'Hallo, Jean. Sorry, I didn't hear you. Daydreaming a bit. Hi, Muffy.' She bent to rub the dog's long, silky ears.

'You on your own for a while?' Jean said.

'Yup. Jeff's gone for three weeks, and I'm on vacation till Monday. A whole week.'

'Going away?'

'No. At least not right now.' Maybe she would be away if it worked out with Roger, or if Kurt threatened to return. 'The forecast's good. I might get my bike out of the garage and clean it up, ride out somewhere, spend some time on the beach taking pictures. And there's a movie I wanted to see.'

Jean glanced at her watch. 'We've got a few people over,' she said. 'Come by if you feel like it.'

'Thanks, I might do that.'

'Any time.' Jean gathered up Muffy's leash and waved goodbye.

Maggie knew she wouldn't go. For once she didn't have to make any plans for supper. She could eat or not, just as she pleased. She would take a half hour to sit on the shaded porch with a cool glass of lemonade and savor her independence. Before any other well-meaning people could disturb her, she gathered her purse from the front seat and slammed the car door.

She ran up the steps to the verandah, her heels tapping on the wooden floor. The flap of the letter box was up, as if someone had pushed something through. She hesitated, frowning, remembering the strange car. Inside the house, she pushed the door closed and looked down. There was no envelope or paper on the floor behind the door. Then she let out her breath in a laugh, remembering Jean's barbecue. The car belonged to one of her guests of course. Goodness, her nerves must be on edge if she was seeing possible intruders on such flimsy evidence

As she dropped her bag on the hall table, a scraping noise came from the back of the house and she froze, listening, her heart beating fast. She felt behind her for the door knob and took a firm grasp on it, ready to twist it open and run. Her car keys were still in her hand, and she fitted the biggest between her fingers as she been taught at the self defense classes. Her mouth was suddenly dry.

As if at a signal, a man appeared at the end of the hallway. The sun was low in the sky, sending beams into the front windows and casting dark shadows so that she could not see his face. She squinted at the stranger, a small clutch of fear tightening her stomach. No one she knew would come into her house while she was out. Her feet felt rooted to the spot, and she willed the muscles in her legs to run. She knew she should get out, but something held her, some intuition, some dreadful knowledge.

Still he said nothing, but moved a step closer. His face suddenly sprang into focus. She gasped and put out a hand to steady herself against the wall. Her heartbeat changed to a rapid thud in her ears, she felt hot and then cold.

'Kurt?' Her voice strangled in her throat, the question no more than a whisper.

Kurt Rainer took another step closer.

'Hello, Maggie.'

'What are you doing here?'

'Not a very gracious way to welcome an old friend. I've disturbed bears in the woods and gotten a better welcome.'

She could see him more clearly now. His mouth still turned up a little more on the left corner than the right. He had always been tall, even in high school, and had reached his full height well before his senior year. But he had filled out, his muscles looked full and supple under the red polo shirt. The unruly lock of black hair still fell over one eye. She couldn't see his eyes because of the sunglasses. They were probably still the same bright blue. One arm was in a canvas support that held it strapped across his chest. He was holding it as if it pained him. He moved another step closer, favoring one leg, then leaned against the wall for support. Her back was flat against the door now.

'Hey, it's only me! It's been a long time,' he said.

It had been twelve years, a long time and a lot of heartache, a lot of changes in her life because of him.

'How did you get in here? What do you want?' she asked again.

'This is still my grandmother's house, isn't it? Where is she?'

'I'm living here. We've been here three years.'

Again that quirky smile. 'We? Married, Maggie?'

As if you care! 'Not anymore.'

He took another step. She could see lines now around his mouth, a white scar running down the jaw. It could be a knife wound. Probably was if Kurt Rainer had continued his old lifestyle. He was pale under the tan and his lips pressed together, making a thin line.

'I have a son,' she said. 'Jeff and I live here. Your grandmother rents it to us.' That wasn't strictly true. They lived rent free in return for looking after the big old house and the grounds.

He was resting one shoulder on the stair rails, looking at her with the old smile that said, 'Come on, Maggie. Level with me'. God, what was she to do? Thank God Jeff wasn't here. They mustn't meet!

She squared her shoulders and edged past him, holding her breath as she moved close to him, feeling the electricity and the warmth of his body like passing through a magnetic field. She went down the hall into the kitchen, trying to make sense of his sudden appearance. He obviously couldn't have received Frieda's letter that she'd only just mailed. He followed her into the narrow space between the counters. Trapped on all sides, she cast around for an escape, something to do with her nervous hands.

'I was going to have some lemonade. Want some?' She opened the refrigerator door.

'Hope you don't mind, I helped myself.' He motioned to a glass on the counter top.

'Isn't Oma here?' he asked again.

She had to smile at the affectionate title

they had all used as children. 'No, she left nearly a year ago. She's at Glenhaven, the retirement home.'

He made a face. 'You must tell me about it. I'll just take my stuff through.' He waved at the duffel bag.

She looked at him over the open refrigerator door. 'Stuff?'

'Yup.' He moved back at last, swung a pine chair away from the table and sat heavily. 'Grandmother always said I could stay here whenever I wanted. I can take my old room.' He rubbed his free hand across his face. He looked tired and drawn.

The room that had been his all through high school and for five years after was off to the side of the house. Maggie and Jeff never went in there. She'd never even cleaned it up.

She put the pitcher of lemonade carefully back in the refrigerator and closed the door. Everything was very quiet and very bright. The hum of the cooling motor was suddenly extraordinarily loud. Kurt's red shirt and black jeans, pulled tightly across his outstretched thighs, stood out in relief against the pale background of the kitchen wall. The pattern on the tiles seemed to shimmer and writhe.

'Hey, Maggie. You all right?'

In a flash he was out of the chair and by

her side, despite his wounded leg and his fatigue. He took her arm and his touch burned ice and fire to the center of her being. She wanted to scream, tell him not to touch her ever, ever again.

She took a deep breath and moved away. 'You can't stay here.'

The ache began as a tiny bud below her breastbone. She held onto the back of a chair, squeezing hard to make herself focus on reality.

He moved slowly back to the table and sank into his chair, watching her with a small frown creasing his brow. 'Thought you were going to faint there for a minute. Can't be that upsetting to see me again, can it?'

If only you knew, she thought, if only you knew.

'I don't want you here.'

He gave a small laugh. 'But I won't bother you. You'll never see me. Besides . . . ' He moved his arm in the sling, ' . . . I'm out of work for the moment. I need somewhere to stay. Oma did always keep a room for me. I'm always welcome, she said. I'm surprised she didn't tell you, if you're that close.'

Maggie leaned back against the kitchen counter. She had no wish to discuss anything with him. Her only priority was to get this unwelcome man out of her kitchen and out of her life.

'Did they release you from the hospital?'

He hesitated a fraction too long. 'I had to leave.'

'You *had* to leave? What exactly does that mean?'

He shrugged, lifted the sunglasses, and pressed a finger and thumb to his eyes. 'I was ready.'

'You don't look good.'

'Thanks. Just tired. I drove all night.'

She'd seen the lines of fatigue drawn tight around his mouth and eyes, the hollowness in his cheeks. She suspected he was in considerable discomfort, if not downright pain.

'Whatever for?' she said. 'Surely — '

'Leave it, Maggie. I can drive all night or all day if I want.'

'Of course you can.' Why was she wasting her time quarreling with him when she never even wanted to talk to him again?

'Where is this Glenhaven place?' he asked suddenly.

'Where Oma is? Down by the harbor. I work there.'

'And she rents the house to you.' It wasn't a question.

Maggie nodded, then decided to explain.

There were enough secrets between them without concealing harmless facts. She ran her fingers over the counter top, picking up a few crumbs, avoiding having to look at him.

'She doesn't charge any rent. I look after the place for her. I lived with her before she went to Glenhaven. So it's quite ethical.'

'I wouldn't have expected anything else.'

She glanced up at him. He was teasing her just like he used to.

'Something wrong?' he asked.

She sighed. He could still read her like a book. There had never been any secrets between her and Kurt, except this huge one that he must never know.

'Is she all right?' he asked anxiously, misunderstanding the reason for her worry.

She sighed again. 'Most likely just old age. She's as feisty as ever, still speaking her mind and reading her newspapers. But she's fading slowly, like an old photograph. It's still her, but only just. Everything was too much for her in this house. I make sure I see her every day if I can.'

He looked at her over the rim of his glass, but he was still wearing those damned shades. She couldn't read his expression.

'I see.'

No, you don't see, she wanted to shout at him. You don't see what I've made of my life

48

since you and Steve turned everything upside down. Between you, you hurt everyone you touched. But I've survived both of you.

'You'd be more comfortable at the motel,' she said through stiff lips.

He took off the glasses, and she saw his eyes again. They were still blue, bright blue, just as she'd expected, more vivid than ever against the deep tan of his skin. A web of fine lines was etched around them. There was a dark bruise high on one cheekbone. She refrained from comment.

'Your room hasn't been cleaned for years . . . '

He brushed the lock of hair back from his forehead. Maggie's heart lurched again, a funny kind of buzz starting low down in her abdomen. Damn you, Kurt, you have no right to still have this kind of effect on me! Go away! And stay away as you have for the last twelve years!

'No problem to me,' Kurt was saying about the room. 'I'm used to camping out.'

'I don't want you here,' she repeated.

'You mentioned that.' He raised one eyebrow. 'This is my grandmother's house, isn't it?'

She nodded.

'She invited me. I'm here for a while until I decide what to do.' He turned the empty glass

49

on the table, not looking at her. 'Don't worry, I won't get in your hair. You won't even know I'm around.' His voice was cold.

She took a deep breath and closed her eyes. What on earth had Frieda been thinking of? Had she been in touch with him all these years without saying a word? Maggie clung to the promise that he'd leave her alone. She prayed to God he meant it.

She took another breath, struggling to center herself, to deal with the tumult of emotions. He wanted his old room! Kurt Rainer wanted to be in his old room, in the house that she now lived in! The man she'd firmly shut out of her life and her thoughts was back in flesh and blood and invading her home. She leaned back against the counter and closed her eyes. The clock ticked loudly in the silence that hung heavy in the kitchen. Through the open window, the chain on the humming bird feeder creaked softly as a bird came down to drink. Whatever she said would be wrong. '*Go away, I don't care if your grandmother promised you the whole house. You can't stay here.*' Or how about. '*Please make yourself at home. Share everything.*' Not! as Jeff would say.

A scraping noise from the table startled her into opening her eyes. Kurt had pushed his chair back and was on his feet, doubled over, his hands pressed to his side. His face was waxy pale, his eyes squeezed shut. His mouth twisted in a grimace of pain.

'What is it?' Maggie thrust herself away from the counter and took two steps to his side.

He steadied himself with the back of the chair, then waved her away and straightened carefully. 'It's okay,' he said in a gasp. 'Don't worry about it.' He let go of the chair and took a tentative step. 'Got to move the car,' he whispered through bloodless lips. He reached the doorway with a visible effort and clung to the jamb for a long moment. Then, quietly and slowly, he slid down the length of the wall and lay crumpled in a heap at her feet.

3

Maggie dropped to her knees beside him. 'Kurt?' she asked. No response. Her hands fluttered helplessly over his shoulders. Dare she touch him?

'My god, Kurt, what is it?' she said again.

She had to see what was under him, what he had been clutching to his abdomen. First, she needed to straighten his legs, move his arm out of the way. Then she took hold of his shoulder and pushed hard to turn him over. He wouldn't budge, he was a dead weight. She thrust her hair back, wriggled lower on the floor, twisting around so that one shoulder was almost under his, and heaved again. He moved with a groan and lay on his back.

A darker, wet patch on the bright red shirt showed where blood was seeping from a wound. She touched it gently and looked in horror at the fresh, bright stain on her fingertips. 'Oh, no,' she whispered.

She leaned over him and tried to pull the shirt up and out of the waistband of his jeans, then hesitated. The leather belt held the material cinched in tight to his waist. She would have to unfasten it. Praying she was doing the right thing, she freed the loose end of the belt. Her fingers struggled with the metal clasp, and she bent over his hips, concentrating on what she had to do.

Suddenly, she was aware of a change in Kurt's breathing and she looked up anxiously. He was watching her through half-closed eyes, a mocking smile on his lips.

'Quite like old times,' he whispered.

She let go of the belt buckle as if it were red hot and scrambled to her feet, feeling the warmth of a furious blush sweep up her neck and over her face.

'I was trying to help.'

'Thanks, I'm fine.' He struggled to sit up, but fell back again with a grimace of pain.

'You don't look fine. What on earth happened?' she asked.

'The wound's opened up that's all. I'll get a fresh dressing when my head clears a bit. Just lost a bit more blood than I thought.' He lay back on the smooth tiles of the kitchen floor and closed his eyes.

'Let me see it.' This time, she undid the buckle with cold efficiency and tugged the shirt free. A large dressing on his side was saturated with scarlet blood.

'I'll get the first aid kit. Don't move.'

He turned his head, and she saw the old

grin. 'I'm not going anywhere. The view's pretty good from here.' Suddenly conscious of her bare legs close to his hand, she turned quickly and left the room.

The wound was clean, but Kurt flinched and clenched his teeth as she replaced the bandages. Maggie dressed it as best she could, then helped Kurt to his feet and steered him to a chair. He sat for a moment with his head in his hands.

Maggie put a glass of water beside him. 'So you have an open wound, a broken arm, and a limp. Anything else?'

He shook his head. 'Just a couple of cracked ribs.'

'Just a — ' Maggie said, waving an arm in exasperation. 'Is that all? What did you do to your leg?'

'A branch kind of dug into it. Tore the muscle. It's a bit sore.' He shrugged dismissively.

'I bet. You need to be in the hospital.'

'No way, Maggie, no hospital. I'll be fine.' He struggled to stand up.

'Sit down. You'll fall down again, and I don't want to have to push you around on the floor anymore.'

He looked at her from under the lock of hair that had fallen across his forehead. 'Kind of fun though, wasn't it?'

'No, it was not fun.'

He moved again as if to get on his feet and sat down with a sigh. 'Damn. I need to move the car.'

'Stay where you are. I'll do it. Where are the keys?'

'In the pocket of my jeans.' He made a small gesture to the front pocket. 'I can't get them out without standing up or leaning on this arm.' He lifted his left arm in the sling.

Maggie gave him a venomous look and took a deep breath. 'Hold still.'

He leaned back in the chair and extended his leg to give her access to the pocket. She tentatively put her hand part way into the opening, feeling the warmth of his body through the cotton lining and the hard muscles of his upper thigh under her probing fingers. The pocket was deep, the keys hard to reach.

She made her hand as small as she could, conscious of the warm bulge behind the zipper. She hesitated, trying to grasp the key ring with just two fingers, fearful of brushing the obvious mound with her thumb. Kurt's eyes were on her, following the path of her hand as it moved into the depths of the pocket. She swallowed. She could have sworn that out of the corner of her eye, she saw movement behind the zipper. She daren't look. What the hell was she doing? Damn him, he was enjoying this, knowing exactly what she was feeling both literally and figuratively. Did she really want to give him the satisfaction of feeling him up? Angry now, she thrust her hand all the way into the opening, grabbed the keys and withdrew them fast.

'Got them.'

'Good.'

She couldn't meet his eyes, sure they would be full of mocking laughter. The keys were warm in her hand from the long contact with his body. She refused to dwell on where they had been and what she'd had to do to retrieve them.

'Put the car round the back,' he said. 'Is the old shed still standing?'

Maggie forced her voice to sound normal. 'It's still there. I'll do it just to keep you quiet, but when I come back you're going to tell me what's going on and why it's so important to get that car out of sight.'

Five minutes later, Maggie dropped the keys on the kitchen table and dusted off her hands. 'All hidden away,' she said.

Kurt looked up at her. His face was still pale and he was nursing his wounded arm.

'The car's in the shed. *You* should be in bed,' she added.

'True.' He rubbed a hand over his face. The dark stubble rasped as his fingers passed over his jaw. 'Thanks.'

'You look terrible.'

'Not forgotten how to make a guy feel good, eh, Maggie?'

'Making you feel good is not one of my priorities. However, I'd do what I could for a wounded dog, at least overnight. Hold on to me.' She stooped until his arm draped over her shoulder. Passing her arm around his waist, she hooked her fingers on the leather belt. 'Stand up slowly.' Well, she guessed she'd made a decision about letting him stay tonight.

She helped him to his feet and heard his sharp intake of breath as she took more of his weight. He was in more pain than he would admit and dead tired into the bargain. What had made him drive here when he should still be in a hospital? That gash in his side looked a lot like a knife wound. Was he wanted by the police? Was she abetting a criminal? He sure had a lot of explaining to do in the morning.

'Lean on me.' Carefully, she steered him across the kitchen and down the short hallway to the door of his old room. Pushing the door open with her free hand, she looked at the bed. The bare ticking of the mattress looked stark and uncomfortable.

'God, that bed looks good,' he said.

She stopped in the doorway, his weight heavy on her shoulder. The room looked terrible, much worse than she'd expected. There was no way she could put a man with open wounds in here with dust and dirt everywhere.

'Could we get on with this, Maggie?' Kurt said. 'Much as I like leaning on you — '

'This won't do,' she interrupted. But there were really only two choices. Jeff's room was under the eaves up the steep flight of stairs. Could she possibly manhandle Kurt up the narrow steps? She could start up the bleeding again. Add to that the lack of a bathroom on the second floor.

Down the hallway was her own room with a large, comfortable bed.

She took a firmer grip of her burden, hitching him closer to her by hooking her thumb even more snugly into his belt loop.

'Hold on for two more minutes, champ,' she said and turned away from his old room.

Still closely linked together, they maneuvered warily down the hall. At the threshold to her bedroom, she took a deep breath, guided him through the doorway and towards the bed. 'Don't say anything,' she gasped. 'This is the best place for you. Just for tonight, until you get some proper care.' She gently turned him round until the backs of his legs were against the edge of the bed. 'Now, sit down slowly. I'll hold on.'

She supported him until he was sitting on the mattress and then gently pushed him back to lie against the pillows. 'God, you're heavy,' she said standing up. She rubbed her shoulder and flexed her arm muscles.

Kurt lay back, one forearm over his eyes, breathing hard.

'Bad?' she asked.

He nodded without looking at her. She could see the twist of his mouth as he fought the pain.

'I'll get you something to help. Right now you need to sleep.' She stood up and bent over his legs to remove his shoes. Then she shook out a couple of the blankets from a pile stacked on the chest under the window and draped them over him.

He uncovered his eyes enough to look at her from under his folded arm. 'Not going to join me, Maggie?'

'Of course not.' How could he even try to joke at a time like this? And his jokes were in very poor taste. Of course she couldn't lie down beside him. Couldn't snuggle her face into the crook of his shoulder like she used to and sleep curled up beside him.

She brought a glass of water and a couple of pain killers, but he was asleep before she got back to his bedside. She stood a moment looking at him lying on her bed, noting the deep lines around his mouth. She saw too the way his face had changed in the last twelve years. The boyish recklessness was gone, replaced by a maturity, a solidness that had been lacking before.

'Oh, Kurt,' she whispered, 'why did you do it?'

She left the room, knowing that she would lie awake in Jeff's narrow bed, worrying about Kurt's wounds, worrying about what he had done, whether she was aiding and abetting a dangerous fugitive. Most of all she would pray that he would soon leave and would never know about Jeff.

★ ★ ★

From long habit, Kurt woke at first light. Cautiously, he flexed the muscles in his legs and arms. Damned sore, but no worse than yesterday. The body is never static. If it's no worse, then it must be healing itself. The wound in his side throbbed, but there were no shards of pain stabbing outwards from the lips of the gash.

He relaxed and lay back, taking in the

furnishings of the room. This had to be Maggie's bedroom. There were a couple of photographs in silver frames on the dresser. One was Maggie with a kid. Must be the son she mentioned. Who had she married? And where was the husband now? She'd said, 'Not any more,' when he'd asked. Divorced? Some jerk who didn't appreciate her and left her alone with a kid?

The other picture was a family group. He thought he could make out Maggie's dad in his clerical collar, her mom and her brother Phil. Must have been taken while she was still in high school.

Three framed scenes of the ocean and a beach at different seasons of the year hung on the walls. They were photographs, but pretty good ones. Someone knew something about taking pictures.

He pushed himself up and folded the pillow to prop his shoulders, wincing at the jab of pain in his arm. He'd never get used to this damned cast. He reached for the glass by the bed and saw the two white pills beside it. Why not? He swallowed them quickly with a gulp of the tepid water and lay back with a sigh.

He'd told Maggie Oma had invited him, and that was true. But the invitation had come barely a month after he'd stormed out of Branscombe twelve years ago, wild with fury and boiling over injustice. Oma had let him know his father had suffered a heart attack, told him he always had a home with her but said nothing about anyone or anything else. He'd never answered, and she'd never tracked him down again. He'd figured there was not much to bring him back. There'd only been Maggie, and she'd made her feelings clear, never answering his letters, never available to come to the phone.

Maggie was the last person he'd expected to see when he did return, and it'd given him some kind of a jolt when she walked into his grandmother's house. He'd supposed she was long gone from Branscombe and would have washed the dust of the place from her feet long ago, just as he had. Only he'd kind of figured at one time they would do it together.

She still looked good, slim and curvy. He let his mind dwell on the shorts and shirt she'd been wearing, revealing her bare, tanned legs and a glimpse of cleavage. God, how he'd wanted her all through high school and college. Could never get enough of her, of feeling her smooth coolness under his hands.

Her hair was still long, but she wore it pinned up. He'd had a hard job last night not to reach up and pull out the pins when she was bending over him, just like he used to. Then that thick, yellow coil would fall forward, separating into golden strands under his fingers, shielding her neck and the upper swell of her breasts.

Years ago, the secrecy of their meetings, the planning and plotting to evade her parents' watchful eyes added spice to every encounter. But it wasn't just the idea of forbidden fruit for him. He'd loved her.

He closed his eyes at the painful admission, turned his head a little, and caught the flowery scent of Maggie's perfume on the sheets. God, that brought her right into the room and into the bed with him. He raised a hand to push the pillow higher still and met something soft and silky. He pulled the material out from where it was tucked under the pillow and shook out the folds. It was some kind of dark blue garment with thin straps. He let the delicate stuff drift over his face and rubbed it gently between his fingers. If this was her room, where had she slept, what had she worn?

He couldn't remember much after she'd pushed him back onto the bed. She must have come back to leave the pills, but she hadn't taken her night clothes. Probably couldn't stand to risk touching him unless she had to. He remembered her feeling for his keys, the color high in her cheeks.

He stirred under the blankets. What was the point of remembering? She'd made it clear twelve years ago that she wasn't interested anymore, and her welcome last night had been cold. Except that she *had* helped him, and he'd swear he'd caught something of the old look in her face when she'd tended his wound. Probably wishful thinking.

He'd resisted letting his thoughts turn to her for twelve years, trained himself to push the memories away because they brought her back too vividly to his mind. He'd spent enough time burrowed into a sleeping bag dreaming of Maggie Robbins. She didn't want him, had always put her family before what he wanted. After she ignored his letters, the angry, jealous child in him wouldn't let him ask any more. The stubborn, unloved child's voice told him if she'd loved him enough, she'd have put *his* needs first.

Lying in her bed, still feeling the pressure of her arms around him, helping him, the analytical adult voice of today asked how he would have felt in her shoes? How he would have reacted to the emotional blackmail he tried on her? Would he have wanted a relationship with the kind of person who would do that? He couldn't blame her for turning her back on him. She'd obviously done okay, found someone else to love her, give her a child even. He frowned. Where was this guy? She'd not mentioned anyone, there'd been no sign of anyone else in the house.

He lay back and closed his eyes. He wasn't going to interfere in Maggie's life. Soon he would be fit enough to move on. He just needed to rest up a couple of days, figure out what to do next, try to contact Joe without giving away where he was. Damn, this wasn't the kind of problem he was used to solving. Give him a Japanese tourist insisting on feeding a black bear and nearly losing his arm, and he would know exactly what to do. But give him a web of deceit, lies and murder, and he didn't know where to start.

★　★　★

Maggie threw out her arm and knocked the baseball glove off the bedside table. It fell with a soft plop onto the pile of dirty clothes discarded at the last minute before Jeff left for camp. She brought the arm cautiously back into the bed and rubbed her face, peering at the clock with the football figures marking the hours. Seven a.m. She had watched the miniature sports heroes crawl around the clock face until two, until sleep had at last overwhelmed her.

The old problem was still there despite the new day. Kurt was downstairs in her bedroom, his car was in the old shed at the back of her house, he was wounded, surely needed medical attention, and she had no idea of what was really going on. She had to find out why he was here and not in the hospital where he belonged.

She swung her legs out of bed and stripped off the panties and bra she had worn overnight. She would shower and dress and face Kurt right away. Naked, she stood in the middle of Jeff's room, suddenly realizing she had no clothes, but what she'd slept in, if she discounted Jeff's dirty track suit on the floor. Her shorts and T-shirt from yesterday were in the linen hamper, stained with Kurt's blood. Her son disdained such unmanly things as bathrobes. But there were large bath towels in the hall closet. With any luck, she could wrap one round her and creep into her bedroom to snag a pair of jeans and a clean shirt without waking Kurt.

With a large towel wrapped sarong-like under her arms, she tiptoed down the stairs and listened outside her bedroom door. No sound. Gently, she turned the handle and eased the door open a crack. She could see the end of her bed and Kurt's head and shoulders. He was lying back, eyes closed, still asleep, thank goodness.

She opened the door a little wider and slipped noiselessly into the room in her bare feet. She edged to the closet door and pushed it aside. It made a small sound as the glass slid open. She held her breath. Nothing from the bed.

She let out her breath and reached in for a pair of jeans.

'I liked yesterday's shorts.' The voice came from the bed.

Maggie whirled, clutching at the towel as she felt it begin to slip. 'You were asleep,' she accused.

'Just resting. The stair still creaks. Amazing what you can see if you stay still and wait.'

She secured the towel and decided to brazen it out. 'I can imagine. How do you feel?' she asked.

He pulled himself up higher in the bed. 'Pretty good, considering. I could do with a change of clothes, though.' He rubbed his hand over the shirt stained with dry blood.

'Don't move, you'll start the bleeding again. I'll get dressed and help you.'

Maggie grabbed the jeans again and blindly pulled a shirt from a hanger. Still clutching the slipping towel, she sped from the room and into the shower.

She let the water drive hard onto her back and shoulders, fuming at her own stupidity. She hadn't thought things through last night when she put him to bed in her own room. Hadn't realized that she would have to enter to get her own clothes, hadn't thought about having to help him out of his jeans and shirt. She lifted her face to the spray, deliberately turning the knob to a cooler setting. Damn him. Why did he have to come back at all?

Dressed and feeling almost composed, she knocked at the bedroom door and waited for his answer. He was sitting on the edge of the bed, one arm free of his shirt and struggling one-handed to pull it over his head. All she could see was his bare chest, adorned with the dressing she had put on last night. The muscles moved smoothly under the bronzed skin as he struggled. A thin line of dark hair traced the upper levels of his chest and snaked down to disappear behind the open snap of his jeans. His head was buried in the shirt, only the tousled black curls showing.

'That you, Maggie?' His voice was muffled.

She swallowed and took a deep breath. 'Who else?' she said brightly.

'Pull this damn thing over my head, will you?'

She stepped forward and took hold of the shirt, warm from his sleeping body. He pulled against her.

'Stop,' she said, sharply. 'I told you to wait. It would help to take the sling off first.' Quickly she undid the support and slipped it off. 'Now hold your arm still.' The shirt came off easily, and she laid it to one side.

'Can you do the rest?' Maggie averted her eyes from his naked chest and shoulders and busied herself folding the shirt carefully

'The zipper . . . ' He motioned with his free hand and stood up. 'This arm . . . ' he waved the cast at his side.

'Of course.'

Refusing to meet his eyes, Maggie bent down and grasped the metal tag of the zipper with the very tips of her fingers. She ran it down to the stop without touching anything else under her hand. He wriggled his hips and thrust his good hand into the waist band. Maggie gave an extra tug and the denim fell to the floor, revealing dark blue jockeys that concealed nothing. Quickly, she stood up and turned away. Damn him again. He could have slid the zipper down with one hand. He'd been toying with her again, and she'd fallen for it. From now on, he was on his own.

'I'm sure you can manage the shower,' she

said. I've put a stool in there in case you need to sit.'

He was watching her closely. She was sure he knew exactly what effect his naked body was having on her, knew that she was remembering the time when she had trusted him completely.

'I still have some of Steve's clothes. Maybe they'll fit, then I'll wash . . . '

His hand shot out and grabbed her arm, interrupting her babble and pulling her close to him.

'Steve? Why Steve?'

'I married him,' she gasped, pulling free. 'He . . . died.'

The heat from his body beat against her like a fire, his fingers dug into her upper arm and she saw the heave of his chest as he struggled to speak.

For a long moment, she held his gaze as he stared deep into her eyes, and she watched the swirling depths change from blue to a cold, icy gray. He really didn't know anything that had happened since he left.

The muscles along his jawline under the dark stubble tightened with a visible effort at control, and he sucked in a deep breath, looked away, and released her arm. He clamped his lips tight together, deepening the lines around his mouth. Maggie stood still until he broke the silence.

'I didn't know,' he said, coldly. 'Let's go for that shower.'

Conscious of every movement he made as he walked slowly next to her, she helped him to the shower and fastened plastic coverings to his cast and his side. She backed out of the room and went to find Steve's things that were boxed away in the attic.

She had one foot on the attic stairs when the doorbell rang. She hesitated. She wasn't expecting anyone. But her car was plainly visible in the driveway, so she couldn't pretend not to be home. The peal came again, louder this time.

With a sigh, she turned back towards the long hallway to the front door. Two large dark shapes were visible through the pebbled glass. Suddenly, she remembered Kurt's wound, his reluctance to tell her what was going on, the newspaper report. Could someone have followed him here?

She stopped on the inside of the door, one hand on the bolt.

'Who is it?' she called.

'Police, ma'am. Just like a word.'

Police! So maybe she had been right. He was a fugitive.

She opened the door a crack, holding it on the chain. 'Do you have ID?' The closer one looked barely older than Jeff and grinned at her disarmingly as he showed his shield.

★ ★ ★

'Come in.' She slipped the chain and opened the door. 'What can I do for you?'

The two men stepped into the hallway, carefully wiping their feet on the thick matting first. 'Just a routine call, ma'am,' said the older one. They politely removed their caps and produced notebooks. Their badges said Jim Hutchins and Brad Taylor.

Brad was the school boy. He glanced up from his notebook like a kid puzzling over homework. 'This won't take long, ma'am,' he said. 'Kurt Rainer. Do you know him, ma'am?'

The repeated 'ma'am' made her feel middle aged.

'I did,' she said cautiously, moistening her lips.

'He's your brother-in-law, right?'

'Was. My husband is dead, and Kurt left Branscombe oh . . . ' She pretended to search her memory. 'About twelve years ago.'

'I see. His grandmother still around? We had this as her address.'

Jim Hutchins was watching her closely and glancing around the hallway. Mercifully, no

72

sound came from the back of the house.

'Yes. I rent it from her.'

Brad made a note, frowning over his book.

'Where is she now?'

'In Glenhaven Seniors' Residence. Look,' said Maggie, 'I'm happy to help if I can, but what is this about?'

Jim Hutchins interrupted. 'Be happy to tell you, ma'am.' He gestured towards the end of the hallway to what was obviously the kitchen. 'Maybe we could sit a bit more comfortable.'

Kurt was probably sitting in the kitchen, waiting for the clothes she had promised to fetch.

'I'm sorry,' she said, 'it's a bit of a mess in there. Please go in the living room.'

She ushered them into the sitting area and perched on the edge of a chair as they took seats on the couch.

Jim leaned his elbows on his knees and consulted his notebook. Maggie waited impatiently. Couldn't they do or say anything without those books? Probably didn't know their own name without them.

'You may know that Kurt Rainer was helping with the inquiries into the death of Johnny Gunn?' Jim began. It seemed that Brad only did the preliminary stuff.

'I saw the newspaper report. What do you mean helping?'

Jim ignored the question. 'Mr. Rainer was hurt in the fall and was in the hospital.' He paused for Maggie's nod.

'Go on,' she said. This was like pulling teeth.

'Kurt Rainer slipped out of the hospital last night. We think he might have been attacked.'

'Attacked? Who by?'

'That's what we would like to know, ma'am.' Brad again.

'Have you seen him, or has he tried to contact you?' Jim said.

Maggie looked at them both as they waited for her answer. It seemed to her that whether or not she had seen Kurt was very important to them. And what did they mean by 'helping with the inquiries?'

'Is he a suspect in something?' she asked.

'Not at the moment, Mrs. Rainer,' Jim answered. 'We just want to make sure he's okay and ask him a few more questions, is all.'

Suddenly, the decision was made as easily as the one about letting Kurt stay and giving him her bed. 'No,' she said. 'I don't think he would come here. Why would he?'

Jim shrugged. 'Family. His grandmother's the only relative he has. And he hasn't been

74

back to the condo.'

Condo? Of course he had a home somewhere. Was there a wife, too?

She licked her lips again and stood up.

'Well, gentlemen, I would be glad to help if I could. Good luck in finding him.'

Brad was nothing if not persistent. 'Nothing at all?' he asked. 'No phone calls even?'

'Nothing.' The lie stuck in her throat like dry bread. She swallowed.

The policemen rose together and simultaneously tucked their notebooks back in their pockets.

'Many thanks, Mrs. Rainer,' Brad said with his boyish grin. 'Here's a phone number in case you remember anything or hear anything.' He passed her a card. 'It would be in Kurt's best interest to contact us.' He looked at her closely.

She nodded. 'Of course. Let me see you out.'

When the police officers were safely out of the house, Maggie closed the front door and leaned against it, blowing a stream of air to lift the tendrils of hair sticking to her forehead.

She sank down to sit on the floor, resting her back against the wood. She had lied to the police! She'd concealed the fact that the man they were looking for was sitting half naked in her house. She'd dressed his wound, fed him, given him shelter, but had denied seeing him. Her hands shook and her stomach felt empty. She'd never lied to anyone like that before. She paid her parking tickets the next day, scrupulously dealt with her bills well before the due date. She felt like a criminal.

A sound from the kitchen made her look up. Kurt was in the doorway, a towel wrapped around his waist.

'I lied for you,' she said.

He looked at her gravely. 'I heard. Thanks Maggie.'

Then he rubbed his arms. 'Are you going to sit there for long?'

'I might. Why?'

He gestured to the towel. 'Just feeling at a bit of a disadvantage.'

'Good. It's your turn.' But she stood up anyway and smoothed her jeans over her hips. 'Put some coffee on. I'll be right back. Then we'll talk.'

4

The attic was dark and musty, dust motes floating in the meager rays of light that edged in through the one small, grimy window. Maggie hated going up there. Spider webs were likely to catch in your hair, and tiny scrabblings made her wonder what might be hiding under the old eaves. The pest controller had assured her she had nothing worse than insects, but even so . . .

She clicked on the hanging light bulb that sent the shadows dancing into the corners. Steve's clothes were all here. When he died, she didn't want to touch them. She'd heard of mourning wives clutching an old shirt at night, taking something to bed with them that held the scent of the dead loved one, deriving comfort from it, imagining the warmth of a living body. Not her. She'd scooped everything into a few boxes, ignoring the crackle of paper in pockets, the jingle of coins. Out of sight, out of her life, that's what she wanted for Steve.

Sometimes she felt a twinge of guilt. Everyone deserved to be mourned, and she did mourn. She wept for what might have been, for the fact that Jeff had lost two fathers, for the weak, vindictive man who was Kurt's half-brother.

Later, when her life was settling down to routine again, she barely gave the clothes a second thought. If she did, it was to acknowledge that the prospect of seeing someone else walking the streets in an outfit she might recognize was more than she wished to contemplate. As it was, even months later, the glimpse of a chestnut head of hair, a jaunty, cocky walk, were enough to send her heart pounding with apprehension, although she knew Steve would never return.

She dragged one of the boxes towards her and opened the flaps. Shirts and sweaters were on top. Quickly, without dwelling on past memories, she selected a few things that looked unworn, stacked the rest beside her and dived deeper for pants. She pulled out a navy cashmere jacket that Steve had bought just before they were married but hardly ever wore. She smoothed the warm fabric with her fingers and shook it out before refolding it. Some papers were stuffed into the pocket, throwing out the tailored line. Probably an old bill, one of many that Steve conveniently 'forgot.' She left the papers where they were and got on with the job.

A few minutes later Maggie pulled the attic

door closed behind her and carried the pile of clothes to the kitchen. This room seemed to have become the center of her life, the neutral space where Kurt and she could meet, circling warily, sizing each other up. She would have liked to trust him again, would have liked to tell him about his son, feel his arms round her, wiping away the pain of twelve years. But he'd disappeared without a word, never tried to contact her, find out what was happening in her life. Twelve years is a hell of a long time, she told herself, a long time to ignore someone you supposedly loved. Now he was sitting in her kitchen, needing her help, having got himself into trouble yet again. This time it could be serious. It would take a lot more than a few suggestive jokes to restore her confidence and trust her son to him.

Kurt was sitting at the table again, his chest still bare, a towel wrapped around his middle. It barely came to his knees, and she could see the firm muscles of his calves, honed by many years of strenuous effort. He had always been the first one to the top of a hill, the one who hauled others up after him, lending them his strength. Why had he abandoned her, this young man who coached eager kids, rescued wounded dogs and loved her like no one ever had or could again?

She shook the thoughts from her mind and showed him the blue outfit.

'Try this,' she said. 'It's a sweat suit. No zippers to cause you a problem.'

He looked up at her, that wicked gleam of devilment in his eye. She had been right — he'd been playing her for a fool, pretending difficulty. He'd always taken every opportunity to touch her, make her put her hands on him. Of course, there'd been a time when she'd been a willing accomplice. He'd always been a sensuous man and had taught her to revel in her own sensuality.

She dumped the clothes on the table in front of him. 'Put them on,' she said, 'and then we'll talk.'

'Thanks, Maggie,' he said, and pushed himself to his feet. 'I'll be back. Coffee's on.'

She poured the coffee while he slipped into the bathroom, emerging five minutes later in Steve's track suit, a little tight across the shoulders and short in the leg. He was looking better, more rested, his mouth and jaw more relaxed. He limped back to the table. The sling no longer held his arm to his side. She could see the edge of the plaster cast beneath the knitted cuff of the sleeve.

Maggie refrained from any comment about the missing sling and put a mug of coffee and the sugar bowl in front of him. 'You still take it black?' she asked.

'No change in the way I like my coffee,' he said. 'Black as night, sweet as love and hot as hell.' He grinned at her.

She refused to meet his eyes, busying herself with the cream and sugar for her own cup and sat down opposite him.

'Now talk,' she said after her first sip.

He took a gulp of his coffee. 'What do you know?' he said warily.

'Only what I read in the newspaper. You were with some film company and the star died in an accident. Some people seem to think you might be responsible.'

He shook his head, pulling his mouth into a grimace. 'No way, Maggie. You know I couldn't kill anyone or anything.'

She watched him over the rim of the coffee mug, holding the drink in front of her face like a shield. What he said had been true once.

Fifteen years ago, they'd found a black and white mongrel dog while driving out one day. A speeding car had hit it, throwing it onto the gravel shoulder. It lay bleeding and abandoned by the side of the road. She remembered how Kurt had stopped, wrapped the shivering animal tenderly in an old blanket, and sat in the back seat with it, stroking it and whispering softly to it while she drove to the animal hospital.

She recalled the tears that had brimmed in his eyes, threatening to spill over and spoil his macho image, when the dog died. She remembered too his white-hot anger against the heartless driver. She also knew that he'd relentlessly pieced together a few sparse clues, found the driver, and thrashed him soundly in a dark car park one night. Kurt Rainer was a mass of contradictions, often wearing the white hat of the good guys but just as capable of losing his cool and lashing out in a vigilante mode. Hadn't he disappeared uncaringly from her life just when she needed him most?

Which role had he been playing when Johnny Gunn died? 'So just tell me what happened,' she answered as calmly as she could.

He settled more comfortably in the chair and clutched his coffee mug in both hands. 'For ten years,' he began slowly, 'I've been a guide and outfitter, mostly in high mountain terrain. Even made a bit of money recently doing stunt work. I don't particularly like the people, and sometimes I wonder about showing the general population how beautiful it is back there in the mountains. It only encourages more people to intrude.'

'That's not why the police are looking for

you,' she said impatiently.

'Bear with me, Maggie. I need to do this my way.' He paused. 'I need to lay it out in my own mind too. You were always a good listener,' he added.

That was a low blow, she thought. She had spent hours listening in fascination both to Kurt's problems with his father and to his plans for making the old man proud of him, always wondering what it was that made ill-used children so determined to prove themselves of value.

'Go on,' she said, ignoring the remark and getting up to refill the coffee mugs. 'I've worked for the Star Company before. They're heavily invested in this new movie, and as far as I could tell it wasn't going too well. Johnny Gunn, the star, is — was — a spoilt macho type. He's made a few Rambo style films, but was scared of heights. Bet you never read that in the ads, hey?' Kurt's lips twisted in disgust. 'Anyway, that's why he needed a good stunt man and a stand-in. Thanks.' He took the fresh mug of coffee and added sugar.

'So Johnny had a stand-in, of course,' he continued. 'But we had to get a shot of him with the ropes in place at the top of the cliff. I checked it all out — twice — and then I went back for a third time. It's not really dangerous. He's just going to dangle in space for a few seconds, screw up his face in anguish — we'll know he's nearly wetting himself, but the audience will think it's courageous concentration.'

Maggie raised her mug and cradled it in her hands in front of her face, watching him over the rim. She tried to picture him in his working environment, the expert among novices.

'There was a lot of tension on the set,' he said. 'I'd had a run in with Johnny, who kept trying to put me down, defying the safety rules, strutting around. I'd also heard there were money problems. They're running over budget and over schedule. Plus the female lead is holding out for some concession — God knows what. I didn't have the patience or interest to follow their squabbles.'

Maggie smiled in understanding. He'd never suffered fools gladly.

'So I see Johnny's strapped in, step back, let him go, and he falls three hundred feet.' Kurt looked directly at her. 'I'll never forget the scream. It was all on film. All that was left at the top was the winch — out of camera range of course — and the end of a cut rope. Yes, cut, not broken or frayed. One of my ropes wouldn't fray anyway. That would be sloppy and dangerous.'

Maggie put down her cup and reached for Kurt's hand. He grasped her fingers tight.

'What — ' she started to say.

Kurt sat up straighter and broke into her question. 'The police arrived and confirmed what I already knew — one of the straps had been cut through. It must have been after I left to get a coffee while the cameras were setting up. All kinds of people were milling around, but only me who will admit to touching the ropes.'

At that instant, the doorbell rang. Instinctively, Maggie pushed her chair back to get up but was stopped by Kurt's hand gripping her wrist.

'If it's the police again . . . ' he said.

'Don't worry,' she replied. 'I won't tell them anything. At least, not until I've heard the whole story.'

There was only one figure visible through the glass of the front door. Not likely to be the law in that case. She opened the door cautiously and found herself face to face with a huge display of roses.

'What — ?'

A cheerful face peered round the extravagant bouquet. 'Ms. Rainer?' the delivery boy asked.

'Yes.'

'For you, ma'am. Enjoy.' With that, he

thrust the flowers in her arms and retreated to his van.

She could barely see over the top of the cream and pink blooms and a stray frond tickled her nose. Carefully, she walked back into the kitchen and placed the basket on the counter. Kurt came out of his old room, looking a bit sheepish.

'Just thought I'd stay out of the way,' he said.

'I see.' She touched the perfect blooms with the tip of her fingers. Their perfume was already beginning to fill the room.

'An admirer?' Kurt asked.

'Maybe . . . ' She could see the card, knew very well who would have sent such an expensive offering. She couldn't deal with that now. She had to hear the rest of Kurt's story.

'Don't you want to know who they're from?' Kurt's voice was teasing.

'Are they from you?' she challenged.

'God, no way. Sorry, I mean — '

'I know what you mean. I'll look at the card later.' In private, she added to herself. I can only deal with one thing at a time. The roses on the counter were an intrusion. She wanted to focus on Kurt's account of the death of Johnny Gunn.

'Do you want to sit outside?' she asked.

She saw him hesitate. 'No one can see the patio,' she added. 'It's well screened.'

'Great. I need to be outdoors. Lead the way.' She carried the fresh cups of coffee and a plate of cookies out to the brick patio. The trellis that shut off the view from the neighbors' yard was thick with dark vine leaves, providing a dappled shade over the chairs and table. The sun was warming the stones, reflecting a welcome heat.

Kurt sank onto a padded lounge with a sigh. 'Not mountain air,' he said, breathing deep, 'but a hell of a lot better than the hospital.'

Maggie picked up her coffee mug again and took a cookie. She'd lost count of how many cups she'd already drunk. The caffeine buzz on top of the lack of sleep was making her lightheaded. Everything was beginning to feel unreal, and looking at Kurt across the table only added to the dreamlike quality of the morning. Never would she have believed she would be sitting on the back deck of her house, talking to Kurt Rainer as if he'd never been away. She needed the whole story so she could figure out how to remove him from her life once more.

'Tell me the rest,' she said. 'How did you get hurt?'

'I was belaying.'

'Holding the rope?'

'That's right. The momentum pulled me over the edge too.'

'So how come the police are looking for you?'

He lay back in the chair and folded his arms across his middle. 'Fortunately the cop who investigated has some common sense. His name's Joe Ventriss. We have a beer together occasionally when I'm working up there. We had a long talk off the record about Johnny's 'accident.' Joe's a good guy, but he likes results. He made me an offer that intrigued me.'

Kurt opened one eye and looked at her. 'You know me,' he said with a wry smile, 'always a sucker for a risk, provided the odds are good. It looked as if someone had tried to frame me — not very well, but the circumstantial evidence pointed to me.'

She listened intently, following the play of emotions on Kurt's face. The shrill ring of the extension bell from the phone jarred her out of her concentration. 'Damn,' she said. 'I won't be a moment. It could be Jeff.'

She took the call in the kitchen, keeping her voice low.

'Hi mom,' Jeff yelled. 'Can you hear me?' There was a din of voices and what sounded like someone beating on a tin tray in the background. 'You'll have to talk louder, mom.' Jeff screamed. 'There's a lot going on here.'

She stuffed one finger into her free ear and held the phone away slightly from the other. She turned away from the open kitchen door.

'How're you doing?' she said loudly.

'I'm fine. Tim threw up after breakfast. I helped him clean it up.'

'Really? That was good of you. Is he sick?'

'Not really. It was kind of my fault. I told him people could survive on worms if they had to. You know, that tribe in South America I read about?'

She cut off the details. 'So, are you having a good time?'

'Great. Hiking today and rock climbing tomorrow. And some kayaking.'

Her heart sank at the images he conjured up. 'Sounds great. Be careful. How's the food?'

'Horrible. It's barf in a bun at lunch today,' Jeff said cheerfully.

'Sounds good to me.'

'Gotta go, mom. We've just finished the dishes.'

She refrained from asking how many were still intact. 'Good to hear from you. Call me again?' she said, not wanting the contact to end.

'I don't expect so. The other guys say it's wimpy to call your mom, so I snuck away just this once. Probably won't do it again.'

'I see. I appreciate it. Love you.'

'Yeah. Say hi to Roger.'

She stood for a moment listening to the dial tone, then hung up the phone. Her heart swelled with love for this cheerful, adventurous boy who had filled her life with such joy despite the emotional pain of the early years. It was as if the four males in her life stood around the kitchen like ghosts as she summoned the courage to return outside. Jeff's voice hung in her mind. She'd opened the box of her dead husband's clothes for the first time in six years. Roger had sent her beautiful roses, and Kurt, the suspected murderer, Jeff's real father, was sitting sipping coffee on her patio. Just another wonderful day in the neighborhood! She sighed and pressed her eyelids with thumb and forefinger. She needed some time to digest the story of Johnny Gunn's murder.

When she stepped out onto the patio, Kurt was lying back, eyes closed, letting the sun play on his face. She watched him for a moment. She hadn't heard the whole truth yet. His story matched what she had read in the paper, more or less. But he still hadn't revealed why the police had called and where the wound in his side came from.

She leaned against the wall, feeling the rough wood under her shoulder blades.

'What else is there to tell?'

'I agreed to work with Joe, that's all.'

'Tell me.'

'I gave my word to keep it under cover.'

Maggie took a step forward so she was standing over him. He looked up at her with that same grin he used when he was telling her the curfew didn't matter and he could sneak her back home without her mom waking up.

'I need to know why I'm sticking my neck out for you,' she said.

He hoisted his body a little higher in the lounge chair. The grin faded. 'Sure, Maggie. I appreciate your help. But if you want me to leave . . . ' he swung his legs to the ground.

'I let you stay last night, but I need to know what's going on. Why are the police looking for you?'

'It's a bit of a long story — '

Maggie pulled over a chair and sat. 'Tell me,' she repeated.

Kurt sighed and rubbed his face with his open hands. 'Did I say Joe was smart and devious? His nose was telling him there was something wrong, but he needed time to probe further without the spotlight on the investigation. He asked me to go along with the story in the paper. Of course, he could have taken me in anyway, but he likes to observe the niceties, so he asked first. Joe could do his thing in peace and unobserved.'

'So it was all make believe?' Kurt nodded. 'Some of it. Look, Maggie, I want to contact Joe, let him know I'm here. Check out what I can tell you. Can I use your phone?'

'Do I have a choice?'

'Of course you do.' He looked her straight in the eyes. 'You always had a choice as far as I was concerned.'

★   ★   ★

She felt the hot flush rise up to her face and stood hurriedly, casting around for a reason to leave. 'I need some groceries,' she said. 'If you're going to stay . . . '

'Thanks,' he said. 'Just a couple of days.'

'No more,' she replied and turned back into the house. The kitchen was filled with the scent of the roses. She grabbed her keys from the hook by the door and snatched her purse as she raced by. She felt as if it was difficult to breathe in the atmosphere of the house. Conflicting memories and loyalties tugged her in every direction. She would drive around a bit, pick up some supplies, maybe take a few photographs.

Did she trust him? Her thoughts swirled in her head. Jeff, Steve, Roger, Kurt. Jeff was her priority. He was the only one who mattered. Whatever she did had to be right for him.

★　★　★

The front door closed with a muffled thud, and Kurt moved to the bedroom window to watch her leave. He winced as she ground the gears, and the engine coughed and groaned. Why did she drive such an old wreck? Surely she earned enough now to get a better set of wheels? Wasn't there any family money left?

He'd like to find out just what was going on in her life — would like to know what Romeo sent the great heap of roses in the kitchen. Of course they had to be from some man. Was she involved with someone? The surge of jealousy that had gripped his gut had been totally unreasonable and caught him by surprise. She'd looked flustered unloading the armful onto the counter, the color staining her cheeks. He knew that look. Whenever she was hiding something, or embarrassed, she would duck her head just so and avoid looking you in the eye. She'd always been a poor liar.

His eyes strayed to the photo of Maggie

and her family on the dresser. That innate integrity was what had made it so difficult for her. She'd been uptight, afraid of embarrassing them all, especially when she was still in High School. Kurt of course was already working for his dad and getting himself a reputation. He was the 'no-good' son who preferred living wild rather than cooperate with his workaholic father. He collected traffic fines like confetti. Anything to rebel against authority.

She'd met him by knocking him off his motorcycle. She'd only had her license a week and she'd turned seventeen a month before. Of course, his family and hers hadn't run in the same circles, his dad's cantankerous, solitary nature saw to that. He'd seen her around before he'd left school, but she'd been just a kid. She'd changed. He chuckled to himself at the memory of her.

She'd run out of her car, her hair all windblown, her face pale with shock, her eyes wide with fear and apprehension. And he'd sprawled ingloriously in the road, beside the bike he'd bought himself for his twentieth birthday, because no one except Oma would ever give him a birthday present. He didn't know what bothered him the most, the damage to the bike or to his pride.

She'd taken the blame for the accident,

obviously relieved that he'd only a few scrapes to show for the encounter. Anyone who'd heard about the mishap would have nodded wisely and muttered about 'that dammed Rainer hot head.' She'd kept it quiet. That's how it had started, and soon she was sneaking out to meet him, spending as much time as possible with him.

Kurt picked up the photo and looked closely at the group. There was Phil, her brother, standing with that furtive expression on his face. He was part of the problem. Funny that both Maggie and he should have such a poor excuse for a brother. Just shows you some of it is in nature. Maggie's parents had been great people. If people thought Kurt was bad, Phil was a disaster. A horrible embarrassment to his family. Kurt was wild, but Phil was downright dishonest.

Maggie didn't want to cause her parents any more grief, and Kurt, who loved her, understood that. He'd wanted her so much, but he'd waited for her, patiently. About the only thing he'd been willing to wait for. He closed his eyes, his fingers tightening on the photo frame, while memories flashed through him, each one searingly vivid. They gripped his heart, squeezing it with an almost physical pain. The first time they made love. They'd been so young. He lay back on the bed, one arm over his eyes. The memory was going to unroll like a film in his mind's eye. There was nothing he could do to stop it. Kurt watched the pictures flowing one after the other as if projected on his closed eyelids.

Every detail of the hike on a lonely trail on a perfect, warm day was etched on his memory. Maggie was wearing flowered shorts that showed her long, lean legs, and a loose blouse that gave tantalizing glimpses of whiter skin at the tops of her breasts. He'd been glad to walk in front most of the way, avoiding having to let his eyes dwell on the temptation. Mind you, his imagination hadn't quit.

She was due to start college the next week, and he'd acted wilder than usual to make her laugh, all the time trying to hide his dread of the misery and loneliness that would be his once she was gone.

He could feel his arms round her, tendrils of her hair blowing across his face. She'd given herself to him at last. Clothes melted away, his hands explored her skin, venturing into unknown lands. She'd smoothed the contours of his body, feeling him with her fingertips, sending quivers of agony down his back and thighs. His problems with his father, the disappointment at not continuing his education, the hatred of the monotonous work he did, all ceased to exist. He lost himself in the touch of her skin, the heat of her hands, the exquisite taste of her mouth.

After that first time he'd made her wait, secretly terrified of possible results of their coupling. He'd not expected to need protection on a mountain hike, after she'd resisted him for so long. She'd reassured him, been the strong one. And they'd been lucky, that time. From then on, his universe had changed. It was as if she'd given him the world on a golden platter. She'd been wonderful. He'd walked on air for days, knew he could conquer mountains. She started college, but they lived for each other, seeking each other's company at every possible moment. They'd had such plans!

He sat up on the rumpled bed and groaned as he recalled his promise to love her forever, never to hurt her.

She never knew, but while she was away, he'd enrolled in a correspondence course, planning to graduate too and surprise her with his education and his intelligence and his ability to earn a decent living. And then came the great blow up with his father, and Maggie's refusal to follow him.

Kurt let out his breath in a long sigh and stood up, still gripping the family picture. Carefully he replaced it beside the others. He rubbed a hand around the back of his neck, trying to relieve the tension, deliberately relaxing the tight muscles. He felt tired and drained.

There was just one other photograph in a matching silver frame. Just Maggie and the boy. Surely there should be more? Where were the pictures of Steve? Strange she wouldn't have a family group. She'd married Steve. 'Stevel the weasel,' Kurt used to call him. Not very kind. Good looking kid of course. Always under big brother's feet when he was little. Whining after him, wanting to do what he did, dressing like him. He was even willing to wear hand-me-downs if Kurt had worn them first. Strange kid, indeed. And now he was dead.

Kurt moved away from the photos with a shrug, tugged at the bed covers to straighten them, and returned to the patio. No point in dwelling on the past. He should stop the masochistic indulgence before it got started. He knew what it did to him.

The restlessness rippled through him. He felt twitchy, on edge. The inactivity was getting to him. He stuffed two cookies into his mouth and carried his cup back inside. First he had to use the phone.

Joe's message came on after only two rings. The policeman wasn't in the office, so Kurt left Maggie's number, hoping that Joe would be the only one to listen to the voice mail.

Kurt stretched his good arm above his head and tried a few shoulder rolls. God, he was stiffening up. But he was feeling a lot better, nearly normal unless he moved too fast. What was he going to do with himself while he was waiting for Joe to call and Maggie to come back? Waiting around for other people was damned frustrating. He paced back through the house.

At the door to Maggie's bedroom again, he stopped and looked around, drinking in everything in sight — the bed where he'd slept on her sheets, the chair under the window, the dresser with the two framed photographs. Her perfume hung in the air. Why torment himself with the unattainable? Thinking about their love in the past was no use to anyone. He would get out of her bedroom right now, out of her life again tomorrow. He turned back to the cupboard under the stairs and hauled out the vacuum cleaner. At least he could make his old room habitable.

At two-thirty, his old quarters as clean as necessary, there was still no sign of Maggie. Maybe the old clunker had broken down. If so, who would she call? Not good ol' Kurt. Probably the roses guy. He paced into the living room and contemplated some more of the photographs that must be Maggie's work. She'd left this morning with a camera bag slung over one shoulder, so it looked to be more than a hobby. Back in the kitchen, he opened the refrigerator and contemplated shelves bare of all but milk, juice and a few staples. 'You did need to shop,' he muttered, closing the door.

He paced back once again through the house and hesitated at the door of the living room. Remembering the old days had left him curious and unsettled. She surely had some pictures of those times. Although it was like being unable to resist probing a sore tooth, he could torture himself a bit more by looking at scenes of his youth. He poured another cup of stale coffee, took the last cookie, and sank onto the couch in the living room. Idly, he reached for one of the albums stacked on a side table.

Kurt turned to the back of the album and began to flick through the pages from the end. There were recent shots of a boy of about twelve, obviously posed by a school photographer, interspersed with others taken on the beach, at a baseball field, by a lake. Kurt checked the label on the spine. 'The Rainers,' it said. He turned back to the last portrait and therefore the most recent, and looked at it carefully. So this was Steve's son,

Jeff, the nephew he had yet to meet. The family resemblance was strong. The Rainer cheekbones and straight nose combined with a mouth like Maggie's. The boy had blue eyes under strong brows. His hair was dark too. He'd obviously missed out on Steve's red or Maggie's fairness. He was a good-looking boy, strong and athletic.

What would it be like to have a kid like that, he thought? What would he do with such a responsibility? Would he know how to handle it, or would he blow it from the start like his own father had done? What did he know about bringing up a boy properly? God knows, Kurt Rainer, senior, had been no role model.

No, he'd decided long ago fatherhood was not for him. He'd be the last of the Rainers because he could never risk making another child as unhappy as he'd been. But a nephew was different. Maybe he could learn about dealing with a growing child. Maybe Maggie would let him get to know the boy, take him up in the mountains, do some backpacking, teach him about the wilderness. He'd like that.

He continued turning the pages backwards and saw the boy getting younger in the pictures, as if he were traveling backwards in time. About half way through, Steve appeared. The boy looked to be about six. Maggie was in a few of the shots, looking thinner and tired. What was going on to make her lose all her radiance? Is that what marriage and motherhood did? Kurt gulped some more coffee and then flipped several pages, arriving closer to the front of the album. Maybe it made more sense to start at the first page. He resettled the book on his knees and opened the cover. There was a wedding picture at the beginning, with Steve smiling like the cat that caught the canary. It was hard to read Maggie's expression. Everyone else looked happy enough.

Only one page later, there were Maggie, Steve, and a fat baby with a dopey grin. What, no honeymoon souvenirs? More than enough pictures of the little guy followed, all neatly labeled with date and place. Kurt's hand froze over a portrait of Jeff, aged three months.

5

Kurt flipped backwards through the pages again to the wedding, checking the captions. Honest Maggie. She couldn't hide anything, even the fact that Jeff was born seven months after her marriage to Steve. What had she told him? Was the baby premature? He didn't look like a preemie, although all newborns have that skinned-rabbit look. What did a guy like Kurt know about babies? Not much, except they normally took nine months.

His hand trembled as he smoothed the pictures on the page. What was he thinking? They'd made love desperately, wildly just before he left. Maggie had clung to him, sobbing her pain and fear because of the car crash and worried sick about her parents. He'd been almost out of his mind with rage because of his father. All they had in the world was each other. Was it possible? Was the child his?

His mind went back to those last days they'd been together with Maggie so distraught about the accident that sent her parents to the hospital in critical condition. What had happened to them? Had her mom and dad survived? What a jerk he'd been not even to ask her how they were.

Right at the time of the crash, his own father accused him of stealing from the company, wouldn't listen, even took the shotgun to him. That was the last straw. He had to leave. And Maggie wouldn't go with him because of her family. At that instant he knew he hated all families. That last night as they lay together, she'd begged him to understand. But he wouldn't. All he could see was the blazing injustice, the years of never measuring up to what his dad wanted. She whispered that she loved him, she'd wait, so he'd believed her, written to her, tried to call several times after he left. She didn't answer his calls, returned most of his letters unopened, until after a while, his pride wouldn't let him try any more.

Was she left with a child? No, she would've told him. She would've found some way to let him know. Wouldn't she? But suppose Jeff wasn't his? Suppose he was Steve's as the captions said? If everyone believed he was Steve's kid . . .

Kurt moistened his lips, reached for the coffee cup again. He put it down with a grimace of disgust at the cold dregs. He wanted to confront her. He wanted to grab hold of her, look her straight in the eyes, and make her tell him that she wasn't bringing up his son to believe another man was his father.

He took a deep breath and leaned back against the soft cushions of the couch. He had to rein in his impatience and his suspicions. If she told him, he wanted her to do it on her own. How would she feel towards him if he forced it out of her against her will? He would make her *want* to confide in him. He would play it cool, recreate the atmosphere of long ago, when they melted into each others' arms as soon as they saw each other. He could do it. He'd follow his instincts — he'd learned to trust them in the wilderness. He began to plan for Maggie's return.

★ ★ ★

Maggie reached the beach and stood for a moment on the populated stretch of soft sand near the parking lot, watching the children splashing in the shallows and building sand castles that would soon be washed away by the incoming tide. Was she like one of those laboriously fashioned constructions, so carefully made and patted into place only to be broken down and easily destroyed?

The arrival of Kurt Rainer and all the emotions that he evoked threatened the underpinnings of her life, so painfully put together over the years. She turned her back on the families enjoying the day together and walked through the woods, climbing up and then down again as she neared her goal. A final scramble over some rocks brought her to a narrow beach, screened by gracefully curved, red-skinned madrona trees with shiny, dark-green leaves, far enough from the main path to deter carriers of picnic chests and folding chairs. This was her favorite refuge. She knew the solitude would soothe her soul.

She sat on a sun-bleached log, listening to the beating of the waves and letting the breeze ruffle her hair. Some gulls fought over a piece of food, and the victor bore away the prize. Slipping off her sandals, she pushed her toes into the damp sand. The equipment bag sat next to her with her precious Canon, a good selection of filters and rolls of film. With a sigh, she took the camera out and started to frame some shots of water, rocks, and wild grasses. Soon she became absorbed in the work of composing, adding a polarizing filter as the glare increased, needing to soften the shadows and define the clouds.

Just as her shoulders were beginning to ache from holding up the camera and her thigh muscles protested at the prolonged crouch, a movement high in the trees caught her eye. She straightened and watched as a full-grown eagle stretched its wings and took off over the water. Instinctively, she lifted the camera, widened the aperture and increased the shutter speed to catch the motion. Snapping one quick shot after another, she homed in on the eagle, following it along and away as it dipped and soared, rising into a climb until she could see it no more.

Exhilarated, she returned to her log to pack her camera away, satisfied with the fitting climax, savoring the glorious moment, the sense of power and freedom the eagle had portrayed. The photo excursion might have begun with a vision of crumbling sandcastles, but it finished with the certainty of empowerment.

While her hands busied themselves with the sorting and packing of her equipment, she made a mental list of her options. Was it right to conceal from Kurt that he was Jeff's father? Objectively, she knew he had the right to know. Yet the nagging voice of doubt persisted. Being acknowledged as Jeff's father meant more than a simple statement of fact. What would he do if she told him? Would he shrug in indifference, use her house as a hideout for as long as he chose, and then disappear from her life and Jeff's again? She didn't think she could bear his rejection a second time.

On the other hand, supposing he was overjoyed to know he had a son? Supposing he wanted to meet him, share in his upbringing, write to him from prison?

Her fingers paused in their work. That was the problem. Had he had a hand in Johnny Gunn's murder? She couldn't provide her son with an accused killer for a father. She had to get him to tell her the rest of the story, maybe wait until the drama played out, so she could judge whether or not she could trust him with her boy.

It was late afternoon when she swung by the supermarket. The bank of telephones stood accusingly by the front entrance. Roger would be wondering if she'd received the flowers. She could have called from the house, but the possibility of Kurt overhearing the conversation made her feel awkward. Was she hiding Kurt from Roger or was it the other way around? Was she not wanting Kurt to know that she was nurturing a relationship with another man?

Defiantly, she stuck a coin in the slot and dialed, closing her eyes in relief when his message machine came on immediately. Feeling a ridiculous sense of reprieve, she thanked him, hoping it sounded sufficiently sincere, knowing she was only deferring matters. He would be certain to call back.

She was wheeling a shopping cart towards the checkout when she met Ellen, making for the dairy case. Her friend greeted her with a wide grin.

'Maggie, hi there. Gotta get milk. Have you heard from Jeff?'

'Yes, he's fine. Having a great time.'

'So what are you doing with yourself?' Ellen looked down into the cart. 'Wow,' she said. 'Sorry,' she apologized, 'but that's a lot of stuff. You'll be eating well.'

Maggie wished she had hidden the steak, fruit, and vegetables more carefully under the bags of milk. She adjusted the bread and rolls over the giant box of cereal. 'Just taking the chance to stock up,' she said casually. 'While Jeff's away, and I have the time.'

'Sure,' Ellen looked at her curiously but refrained from comment. 'Good idea. Thought maybe Roger was coming to dinner. Is someone hurt?' Ellen never let discretion stifle her curiosity.

Maggie glanced down at the package of bandages, the antibiotic cream, and the tape. Ellen's eyes were too sharp by far. 'No, my first aid kit got a bit low.'

Ellen nodded. 'Look,' she went on,

'Jennifer goes to camp next week. Shall we go for lunch?'

'I'd like that, but I'm not sure what — '

'Don't worry. I'll give you a call. Got to run.' With a cheerful wave of her hand, Ellen turned towards the doors of the market.

Maggie stacked the plastic bags in the back of the car and slid behind the wheel. Ellen thought Roger was coming to dinner. She noticed the first aid supplies. One small deception was leading to another. Maggie decided she was not cut out for a life on the run. No one could know Kurt was with her, so Roger couldn't possibly come to dinner, at least not until Kurt was gone. At least she'd called and thanked him for the flowers.

She turned the key and revved the motor and sighed as smoke poured out of the exhaust pipe. Only a few more months until her commitments were done, Phil was settled and she could think about saving for a new car. Her whole life was lived according to a series of due dates. So long before this or that happened! The first mark on her mental calendar was Kurt's departure. She'd said two days and meant it. With Kurt gone, she'd feel free to see Roger, pick up where they'd left a promising relationship.

Maggie drove carefully back to the house, observing all the speed limits and stop signs.

Not that she wouldn't always be careful, but she couldn't afford an accident or any interest from the police. She hated the situation Kurt was placing her in.

As she drew closer to the house, her mood began to change. The idea that Kurt was there waiting made her heart beat faster. All those years ago they'd talked constantly about living together, about spending every night under the same roof, in the same bed. She pulled back from that thought. The same roof now, maybe, but only from necessity. He would be there now when she arrived, would glance up as she came in, would take the groceries from her. He would stand close as she put them away . . .

★   ★   ★

There was no sign of life around the house when she pulled into the driveway. The sun was lower now, casting long, purple shadows over the path and the front of the house. She slung her camera round her neck, looped the handles of the shopping bags over her fingers, and trudged up to the door. Dumping the bags on the floor, she put her key in the lock and hesitated. Maybe Kurt was sleeping? Maybe his wound had started to bleed again? She shouldn't have stayed away so long — he might have needed her. She shook herself. Like hell he needed her. Not twelve years ago and not now. She pushed open the door and grabbed the bags.

The house was cool and dim. Soft music was playing from the stereo in the living room and a delicious smell of garlic and tomato sauce wafted from the kitchen.

Kurt popped his head round the kitchen door and waved a spoon at her. He looked very warm and decidedly ridiculous in a flowered apron. A streak of red stood out on his tanned cheek like a wound.

Maggie lugged her purchases into the kitchen and caught the scent of pine cleaner over the aroma of whatever was cooking. Kurt had limped over to the stove by the time she unburdened herself and turned towards him again. He was busy stirring something in the pot with the spoon. Suddenly, she realized she hadn't eaten since the coffee and cookies that morning, and she was ravenous. Her stomach rumbled to prove it.

Kurt put down the spoon and untied the apron. 'Glad you're back,' he said, and reached for a wine glass. Carefully, he poured a measure of red wine from an open bottle and presented it with a flourish. 'Madam,' he said, and gave a little bow.

She took hold of the stem of the glass and

brought it to her lips. 'Thank you. What have you been doing in my kitchen?' she asked with a small laugh.

'Well, let me see.' He pretended to consider carefully. 'After you left seven hours ago to get some groceries, I finished the coffee and all the cookies. Then I rested for ten minutes, then I decided I would go out of my mind without something to do, so I swept the patio.'

Maggie looked out the window. The patio was neat and clean.

'Thank you,' she said again.

He waved an airy hand. 'Then I came indoors and decided that I couldn't take your bed anymore, especially if you weren't going to be in it.' He hurried on, ignoring her movement of protest. 'So I cleaned up my old room.'

Maggie gasped. 'But your side — '

'No problem. All nicely packaged and causing no concern.' He patted the area around his ribs. 'I will admit I leaned heavily on the handle of the vacuum cleaner for support and swallowed a couple more pills. I heal fast. Then ask me what I did next.'

'What did you do next?' She felt her lips twitch at the sight of him, so pleased with his day's work.

'For a while I considered making a missing

person report on you. But no — ' he raised a hand at her indignant movement. 'It could turn into one of those mysteries — ' He assumed a blank face and stiff lips imitating a TV show, ' — ten years ago, a woman left the house for groceries and never returned. Do you recognize this computer-aged photograph?' He allowed his face to relax. 'But I decided to wait a bit longer. That didn't change the fact that I was hungry. You have nothing in your refrigerator.'

She gestured to the grocery bags.

'Too late, woman, too late. Fortunately you have a freezer and a microwave. I found all I needed for a campfire meal.'

'Really?'

'Absolutely. Plus a very dusty bottle of wine.' He raised his glass.

'It must have been left from when Frieda was here.'

'Whatever, it will do. So, milady.' He looked at his watch. 'You have half an hour to dress for dinner.'

Maggie took another sip of the wine and put down the glass. 'There's something I must do first,' she said. 'Come here.'

He stepped very close to her so that she could see the fine lines around his eyes and mouth, could feel the warmth radiating from him, could sense the tautness of his muscles beneath his clothes. She breathed in the strong, masculine scent of him, mingled with the cooking aromas clinging to his shirt. Quickly, she pulled a piece of paper towel from the roll and made a pad in her hand. She cupped his chin with the tips of her fingers and gently wiped the streak of red sauce from his face. 'There,' she said softly. 'That's better.'

He stood for a long moment in front of her, their bodies only inches apart, her face lifted to his. Very slowly she moved her hand from his face and let her arm drop back down to her side. His hands came toward her shoulders and hesitated. She held her breath, not knowing what she would do if he kissed her. He looked steadily into her eyes, a small smile lifting the corner of his mouth as his hands dropped to the camera strap around her neck and lifted the apparatus over her head. He still stood, as if considering something, and then sighed and moved back a step. Maggie let out the breath she was holding. The spell was broken, and she didn't know if she was glad he'd moved away.

'Your bath awaits,' he announced.

'My what?' For the first time, her mind consciously registered the sound of running water mingled with the music and the bubbling of the pot on the stove.

'One moment, madam.' He brushed past her, stepped into the hallway, and opened the door to the bathroom. A cloud of fragrant steam floated out, settling around his head and shoulders. 'Voilà or, as we say in the best hotels, may I wash madam's back?'

She was almost speechless. 'No, thank you,' she blurted. 'I can manage very well on my own. This is — amazing.'

'Amazing, indeed. The man can cook and clean. Quite a prize, eh?'

Before he could expand on that thought, she walked down the hallway to her room. 'This is incredible, but I won't say no. I'll see you in a half hour.'

She didn't hesitate for long about what to wear. Quickly, she selected a long flowered dress with a scoop neck that she'd bought for a party but hardly ever worn. The swirling colors of fuschia and teal would look good against her light tan. She refused to think about exactly why she would care about looking good and hurried out of the room. Kurt was standing at the door of the bathroom, holding her forgotten glass of wine.

'Take it in with you,' he said. 'It will help you relax.'

She lowered her eyes so as not to see his teasing smile and the light in his eyes. She didn't really want to relax around him. She couldn't afford to relax around him. 'Thank you,' she said yet again and closed the door.

He'd laced the water in the tub with a generous helping of the bath oil that Frieda had given her last Christmas. She stripped off her clothes, pinned up her hair, and stepped into the warm softness. She lay back, luxuriating in the scented water, stretching her limbs, and sipping on the wine. All the time, she was conscious of Kurt on the other side of the door, of the meal that awaited them, of the evening that stretched out before them.

★   ★   ★

She brushed her hair so it was lying smooth and shining on her shoulders and touched her mouth and eyes with a little color. Not that she needed much. Her cheeks were glowing, and her eyes had a sparkle that had been missing for a while. But that had nothing to do with Kurt or what was waiting for her on the other side of the door. She was showing the effect of a day in the sun and wind, that was all. Not to mention the glass of wine on an empty stomach!

She frowned at her reflection in the misty mirror. Be careful, she told herself. All her senses were alert, wary of the danger that Kurt represented. He'd taken over her house, her kitchen. No way would she allow him to take over her life again. She took a deep breath, squared her shoulders and stepped out of the bathroom to the kitchen.

'No, this way,' Kurt said. He took her hand and led her to the living room where he had set up a table. The windows were open, allowing in the cooler evening air, but all the shades were lowered. Candles flickering on the table concentrated a pool of light, throwing the corners into mysterious shadow. The whole room became a magical place, offering peace for her mind, food for her body, loving companionship for her soul. Why was she so sure of that last truth?

Kurt's voice interrupted her thoughts. 'Sit here,' he said, gently guiding her with a hand on her shoulder. A shiver went through her at his touch. Her skin was both fiery hot and ice cold where his fingers lingered. Without a word she sat where he indicated and allowed him to pour more wine. She resolved to make this glass last the whole meal and keep all her wits about her this evening.

Kurt placed a plate of food before her and sat down opposite. As if in a dream, she picked up her fork and tasted the dish. Kurt's eyes were on her from across the table, watching as she raised the morsel to her mouth. His gaze lingered on her lips, and she felt them tingle and swell as he watched.

'This is wonderful,' she said, swallowing the first mouthful. 'What did you do?'

Kurt shrugged. 'Just chicken and a few cans of this and that.'

'When did *you* learn to cook?'

'I've learned lots of things over the years, some good, some bad.' He paused. 'When you take a party of tourists out for a week, you have to feed them.' He tasted his own meal. 'Now it's your turn,' he said.

'I couldn't possibly cook like this — '

'No, I meant your turn to fill in some of the gaps.'

She put down her fork and took a sip of wine. Here was the danger flag. What did he suspect? 'Could I have some water too?' she asked.

'Of course.' Kurt sprang to his feet and brought a glass of iced water. 'Your wish is my command,' he said humorously.

'Thank you.' She drank some of the water and put down the glass. He was still watching her expectantly.

'What exactly did you want to know?'

'How you came to marry my brother.' His voice was tight, a hoarse rumble in his throat.

'Steve? Well, Steve was always there.'

'I'll bet he was, the little weasel.'

She saw the taut muscles along his jaw. The candles threw his cheekbones into relief, leaving shadows around his eyes.

'Whatever possessed you to marry him?'

Well, she wanted to say, you weren't there, were you? And I was pregnant and the local minister's daughter. And I had disobeyed my parents and flouted every rule in their book with you for years. Dad and mother were recovering from the car crash. There was no word from you. How could I give them that news as well?

'Steve was very good to me after you left,' she said carefully. 'He was there for me. He helped me a great deal while mom and dad were recuperating.'

Kurt had the grace to look a little shamefaced. 'How are they?' he asked.

'Dad died about ten years ago. He never really recovered from the crash and my mother followed him a year and a half later. I don't think she knew how to live without him.' She bit her lip at the memory of the pain and loss of those years.

'I'm sorry,' he said and squeezed her fingers. She withdrew her hand, unable to trust herself not to clutch at his fingers and blurt out the whole story.

'And you had your son,' he said.

She nodded. 'Jeff.'

He looked at her closely. 'So I'm an uncle. What does he like?'

She wanted to leap up and run from the room. How could she answer these questions? She pressed her feet to the floor, forcing herself to remain calm and stay in her chair. 'He's a normal boy. He likes sports, the outdoors.' Her jaw ached with the effort to stop the betraying quiver of her lips.

'Not like his father.'

She raised her eyes to his face in surprise. He was leaning back in his chair, turning the stem of his wine glass. 'Steve wasn't exactly an athlete.'

'Maybe not.' When would he stop this torture?

He sat forward and leaned over the table toward her. 'I didn't know he died,' he said softly.

She nodded. 'A plane crash. He flew his own plane.' Now she could let her mouth tremble, allow the tears to gather.

'The news was a shock. I'm sorry to hear it. So, you were happy with him?'

'What do you think?'

Kurt was silent for a moment. 'I didn't mean to make you cry,' he said. 'I just feel I need to know what's happened since I left.'

'What made you suddenly so interested?'

'Suddenly? I've always been interested. It was never my intent to cut myself off — '

She could stand no more. She thrust her chair back and stood facing him defiantly. 'That's enough with your questions. I've made mistakes in the past like everyone else and some of them I'm not proud of. Can't you see what you're doing to me? I'm no masochist, Kurt. I take no pleasure in opening old wounds. Just do what you have to do and get out of my life.'

'Well, that's blunt enough. You'll be pleased to know I called Joe.'

For a moment she couldn't think who he meant or what it had to do with them both.

'Joe's the police officer I told you about.'

'Yes, the one who connived with you to spread a false story.'

He let that go. 'I need to go back. Joe's made progress. I'll leave tomorrow.'

Suddenly her heart was empty at the thought of him really going away.

'As you please.'

'I want to ask you one thing.'

'Yes?'

'I would like to see Oma. Will you take me? Later tonight?'

★　★　★

The restlessness was back, competing with the drip of corrosive anger at his own clumsiness. It drove Kurt outside to wait for Maggie while she changed out of the dress she'd worn for supper. He paced to and fro, unable to rid his mind of the recent images.

He'd set it all up pretty well, music, subdued lighting, wine, and food — it was all there. Of course he wanted to get to the truth, but he'd thought about what would please her, shoving his impatience to one side. He'd been sure the evening would go according to his plan.

When she'd come out of the bathroom, her hair all silky and shining, his mouth had gone dry and his stomach tightened at the sight of her. The colors of the dress she wore blended and merged like an impressionist painting in the candlelight, and the scoop neckline showed a glimpse of the swell of her breasts. He'd caught a trace of the scent of the bath oil as she moved towards him. He could imagine what it had done to her smooth, sun-warmed skin. He'd had trouble stopping himself from folding her in his arms, covering her face and eyes with kisses. Later, he'd promised himself, later.

Dream on! he thought, bitterly. He'd started off fine and then blown the whole thing by pushing too hard. He hadn't expected the twist in his gut, the urge to ask the all-important question about the boy. He'd rushed in like some damned tourist trying to get close to a wild animal. She'd taken fright, like a fawn, and raced for cover. He sure wasn't going to learn much more tonight, he decided, kicking a stray stone back to the edge of the path. He was mad with himself, mad with Maggie for the secrets he suspected she was hiding, mad with the whole situation.

He sank onto a wooden bench under a tree, but only seconds later sprang back up. He couldn't settle. Since gentle persuasion hadn't worked, maybe he should try direct confrontation. After all, that was more his style. He didn't know any more how to handle this. He wasn't used to hesitating, wondering. In his job, he just took care of things, no matter what. Things were usually pretty straight forward, you followed good procedures, solved the problems with well-tried solutions.

He strode down the gravel path, out to the road and back, listening to the crunch of his footsteps and the faint sounds of the neighborhood. There were many things to do, decisions to make about the future. One, clear his name of the suspicions around the Johnny Gunn murder. Then he would find out if Jeff was his son. To do that, he would need Maggie's trust and cooperation. Not much unnerved him, but figuring out how to get to that point scared the daylights out of him. One thing he did know — this was turning out to be damned important, more important than some of the other plans he'd been toying with.

Kurt stopped by the car and stood with his arms folded. How long did it take a woman to change anyhow? Had he been a rogue male in the bush too long to remember such details? Maybe it was time for him to return to civilization. Suddenly, he saw a large, white smear on the windshield, where a bird had left its opinion of the whole mess.

He grimaced in distaste. 'I'm with you, buddy,' he said and turned back into the house for something to clean it off. It would fill the minutes until she deigned to appear.

He met Maggie in the front hall. She'd put on dark slacks and a black cotton wind-breaker.

He tried for an easy grin. 'You look ready for a commando raid,' he said, reaching for some levity to break the tension. 'All you need is a mask.'

She rolled her eyes, pointedly ignored his comment, and moved on toward the door.

'Just a moment,' he called. 'We need some cleaner.'

'What — ?' she began, turning back. Then she shrugged and continued on her way.

'Well, make it quick,' she said over her shoulder. Kurt opened his mouth to protest and then shrugged and continued on his way.

He made a quick job of the one handed clean-up while she stood in silence by the driver's door. The hostility vibrated from her in waves he could almost touch. Maybe he did need to get out of there as soon as possible. But then what?

When the windshield was clean, she climbed into the car.

'I'll drive,' she said.

'Fine'

He recognized her need to feel in control of something, to have a reason for not looking at him or speaking. Most likely she resented the hell out of him for calling the shots on the agenda since he arrived. He had coerced her into helping, made fun of her, tried to manipulate her into opening up to him about her marriage. *So, sue me,* he thought. What was a guy supposed to do when he was used to running things his way, being in charge.

Kurt cleared his throat and settled more comfortably in his seat. A stab in his side reminded him he should change the dressing

126

on the knife wound. Later. If he was honest about it, it was clear that at this moment he needed to try and mend some fences. He'd learned patience and careful planning. Time to put those skills to use in his personal life as well as on the job. After all, he did care about Maggie, did want to know about the boy. He would just have to find another way to get her to tell him.

'Thanks for agreeing to take me to see Oma,' he started. That was surely a safe remark.

She gave a kind of grunt in reply.

He needed to risk a bit more. 'I didn't mean to upset you,' he continued. Still nothing. He tried again. 'I didn't realize how many losses there were in your life. Your parents, Steve . . . '

Her eyes were fixed on the road, her hands tight on the wheel.

'What about Phil?' he asked. He prayed her brother was a good choice of subject, that Phil was still healthy and functioning.

To his relief, she spoke at last. 'Phil's still around. Still trying to beat the system.'

'How's that?'

She changed gear with a scraping noise. 'It's a long story. He still has debts to pay off.'

'Are you helping him?' He knew the answer to the question before she replied.

'A bit.'

Kurt sighed. 'A bit' most likely meant 'a lot.' So that was why she was driving this wreck and her furniture looked like something from the Goodwill store. 'Still bailing him out, eh?'

'Phil's family,' she replied stiffly. 'In a family, there are no disposable people.'

How about that for a cliché? he thought. 'Generally speaking, I don't share your faith in families,' he said, leaning an elbow on the window ledge. 'Seems to me, the less one sees of one's relatives the better.'

She glanced at him, and he saw her nod, as if in confirmation of a thought. 'You've made that clear.' Her voice was cold and distant.

'Well, I'm not that bad. I do care about Oma — and I would like to get to know my nephew,' he offered, kicking himself for sounding too harsh.

'Jeff won't be back for two more weeks. You'll be long gone by then.' Her tone indicated the end of the discussion. She maneuvered into a parking space in front of the residence. 'We're here. We shouldn't run into anyone.'

6

Just as Maggie and Kurt approached the wood and glass door of the entrance, two figures emerged, a man and a woman.

The girl was a stunner, with a cap of sleek, dark hair and a petulant expression. The light from the foyer shone full on them both as they came out.

'Damn,' Kurt muttered under his breath. It was too late to pretend they weren't going into the building. No choice but to brazen it out.

'Good evening, Dianna,' Maggie said brightly. 'You're late going off shift. Everything okay?'

'I was talking to Mrs. Haydon,' Dianna answered. Kurt realized from the ugly set of her mouth and her frown that she wasn't just petulant, but downright angry. He was getting more exposure to female fury than he ever wanted.

'I see.' Maggie glanced at the girl's companion who stood by her side. The man had not spoken but was looking curiously at Kurt. Suddenly he grinned.

'It's Kurt Rainer,' he said. 'Thought I knew

you. Couldn't place you for a minute. How're you doing? Long time, no see.' He grabbed Kurt's hand and pumped it vigorously. 'We played football together,' he said. 'Remember me? Dave, Dave Hirsch.'

'Of course,' Kurt answered. 'Good to see you. How are you, Dave?' Of all people to run into, it had to be a guy who'd been around all through his school years — and who probably recalled all the escapades etched into the town's collective memory.

'Doing great,' Dave answered. 'I'm in real estate and looking to settle down any day now.' He put an arm round the girl, who stiffened and moved away.

Dave seemed not to register her coolness. 'Dianna, sweetheart, this is an old school buddy of mine, Kurt Rainer.'

The girl looked up with interest. Almost immediately, she seemed to perk up and gave Kurt a seductive smile. He smiled back. She had eyes like a cat, large and almond-shaped.

'Really?' she said. 'I'm very pleased to meet you.' Her angry mood seemed to have dissipated, and she now was sweetness and charm.

Dave slapped Kurt on the shoulder. 'Now that you're back, we'll get together and catch up over a beer,' he said enthusiastically. 'I'm in the book.'

'Sounds good, but I'm leaving tomorrow,' Kurt answered. 'Give me a raincheck on that,' he added as cheerfully as he could. Damn, he didn't need an old school chum to put two and two together before he made it back to Joe.

They met no one else as Maggie led Kurt down the brightly-lit, silent corridors of the residence. Sounds of music and TV shows filtered from behind some closed doors. Most of the old people had tacked flowers, a plaque or a picture to their door in an attempt to provide a personal touch. She strode quickly, anxious to get this over. She'd seen how he'd responded to Dianna's smile. Not two hours ago, he'd been trying to charm her, wanting to worm every part of the last twelve years from her. He was still fickle and unreliable. She couldn't wait for life to get back to normal.

Frieda occupied two rooms on the second floor. She was waiting for them, wrapped in her green and red shawl, comfortably established in a padded rocking chair.

She stretched out her thin hands at the sight of Kurt and drew him to her. Her eyes scanned his features, and she put out her fingers to lightly trace the planes of his face.

Without a word, he buried his head on her shoulder, and she gently patted his back like a small child. 'My boy, my boy,' she crooned. 'You're back at last.'

Maggie cleared her throat, feeling like an intruder on the reunion. Seeing the love between the old lady and the powerful man made her uncomfortable. Tears pricked at the back of her eyes, hot and salty.

'I'll just check in the office,' she said. 'Be back in a few minutes.' She retreated before either Frieda or Kurt could protest, asking her to stay.

In her office, she read a few messages that had come in that day, wrote herself a couple of notes, and straightened the objects on her desk that were already neatly arranged.

She stepped to the window and looked out over the dark lawns to the metallic gray sheen of the water. A slim moon gave just enough light for her to make out the shape of the gazebo. It was only a few days since Frieda gave her the news about Kurt, but she'd lived on an exhausting roller-coaster of emotions since then. She still hadn't developed the pictures from that day, nor from the trip to deliver Jeff to camp. Kurt would be gone tomorrow. Then she would fill the emptiness with work in the darkroom.

She sighed and glanced at her watch. Fifteen minutes. Was that enough? Better give them a bit longer.

Twenty minutes later, her files checked, her drawers tidied yet again, Maggie made her way back to Frieda's small apartment. Kurt was standing in the open doorway, saying goodbye. He turned as she approached and visibly squared his shoulders.

'It's good to see her again,' he said, with a break in his low voice. 'She wants to speak to you. I'll walk around outside.'

Maggie found Frieda wiping her eyes with a delicate handkerchief. The scent of lavender wafted in the still air. 'Thank you for helping him,' the old lady said. 'He told me what you've done for him. You're a good girl.'

Maggie thought guiltily of her comment to Kurt about doing the same for a wounded dog.

Before she could find a suitably noncommittal response, Frieda tucked away the scrap of lace, continuing to talk.

'He'll get all this sorted out in no time,' she said, readjusting her shawl. 'Then he can think about that wonderful job offer he got. Just help me up, dear. I'm all ready for bed.'

Maggie gave her an arm, and they moved towards the bedroom. What job offer?

'So I've given him the key,' Frieda went on.

'What key?' Maggie asked, steering the old lady towards the bed.

'To the cabin of course. You remember the

family cabin, don't you?'

'Yes, yes, I do.' Maggie remembered it mainly for some delightful afternoon hours she and Kurt had spent there, hidden away from everyone. Another place she was now careful to avoid.

'So he can come back whenever he wants,' Frieda said.

Great! Despite the sinking feeling, she smiled at Frieda's obvious pleasure.

'But that wasn't what I wanted to talk to you about,' Frieda said, settling back against the pillows. Maggie pulled the comforter over her and smoothed it out.

'You have to speak to Roger Saint George about Dianna.'

'Dianna? What's the matter?'

'She has to go. That young lady has been extracting money from people. I've been watching and I'm sure.'

'Extracting? What does that mean?'

'Basically, blackmail. Threats. Here,' she thrust a package of papers at Maggie. 'It's all here. I've already spoken to her, so she knows what's coming.'

'I can't believe — What did she say?' Maggie now understood why Dianna had a face like thunder and was leaving so late.

'She sneered at me. Read this and then give the papers to Roger,' Frieda commanded.

Maggie took the package and thrust it in her pocket. Frieda was dropping too many bombshells on her these days. What was all this about? The last thing a place like Glenhaven needed was confrontation and scandal. She kissed Frieda gently, keeping her misgivings to herself.

'Goodnight,' she said. 'Do you have everything you want?'

'I do now that my grandson's back.'

Maggie moved to the door.

'Read it!' Frieda said sternly.

'Of course. I'll see to everything,' Maggie replied, hoping she sounded reassuring. What on earth did Frieda think she'd found?

She walked quickly back to the front of the building. Flashing lights spun on two police cars parked immediately outside the main entrance doors, sending alternate blue and red beams over the dimly lit foyer. Surely Frieda wouldn't have called them about Dianna, even if she'd had time. Was Frieda's discovery really a police matter? After a moment's hesitation, she strode purposefully toward the door. Whatever they were here for, they needed to turn off the lights before someone raised the alarm and the halls filled with anxious people.

Maggie stepped forward, her mouth open to deal with any questions just in time to see a police officer push Kurt's head down and thrust him into the back of one of the cars. The doors slammed and both vehicles left, spurting gravel from their tires.

★ ★ ★

Maggie drove home in a daze. How had the police known where to find him? Had they been watching the house? No, that made no sense. They would have picked him up right away. Someone had betrayed him, and the only person besides herself and Frieda who knew who Kurt was, was Dianna. She'd taken note of the newspaper that evening in the gazebo. If Frieda had stumbled upon a scheme to defraud people in Glenhaven and then challenged Dianna about it, the girl would have known how to get her revenge. She only had to call the police after running into Maggie and Kurt and pass on the information that the wanted man was in the building.

Now the police knew he was in Branscombe, where would that leave her, she thought, after she'd lied to the two officers? She swung round the corner, vehemently wishing she'd never heard of Kurt Rainer.

She pulled into the driveway, not remembering anything about the road home. The

136

house felt empty, devoid of both Kurt and Jeff. The solitude she'd so looked forward to when Jeff left for camp now hung around her like a wet, clinging fog. She flung her purse on the hall table and made for the kitchen, switching on all the lights as she went. The candles still stood in their saucers in the living room, a mute testimonial to the romantic meal and the feelings that ran like raw nerves just below the surface of the skin.

So he'd been arrested. He'd said he'd contact his friend, the policeman, and probably return to the area where it had all happened. He'd intended to go back, but not like this. He'd claimed he was innocent. Was he? Or was he just a clever prevaricator? His feelings about families hadn't changed. He wouldn't be interested in making a life for Jeff even if he were innocent of the murder charge.

There was a message on the machine from Roger asking her to call him back no matter what time she came home.

She looked at the clock. Ten thirty. She was nervous, on edge, her mind racing, with no taste for talking to Roger tonight. She'd get a good night's sleep if she could and start everything new tomorrow. Then in the morning she'd close up Kurt's room again, leaving his stuff out of sight and put it all out of her mind.

She poured a glass of water and clicked off the light in the kitchen. The phone rang. Roger again? Or a message from the camp about Jeff? For a moment she hesitated, then picked up on the third ring, fearful it might be a message from the camp about Jeff.

'Hello.'

An unknown man's voice answered. 'Hi. Sorry to call so late. Is Doc there?'

'There's no doctor here. You have the wrong number.'

'Hey, no, don't hang up.'

She hesitated.

'You must be Maggie,' the man said. He went on quickly before she could break the connection. 'Sorry if I scared you. You must have thought it was some creep calling at this time of night. I'm Joe, Joe Ventriss. I'm with the police, investigating the Johnny Gunn case.'

Maggie relaxed a little, still unsure of how to deal with this. 'Kurt mentioned you,' she said.

'I wanted to talk to him,' Joe replied.

'You're too late.' Maggie explained what had happened.

Joe gave vent to a couple of expletives. 'I'll get onto the local boys as soon as I can.'

Maggie wanted to ask if Kurt was guilty but feared the answer too much. Instead, she frowned, recalling Joe's greeting.

'Why did you call him Doc?' she asked.

Joe laughed. 'Just a joke between us. Most people up here barely got through high school. Kurt got a doctorate in Environmental Studies — oh, about five years ago. I kid him about it.'

'I see.' More and more she was realizing how much Kurt had grown from the wild young man she'd once known.

'How's he been doing?' Joe asked.

'Pretty well, considering,' she answered. *But I'm a basket case*, she nearly added.

'Well, thanks for everything you did for him. He told me an old friend took him in.'

'Don't go.' She shifted the receiver to the other ear. 'How did he get stabbed?' she asked in a rush.

'Wouldn't tell you, eh? Sounds like Doc,' Joe said. 'It was my fault, I guess. I let it be known he might be involved and maybe had some information about the killer.'

'The killer!'

'Yeah, there is one. Did you think it might be Doc?'

'No, but the newspapers . . . '

'You can't believe everything you read. The perps forgot that too. Someone didn't like the idea that Doc might know too much. They got to him right in the hospital.'

'My god!'

'Well the Doc's got pretty good reflexes, have to have in his kind of job. He moved fast, and they just got his side.'

'*Just*' Maggie thought. Why were men so cavalier about physical danger? 'Who was it?' she asked.

'Don't know for sure. Got a few ideas, though.'

'So whoever it was is still on the loose?'

'They think so. But we'll get them.'

A cold hand clutched at Maggie's heart. 'Will they be sending Kurt back to you? To the same area?' she whispered.

'Yup, 'fraid so,' Joe said. 'That's why we put out the alert. The whole idea was to keep him safe. Don't you worry,' Joe said reassuringly. 'We're working on some good leads, and we'll keep a good eye on him this time. Talk to you later.'

Somehow, Maggie was now reluctant to let go this link with someone who knew Kurt and obviously cared about him. 'Wait. Can I have your number?'

Joe gave the number. Maggie's hand was shaking as she hung up the phone. 'Perps,' 'leads' — what crazy situation had Kurt dragged her into?

But he was innocent — that black cloud was gone. She need have no fear of presenting Jeff with a criminal for a father.

★   ★   ★

The raucous shrieks of two crows brought her abruptly awake the next morning. She peered at the clock. Seven. Much to her surprise, she'd slept long and deeply. She lay for a moment, clearing the fog of sleep from her brain. This was her own bed, her own room. She put the back of one hand over her eyes, resolutely determined not to think of its last occupant. Kurt was gone. Wasn't that what she'd wanted? He'd vanished once more from her life . . .

The hollow feeling in her stomach, the tears that threatened at the back of her eyes, were nothing more than a reaction to the stress of the last few days. She must keep busy, prevent any unproductive musing about the 'might have beens.' Her darkroom was waiting. She would take Ellen up on the suggestion of a lunch date. She'd lots to do, including packing up his things.

Quickly, she summoned up a burst of energy that drove her out of bed, telling herself it was much too nice a day to spend luxuriating between the sheets. She plugged in the coffee maker to perk while she dressed.

The package of papers Frieda had given her about Dianna lay on the kitchen table where she'd tossed them last night. She'd promised to read them. Frieda's last lot of news had led to Kurt. She hoped these would prove easier to deal with as she unfolded the first sheet.

Ten minutes later, she looked up to stare through the window and let her breath out slowly.

Wow, she said to herself. *This is serious stuff*. If Frieda's evidence held water, the girl really *was* extorting money from the residents. Frieda had documented times, dates, even amounts. There were copies of threatening notes with words cut from newspapers. It all sounded highly dramatic and out of character for the quiet town where they all lived. Frieda must have been working on this for weeks. Maggie knew she had to do something about it.

She reached for the phone and dialed Roger's office. His secretary picked up on the second ring.

'Hi, Carol,' Maggie said. 'Is he there?'

'Sure thing, hon. I'll put you through.' But as usual, Carol wanted to chat. 'How're you enjoying your time off?'

How, indeed? 'I'm looking forward to

getting some stuff done. Jeff's enjoying camp.'

'Great, that's great,' Carol said with enthusiasm. 'Roger's here now.'

Roger's deep voice filled her with reassurance. Here was stability, reasonableness. No wounds, physical or emotional, no family baggage, no tearing memories.

'There's a problem we need to deal with,' she said after the usual niceties. 'I can't tell you over the phone. Can I see you today?' She pushed her hair back behind her ear.

'Any time,' he replied. 'I was hoping you'd call. I wanted to ask you — '

He broke off, and she heard his muffled voice responding to Carol. She drank her juice while she waited.

'Sorry about that,' he said. 'I was saying, we never did have that dinner we planned.'

She averted her eyes from the pile of plates waiting to be stacked in the dishwasher from last night. 'No, we didn't.'

'Can we still do it?'

She smiled. 'I think so. Let's talk about it later.'

She stretched her arms over her head and leaned back. She could make her life return to normal again. Roger was still there, like a comfortable security blanket. She could count on him. She giggled silently. How would smooth, sophisticated Roger Saint

George like to be compared to a threadbare blanket, however loved and cherished?

The crows shrieked again as they continued their quarrel outside the window. Yes, everything was back to normal.

★   ★   ★

When she left the house, a tiny bird lay lifeless on the path, right outside the front door. 'Oh no, you poor thing.' Maggie knelt down on the gravel. A movement from over her head made her look up. The two crows sat side by side on a low branch, watching her.

'You did this, didn't you?' she said. 'You're just a pair of bullies. As if you don't have enough to eat.' The silence in the trees meant the other birds were keeping a wary distance.

She fetched some newspaper and gently scooped up the limp little body. The wee thing had never had a chance.

She was supposed to be on vacation, had intended to make a complete break with work, yet here she was driving once again towards Glenhaven. With a sigh, she disposed of the bird's body and pulled out her car keys.

The poor old car clunked and shuddered as she carefully pressed the accelerator to keep the engine going. Only a few more months, and Phil's debts would be cleared. She promised herself one of the first things she would do when she had some cash again would be to shop for a 'new' used car. But she was glad she'd helped Phil out when he needed her. Who else could you turn to in trouble but one of the family? That's what families were for.

The throaty growl softened, and she prepared to put the car into gear, praying it wouldn't stall. It didn't like this hot, humid weather. Come to that, it didn't like rain, cold, or any other climatic conditions. It was just too far gone.

A police car swerved into her driveway and came to rest with its grill no more than two feet from her radiator. In surprise, she took her foot from the gas, and the engine choked and died.

'Damn,' she whispered. Now she would have to go through the whole process again.

The young policeman who had visited only two nights before emerged slowly from the car. He adjusted his cap and hitched his weapon to a comfortable position on his hip. What was his name? One was Jim and one was Brad. She thought this was Brad.

Maggie watched him, her heart beating faster in her throat. It was stupid the way law-abiding citizens felt guilty if a police officer approached them. It was always: what did I do? He was taking his time, looking around. What did he want? Had he found out she'd been hiding a fugitive all the time she was answering their questions with half-truths? She'd never so much as had a parking ticket. How did the police operate? Was what she'd done a serious offense?

The officer approached the open window of the car, but he was still moving slowly, taking in every detail of the house and the gardens. Was he looking for clues, something to betray her complicity? Like what? *Pull yourself together*, she told herself. *No one's going to put you in jail, even if they know. Besides, Joe says he's innocent.'*

The young policemen bent down towards her. She could smell peppermint gum.

'Good morning, officer Taylor,' she said, smiling brightly after a quick glance at his name tag. 'How can I help you?'

He put a finger to his cap. 'Morning, ma'am,' he smiled. 'We were here the other evening, my partner and I.'

'Jim,' she said.

'That's right, Jim Hutchins. Well, we got to talking about you after we left.'

She swallowed hard. 'Really?' she said breezily. 'Whatever for?'

146

'I guess you heard we found that guy, your brother-in-law?'

'Yes, I did hear something about that.'

'Well, you don't need to worry about him any more.'

Brad Taylor squatted on his haunches. He'd shaved recently, but his skin was still soft, the skin of an adolescent. He was young and eager to do well. What had Kurt told them? Innocent or not, she preferred not to be publicly associated with him.

'I suppose that's good,' she answered. Would he never get to the point?

'Well, I had a look around as we left the other evening.'

Her heart gave a lurch. Had he heard or seen them in the kitchen? Brad went on, still taking his time. 'I don't want to offend you, Mrs. Rainer, but I think you need a security check around your house.'

She frowned at him. 'I don't know — '

Brad was warming to his topic now. 'You see, ma'am, your outside lights aren't good, you've got thick bushes up around your windows. Now, your brother-in-law obviously didn't make it to the house, we picked him up at the place where his grandmother lives now — '

'How did you know he was there?' she interrupted.

'Informant,' he replied casually. 'Anyhow, Mrs. Rainer, I wanted to tell you we can come and do a full security survey of your property. Give you a few pointers. A lady living on her own, you can't be too careful.'

She smiled at him in relief. Kurt and Joe had kept their secret. They'd protected her. 'Thank you, officer,' she said. 'I think that might be a good idea sometime.'

Brad stood up easily from his crouch. He passed her a card. 'Just give a call when you're ready. Don't leave it too long, now.'

'I won't. Thank you.'

He readjusted his cap again and laid a hand on the hood of the car. 'Doesn't sound in good shape,' he remarked.

'It's old.'

'Yeah, I see that. You should get it checked out. Wouldn't want you in an accident, would we?'

'Thank you so much for coming by,' she said.

'No problem. Good day to you ma'am.'

With another polite movement of his finger to his cap, Brad Taylor returned to his vehicle and smoothly pulled out of the driveway.

Maggie waited until he disappeared before turning the key and starting the laboring engine. Next stop Roger.

Roger rose hastily from behind his desk to meet her in the doorway of his office.

'Come in, come in,' he said, and placed his hand on her arm, drawing her towards him.

Bars of buttery yellow sunlight lay on the dark rug, filtered through the slatted blinds. Roger's desk gleamed with polished wood, a gold pen and pencil set lay where he had left them. A computer hummed discreetly in the corner. The screen saver showed a dizzying pattern of lines and color.

Roger's arms went round her, and he kissed her. Maggie could see their reflection in the glass of the print on the wall opposite the window. As kisses went, it wasn't bad, although her kissing experience had admittedly been limited for a while. Roger stood half a head taller than she, and he had good, broad shoulders. The warmth of him against her was solid and reassuring. Their blonde heads were close together, and Roger's hands held her discretely halfway down her back. His lips were cool and firm.

It was a nice kiss. A competent kiss. A thoroughly unexciting kiss. She wondered why she hadn't ever thought that before when Roger kissed her. Because the arrival of Kurt Rainer had recalled a totally different kind of

kiss, that was why. Kurt's kisses were
— would be — she wouldn't go down that
path. She concentrated on enjoying the
comfort of Roger's arms round her.

Roger lifted his head and leaned away, still
holding her with his hands clasped behind
her back. He smiled. 'What's up?'

Maggie sighed, rubbing her hands appre-
ciatively over the silky cotton of his sports
shirt. She gave him a peck on the cheek,
hoping he wasn't wondering about her lack of
response. He didn't seem to have noticed.

'Sit down.' Roger guided her to the leather
couch against a side wall and sat next to her,
keeping hold of her hand. 'Nothing wrong
with Jeff?'

Maggie shook her head. 'No, he's fine.'
She released her hand gently from Roger's
grasp and fished in her shoulder bag for the
papers Frieda had given her. 'I think you
should take a look at these,' she said, handing
them to him.

He took the small package with a puzzled
frown and slid off the elastic bands. Maggie
got up from the couch and took the few steps
to the window while he read. She could hear
the rustle of the papers as he unfolded them
and then laid them aside. She was now sure
that it was Dianna who had called the police
about Kurt. She tried to recall the details of

her conversation with Joe. Certainly the police officer's comments and tone had seemed to support Kurt's contention that he was innocent of any complicity in Johnny Gunn's death. If so, then she should tell him about Jeff. Without a murder rap hanging over him, he might be a suitable person to reintroduce into her son's life. A man deserved at least to know he had a son.

But that still didn't wipe out the pain of his desertion. It didn't explain why he had stayed away so long with never a word, despite her desperate attempts to reach him. She would not risk Jeff suffering the same betrayal.

How could she be sure if she let Jeff know his father that Kurt wouldn't abandon the boy again when some other interest grabbed his attention? Kurt seemed to live a fairly unrooted existence, although the news of his academic degree had been a surprise. She wondered when he had found the time and the motivation for such an impressive qualification. He'd been a bright student in school but preferred to use his talents elsewhere than in the classroom.

She pushed the thoughts of Kurt away and turned back to look at Roger. Her future was here. Kurt had flashed in and out of her life once more like a lightening strike and was now gone. She'd learned to value what she had, if nothing else. He'd reminded her of instability, recklessness, and unfaithfulness. What she and Roger had here and now was infinitely better.

7

Roger looked up from the papers, carefully folding them back into their original shape.

'So,' he said.

'What do you think?'

'I think Frieda has a good imagination.'

'Don't you believe it?'

He tapped the package on his thigh. He was wearing an expensive, light weight suit with a faint check. Maggie thought he looked as if he belonged in an ad in an upscale catalog with the sun on his blond hair and his tailored shirt. She'd always liked his carefulness, his attention to detail.

At last he spoke. 'I think this has the potential to do us a lot of harm.'

'Us?'

'The organization. Our good name is worth millions.'

'Of course. But the residents also have to know that we're here to protect them, to look after their interests — '

Roger waved a hand to interrupt her. 'Whether or not all this — ' he indicated the bundle of papers, ' — is wholly based on facts is beside the point. We must minimize the damage and the publicity. Our reputation is at stake. Word cannot — must not — let it get out that there is any such activity going on in Glenhaven.'

Maggie sank into the leather chair opposite him. 'What do you want to do?' she asked.

'I'd like you to look into it, as discreetly as you can.' He stood up, thrusting hands into his pants pockets.

She raised her eyebrows. 'Sweep it under the rug?' she asked, feeling the glow of heat mounting to her face. She desperately wanted Roger to be honest and forthright. Surely he was not telling her to hide the extortion, pretend that nothing was going on?

He turned away and paced to the window and stood with his back to her. 'The girl will have to go.' He swung round and leaned both hands on the back of his desk chair. 'I'm relying on you, Maggie,' he said. 'Damage control. Say as little as possible. Clean it up quietly and quickly.'

She nodded, keeping her eyes on him, as if watching him closely would help her understand what he was thinking. 'I can do that, of course. Then what?'

He frowned. 'What do you mean?'

'What about the money she's taken?' Maggie pointed at the papers still in his hand. 'She's extorted thousands from Mr.

Blacklock. Mrs. Swindon — '

'Yes, yes, so Frieda claims.' He stood straight and threw the package on his desk. 'We'd need a lawyer and an accountant to determine for sure the extent of the — ' he hesitated, 'misdeeds.'

'Misdeeds! That's a strange word! Wouldn't you call it fraud, blackmail — ' she made an effort to lower her voice, ' — even criminal activity?'

Roger sat in the chair behind his desk and ran a hand through his hair. 'Of course you're shocked,' he said. 'I'm shocked. Any reasonable person would be shocked. But I need to think about this. Do what you can with Dianna. Get rid of her. Talk to Frieda again. See if she's certain about all this, or if there's some imagination at work.'

'That's the second time you've mentioned Frieda's imagination. She was a first class journalist, you know. She knows how to put together a case — '

'That may well have been true.' Roger interrupted her again. 'But I can't risk my whole investment, my career, on the say-so of an eighty-year-old woman who may or may not be seeing burglars under the bed.'

Maggie pressed her lips together. She didn't want to hear Roger putting his business interests before straight dealing. On the other hand, he did have many thousands of dollars invested in this seniors' home and in two others he owned and operated. Of course he would think of the implications of a scandal.

'It's not only the money,' Roger said as if reading her thoughts. 'Don't forget all the staff who rely on me for their jobs, the residents who are happy and settled. What would a scandal and a decrease in our income do to them? We'd lose clients — there'd be repercussions . . . ' He waved a hand as if to include the whole elegant setting around them.

'I understand.' She managed a small smile to show she was glad to know Roger was thinking of someone other than himself. She told herself she felt better about the way he wanted to handle the affair.

'I'll pass all this on to my lawyer,' he said as she rose to leave. 'Between us we can settle all this. If and when we determine the losses to residents, I'll make it good, don't worry.'

Maggie felt an enormous sense of relief and nodded thoughtfully as the tension went out of her back and shoulders. 'I'll get right on it,' she said, 'and report back to you.'

Roger smiled benignly at her, waved a hand in acknowledgment and picked up his gold pen.

She walked through the hallway to the residents' lounge. A murmur of voices came from one corner, and she spotted Frieda talking to a tall brunette. With a quickening of her pulse, Maggie recognized the visitor as the morning anchor of the local TV program. Surely Frieda wasn't going public with the story about Dianna?

She strode past the grouped armchairs and small tables and stood by Frieda, feeling slightly out of breath. Talk about stress! Kurt and his problems, the issues from the past, blackmail in Glenhaven, Roger. She filled her lungs with air and put on a carefree smile.

'Good morning,' she said. 'How are you feeling this morning, Frieda? How are you Jane? Nice to see you.' Branscombe was not a large place, and Jane was often present at social and civic functions. The last time Maggie had met her was when she and Roger had attended the Valentine's Ball. Frieda, of course, had a wide network of friends, excolleagues, and acquaintances that she maintained assiduously.

Jane Wentworth gave a friendly smile. 'Just great, thanks Maggie,' she said. 'I called in to say hi to Frieda and do some catching up. We're having a really good chat.'

'Are you?' Maggie rested a hand on Frieda's shoulder. She didn't know how to ask what they were talking about. She searched Frieda's face for signs of anxiety. The old lady looked tired, and she was breathing slowly and carefully.

Frieda raised a thin hand to pat Maggie's fingers. 'Oh, yes,' she said. 'We're destroying a few reputations, aren't we Jane? Letting a few skeletons out of the closet and a good few cats out of the bag, to coin a couple of well-used phrases.' She chuckled delightedly.

Maggie hesitated. 'Sit down, girl,' Frieda said. 'Can't stand people hovering behind me. Reminds me of the Grim Reaper — and that creepy girl, Dianna.' She nodded knowingly at Maggie.

Maggie felt her stomach tighten with apprehension. 'So,' she said as lightly as she could, 'whose skeletons are you examining?'

Jane laughed. 'Frieda's in a reminiscing mood,' she said. 'I caught her at a good time. She remembers a lot about the early days of the *Branscombe Gazette*. I'm thinking of doing a piece on their fiftieth anniversary.'

'An exposé!' Frieda interjected.

'Not quite,' Jane replied. 'I don't want to get sued or lose my job.'

Frieda gave a delicate snort. 'All wimps, these days,' she said. 'No guts to go for the roots.'

'Well, we try our best.' Jane picked up her

purse, readying herself to leave.

Maggie let her breath out in relief that the conversation wasn't touching on matters closer to home. She smiled in sympathy at the other woman. Jane was a good reporter, honest and fair. It wasn't her fault that modern life was hemmed in by lawyers and accountants and fears of litigation and thus became a balancing act. She felt a little more empathy for Roger's dilemma. It was easy to take the high moral ground when your livelihood wasn't at stake.

Jane bent to kiss Frieda on her cheek. 'Take care,' she said. 'I'll let you know whether I get the okay to do this. I want to have a word with Roger about the police activity here last night.'

She waved cheerfully at Maggie and left in a wave of flowery perfume.

Frieda sniffed. 'Uses too much of that stuff,' she complained. 'She's a nice girl, but she makes me want to sneeze.'

Maggie turned towards her. 'You didn't answer my question,' she said. 'How are you feeling?'

'About the same,' Frieda answered. 'Don't fuss around me. I'm well enough. Now, first off, did you talk to that boss of yours?'

Maggie nodded and sat forward, lowering her voice. 'He's very concerned,' she began.

'I should think so! Nearly fifteen thousand dollars she's taken. Eight from that poor Mr. Blacklock who hardly knows what day it is and depends on her for nearly everything!'

Maggie willed Frieda to keep her voice down. 'I know,' she said quietly. 'Roger will look into the details. I just wanted to let you know that I believe you.'

'Why? Doesn't he believe me?'

Frieda was still too astute. 'It's not exactly that.' Maggie struggled to find the right words. 'He needs to check everything out. He promises that he'll put everything right as soon as he can.'

'Hmm.' Frieda looked at her searchingly. 'That's a lot of every things. Sounds a bit like a cover-up brewing to me.' She suddenly sat up a little, and her tone became brisk. 'I'm going to leave all that to you,' she said. 'Now, second thing. How's Kurt?'

'He's well.'

Frieda looked at her with the same searching gaze. 'Where is he? Still with you or did he go to the cabin?'

'He's not at the cabin.'

She really didn't want to break the news about Kurt until she knew what was going on. She groped in her mind for something to say, hoping Frieda would let the subject drop. 'He still needs to rest up of course. His side is better, but he had a lot of cuts and bruises. There's a big gash on his leg — '

'So where is he? What was all that Jane said about police activity?'

Maggie cleared her throat. 'Yes, the police were here.'

'Was it about Kurt?'

Maggie moistened her lips. 'Yes.'

Frieda frowned. 'Why?'

Maggie couldn't avoid the truth any longer. She took Frieda's hand. 'The police picked him up,' she said gently, 'as we were leaving here last night. They've sent him back to the mountains, to Wellington, the small town where they're doing the investigation.'

She felt Frieda's thin fingers tighten their grasp. 'Arrested?'

Maggie shook her head. 'I don't think so. He seems to have been working with the police and letting people think he was a suspect while they carried on the investigation. They appear to have believed this would allow them to find out the truth. That's why he was attacked — by someone who thought he knew too much.'

'He told me about that,' Frieda said. She shifted impatiently in her armchair and adjusted her shawl. 'Men! They make these convoluted plans and play at them like little boys with a war game. Kurt always had too much imagination for his own good.'

'That's true.'

'What will happen to him now?' Frieda's voice showed her anxiety again.

'Joe — that's his policeman friend — says he'll be safe. They'll sort it all out now.'

'You worried about him?' Frieda lifted her handkerchief to suddenly pale lips.

Maggie noticed the tremble in her fingers. 'A bit,' she confessed.

'So am I.' Frieda's voice faltered. 'What makes them think that the man who stabbed him before won't try again?'

'I don't know what they think.' Maggie looked more closely into Frieda's face and noted the shallow breathing. 'Frieda, are you feeling all right?'

The old lady leaned back in her chair and closed her eyes. 'No,' she whispered through bloodless lips. 'I think I need some help.'

Maggie sprang to her feet and stepped quickly to the bell push on the wall, summoning the nurse on duty and activating the direct line to the ambulance service.

*   *   *

Several hours later, Maggie closed the door of Frieda's room and slipped into the small staff office at the end of the hallway to use the phone. It had been a harrowing time from when the ambulance bore Frieda off to the hospital until she was declared out of danger. Despite her protests, Frieda was to stay under observation.

As soon as she could talk, she'd dispatched Maggie to fetch a change of clothes and slippers. 'Don't forget my library book,' she'd said as Maggie left. Whatever would they do without Frieda to keep them going with her intelligence and her zest for life? Maggie breathed a prayer of thanks that she would be with them for a while longer.

She wanted to phone Wellington, and a quick call from here would save her the walk down to the administrative area where she would risk being trapped in long conversations with well-meaning people. She placed the bag with Frieda's personal items on the desk. The rooms on this floor were deserted, all the residents downstairs for lunch.

The number Joe had given her was tucked into her wallet. She'd told herself she would never use it to contact Kurt, that she would know soon enough whether or not he was still being held in connection with the murder. But she'd seen in the last day or so the depths of feelings in the man, under the tough, extrovert exterior. She knew he cared deeply for his Oma. He would never forgive her if she failed to let him know about the heart attack. What was worse, she would never forgive herself if Frieda didn't recover or had a relapse, and she'd left Kurt in ignorance. Much as she wanted never to reach out to him again, he had to be told and be given the chance to see Frieda again.

The phone was picked up on the first ring.

'Wellington Police. Joe Ventriss speaking.'

'Officer Ventriss — Joe,' she began, 'it's Maggie Rainer.'

'Anything wrong?'

Joe was another one who picked up quickly on undertones.

'No, yes. Is Kurt there?'

'Not yet. Should be pulling in any time now — say in thirty minutes.'

'Are you going to — keep him there?' She didn't know how else to ask if Joe had changed his mind about Kurt's innocence.

'Who? Kurt?' Joe laughed. 'No way. We just need him to tie up a few loose ends. That attack in the hospital was a blessing in disguise.' Maggie revised her opinion of Joe's sensitivity. How could a vicious, life threatening attack be a blessing?

'It gave us a few more leads,' Joe continued. 'We've got the guys who did it.'

'It looked as if he was arrested.'

'Nah. Sorry if it bothered you. I wanted

him back where I could keep an eye on him and where he could help us. The local boys got a little carried away.'

Maggie suspected that the bulletin Joe sent out had been couched in terms that made the 'local boys' think they were looking for a suspected murderer rather than a consultant.

'So,' Joe said. 'Want me to have him call you?'

'No, just give him a message. Tell him his grandmother's had a minor heart attack. She's okay now, but she is over eighty and rather frail. I've just come back from the hospital to pick up a few things for her. Tell him they'll be keeping her in for a couple of days. She's not in any immediate danger, but I know he'd want to know.'

'I'll see he gets back down there as soon as possible. Shouldn't take too long to clear up the loose ends. Then he's free as a bird.'

'Thanks, Joe.'

Maggie replaced the receiver. Kurt was definitely cleared. He'd told her the truth. It had all been some plot cooked up between him and Joe to flush out the real criminals. Now she must figure out how and when to let him know about Jeff. It would be a relief in many ways to be free of the secret. She'd never realized the burden of it until now that it would be lifted from her. Still, it was a big step — a new chapter. She'd need to plan it carefully, not be taken off-guard.

She put her wallet back in her leather shoulder bag. The purse was growing heavier. Time to clean out the accumulation of debris. Time to do a lot of things that were part of a normal, daily routine. Frieda would do as well as anyone of her age and frailty could after a trauma. Maggie would keep in contact with the hospital, visit as often as she could.

She pulled the zipper closed on the purse and looked around the small office. It was rarely used. A small desk with a phone and a supply of notepads sat under the window. A few lists of duty rosters and reminders were pinned to the cork bulletin board. The waste basket under the desk was filled with torn up newspaper.

Suddenly, the sound of wheels came down the hall, a murmur of voices drew closer. Without quite knowing why, Maggie moved quietly to the door that was not completely closed

The slight squeak of rubber wheels drew closer, and the voices became clearer — one rising above the other. Although it was not possible to make out the individual words, Maggie could hear the querulous tone belonging to an elderly man apparently complaining.

The answering voice, although pitched low, was clear. She recognized Dianna's clipped speech.

'Now, Mr. Blacklock, you have to behave if you want me to give you your treat. Now look what you've done — you've dropped all your papers!' The sound of the wheels ceased as the resident and nurse stopped outside Maggie's office. She heard the rustle of Dianna's uniform as she stooped to pick up the papers.

'I'll get very cross with you,' the girl said irritably. 'You know what will happen if I'm angry.' A low mumble came back in reply.

'I don't know what you're saying, you silly old fool. Just do exactly as I tell you, and I'll look after you.' Another spate of muttering. 'Yes, I've told you that I'll see that other nurse you don't like doesn't come near you — although sometimes I think I should, just to pay you back for aggravating me. Now be quiet and hold on to these things for me. You just write me another nice check when we get back to your room, and you'll be all right. You know what happens to old people if no one bothers about them. Here are your papers — your check book is right there . . . ' The squeak of the wheels started up again and faded down the hallway.

Frozen in disbelief, Maggie stood looking

167

at the door as if willing herself to see through the wooden panel and follow Dianna and Mr. Blacklock down the corridor. What had she heard? It all tied in with what Frieda had told her. This was surely grounds enough for dismissal?

She felt her throat tighten in anger. She would have to go down to the main floor after all. Roger had to be told, and then she would deal with Dianna. She turned to the desk to pick up Frieda's bag and her own purse. Footsteps sounded in the corridor, and the door flew open with a crash. Maggie whirled to see Dianna on the threshold, obviously startled to see someone. The nurse recovered quickly and thrust a small piece of paper in her pocket.

'Mrs. Rainer,' she said, 'what are you doing in here? Can I help you?'

Maggie picked a piece of newspaper out of the basket on the floor. It was lacy with holes where words had been cut out. 'I think this and what I just overheard are sufficient. I've seen some of the anonymous notes you left for some of our residents. What you've been doing is despicable.'

Dianna's pretty mouth curved into a sardonic grin. Suddenly, she looked far older than her years, with a cynical glint to her eyes. 'I knew it was time to move on,' she said. 'I'll be gone tomorrow.'

'Dr. Saint George — ' Maggie began.

'Won't do anything about it,' Dianna broke in harshly. 'What can he prove without a lot of expense? He'll eat the losses and hope nothing comes out. Just like all the others.'

She pushed past Maggie, unlocked a drawer, and took out a notebook. 'This is all I need,' she said.

Maggie tried to grasp her wrist, but Dianna was too quick and strong. 'Don't worry,' she said, 'your precious reputation is safe, if you know how to keep your mouth closed. I've already written my resignation. I've gotten all I could out of this job.' With that ambiguous statement, Dianna took the newspaper from Maggie, crumpled it and tossed it into the waste bin.

Maggie found her voice. 'You're wrong about Dr. Saint George,' she said. 'He's consulting his lawyers. I can't stop you physically, but we will pursue this. You won't get away with it.'

Dianna laughed. 'You people! He'll think twice about letting anyone know,' she said. 'Mud sticks, you know. Now, if you'll excuse me, I have some loose ends to see to. Here's the letter you want.' She tossed an envelope contemptuously onto the desk. It slid across the surface and fell to the floor.

'That old witch found out,' she said harshly. 'I knew she'd been watching me, crafty devil.' She took a jacket from the coatrack behind the door. 'But I got back at her, didn't I? Her precious grandson, wanted for murder! Gives herself such airs, holier than thou old cow!'

She swung a shiny black purse onto her shoulder. 'Don't know what to say, Mrs. Rainer? My advice to you,' she stepped closer and thrust her face forward, lowering her voice to a hiss, 'is to do nothing, say nothing. Otherwise that boy of yours might find out he has a killer for a daddy!'

She laughed at the look of shock on Maggie's face. 'You're like all the rest. All goodness and light with a dirty secret to hide. Not hard to find out or put two and two together. I've got plenty of connections. I'm sure a guy in prison would like to know he has a family on the outside, would be anxious to keep in touch with his son.' With a final laugh, she flung out of the room.

Maggie took two steps to the door and caught it before it closed. Dianna was already out of the hallway — she must have run to the stairs. Pursuing her would be futile. What would she do to prevent the girl from leaving?

She sank down onto the hard wooden chair to collect her thoughts, shaking from the rush of adrenaline and her anger at Dianna's callousness and duplicity. She took deep breaths, and gradually her heart rate slowed, and warmth flowed back into her hands and feet. There was an added dimension now. Dianna knew about Kurt, about Jeff. Everything was conspiring to bring her to the point of revelation, which would change her relationship with Kurt. But there were ways to acknowledge his rights without binding herself to him. She was an independent, capable woman and could choose her own path without being dictated to by someone like Dianna. All Dianna had done was make the agenda much more urgent.

Dianna was wrong about one thing, of course. Kurt wasn't a murderer. Maggie was thankful to have spoken with Joe before listening to Dianna's tirade. Otherwise she would have been even more alarmed at the promise of exposure. Nonetheless, she didn't trust Dianna not to make good the threat of spreading rumors just out of spite. How would Jeff react to the whispered conversations, the innuendo?

The question she'd wrestled with was answered for her. She'd known in her heart what she had to do, but it had been hard, so hard. The news had to come from Jeff's mother, not from a vindictive stranger. She would tell Kurt as soon as possible Jeff was his son and salvage what she could of her control over her boy's life. At some point, she and Kurt would tell Jeff the truth together.

With a new sense of resolve, she picked up the envelope from under her feet She supposed it contained a carefully worded resignation. She felt the anger rise again at the girl's nerve. She gathered her purse and Frieda's bag once more. So much for saving time by making a short phone call! She would have to talk to Roger again.

★   ★   ★

'How's Frieda?' Roger asked. He turned towards her as he shrugged into his jacket. Maggie took two more steps into his office and sank into the leather chair. She rubbed her fingers across her forehead. Why did every day feel like a hundred years? She felt as if she was in an action movie where everyone but she knew what was going on.

'She'll be okay,' she answered. 'I took her some things she wanted and called her grandson.'

Roger frowned. 'I didn't know she had a grandson. I thought your husband — '

Maggie nodded. 'I know. Steve and Kurt were half brothers. Same father. Frieda is

Kurt's real grandmother. Her daughter was Kurt's mother and died when Kurt was three. Frieda always treated Steve like her own family when he came along. She was good to old Will Rainer's second wife and to both the boys.' A very short history of many years of a dysfunctional family.

'Bit of a tyrant, wasn't he, the old man? Or so I've heard.'

Maggie twisted her mouth into a grimace of distaste. 'He was a dreadful man. If you're charitable, you could say he never got over his first wife's death. He resented Kurt. His son could never do anything right. And he spoiled Steve for some reason. They were a pretty dysfunctional family. His second wife left him, poor woman. Frieda held them together.'

Roger came to sit by her. He put out a hand and stroked her hair. 'You're tired. This has been a bad day for you.'

She closed her eyes and sighed., leaning into his hand. It felt good and strong. She breathed in the peace and solidity of Roger's presence.

'I just wanted to tell you that Dianna's gone,' she said.

'Gone? Already?'

'I didn't even have to fire her. She quit.'

Quickly she gave Roger the details of the

encounter with Dianna, leaving out the threats about Kurt and Jeff.

'So you have the evidence,' Roger said.

She nodded. 'It seems clear-cut. Did you speak to your lawyer?'

'I did. He wants to take a look at all the papers, but after your news, it seems as if we won't need to follow through.'

Maggie frowned in puzzlement. 'What do you mean, not follow through? What about warning other seniors' homes? From something she said, it seems she might have done this elsewhere.'

'I'll make a few discreet inquiries,' Roger assured her.

'But you're not suggesting we won't prosecute her?

'Let's leave it to the legal guys,' Roger said soothingly.

Maggie shifted uneasily. 'I won't let it be swept under the rug.'

'Of course not. Now, what are we going to do about you?'

She looked at him in surprise. 'Me?'

He stood up and pulled her to her feet, keeping his arms round her. 'You're supposed to be on vacation, but you're spending as much time here as if you were working. You're exhausted. I don't think I've ever seen you so wiped out.' He placed a soft kiss on her forehead. 'Let's do what we promised ourselves. I can take some time. I'll make reservations at Golden Point Lodge. We'll drive up, have dinner, spend a couple of days relaxing. Will you come with me?'

Golden Point was an exclusive, elegant resort on a deserted strip of beach. Maggie had never been there, but Ellen and Cliff had spent an anniversary weekend at the Lodge last year. Ellen was still talking about the food, the pampering, the atmosphere. It was one of the most romantic places she'd ever seen.

This was the moment of decision, if she was going to take her relationship with Roger anywhere at all. She and Roger could cement their relationship, she could have the happy family she wanted, provide properly for her son. Someone would care about her, would be there for her through good times and bad. She would tell Kurt about Jeff, but that didn't mean she had to give up her own life. Kurt didn't want a family anyway. He'd as good as said so.

She craved the reassurance of someone who loved her, someone to share her hopes and fears. Agreeing to what Roger wanted — what she wanted too — would make it impossible for Kurt to have any claim on her. She would clothe herself in the armor of a new relationship that would allow her to resist all Kurt's attractions. When a man and a woman did what she and Roger were contemplating, when they sealed their relationship with an intimate, physical bond, it closed all the doors to other temptations. They would have thoughts only for each other, would become the center of each one's world. She took a deep breath. 'Make the reservation for tomorrow night,' she said and lifted her face to his for his kiss.

8

The afternoon shadows were lengthening when Kurt trudged up the bark covered path to the door of the Wellington police station. The days were long at this time of year in the north country, but the sun dropped early behind the high peaks and cast shadows over the sheltered valley bottom. The young officer who'd escorted him on the eight hour trip from Branscombe hurried to catch up.

The building was small, made of round logs mortised together at the corners. Colors gleamed in the bright sun, the blue of the door and the pansies Joe's wife, Betty, made a point of planting outside. It looked exactly like what it was: a friendly center for helping the community and keeping law and order over a vast tract of land. The inhabitants were few, but they still got into trouble. Drinking, logging accidents, domestic abuse, theft, — the human condition made no exceptions for pristine wilderness and isolation. A few yellowed, curling notices on gun laws and hunting permits were tacked inside a glass display case.

Kurt stopped under the flagpole, turned

towards the mountains, and inhaled deeply, holding his breath a moment. The air tasted good, crisp and clean with a hint of green things bursting into life, taking advantage of the short summer. There was still snow on the high crests, but the late runoff was bouncing down a couple of the waterfalls into the lake. He could hear the chuckle of the water as it fell and splashed and filled in the dry, rocky stream beds. He thought of bringing Maggie here — he could show her secret, magical places where her camera could capture the elusive, beautiful soul of the back country.

'Gotta go, buddy,' said the officer accompanying him. 'Let's get inside.'

The young policeman had let him doze most of the way, mercifully not trying to make conversation, and had even kept the radio turned to low. Kurt nodded and opened the door.

Joe was waiting in his office, his feet on the desk, a cup of coffee steaming on a pile of papers before him. Kurt paused at the threshold, taking in the scene through the open door. Joe was tall and lean, his face weather-beaten, creased as much by smiling as by squinting into far distances. He and Kurt had enjoyed exchanging many an anecdote about the unbelievable antics and comments of the film crews.

Joe swung his feet to the floor as he saw Kurt in the doorway and stood up.

'Come in, Doc,' he said. He nodded to the escort who carried a sheaf of papers. 'Just give me the documents and go get yourself a cup of coffee across the street, my boy,' he said. 'Good donuts too.' The coffee shop was a tiny extension to a gas station with two pumps.

The young man started to protest.

Joe waved him away. 'I'll be responsible. You did a good job,' he said reassuringly, standing up to his full six feet four. 'Good to know we can rely on you guys down there.' He clapped the fellow on the shoulder, gently pushing him to the door. 'Don't you worry about a thing,' he said. 'I'll see everything's okay.'

When they were alone, Joe threw the envelope on the desk and poured a cup of coffee from the machine under the window. He stood for a moment in silence looking out. Kurt knew better than to jump in ahead of him.

'Gonna get rain,' he said and turned to pass the steaming cup to Kurt. 'Just been talking to a friend of yours,' he continued, sliding into his chair and tilting back.

Kurt sipped at the thick, black brew and raised an eyebrow.

'Yeah, spoke to Maggie last night and again this morning.' Joe grinned at him. 'She as cute as she sounds?'

'Cute' was never a word he'd applied to Maggie, but he knew what Joe meant. 'Better,' he said.

'Thought so. She's worried about you, so I told her I wasn't going to lock you up and throw away the key — not this time anyway.' Joe grinned easily at him again and picked up his coffee. He sat forward, a small frown adding to the lines on his forehead. 'She called back not an hour ago,' he continued, 'wanted me to give you a message. Here — ' he shuffled some papers, ' — I wrote it down because I knew you'd want it right . . . ' He picked up a scrap of pink out of the jumble. 'She said you're not to worry, there's no immediate danger, but — '

'Spit it out Joe, what's happened?' Kurt sat up straight, the taste of the coffee suddenly bitter and burning in his mouth. Someone was hurt but who? Was it Jeff, or Oma or Maggie herself? God, had he found people to care about again only to lose one or more? Wild thoughts of car accidents, fires, falls whirled through his head while Joe took his own sweet time telling him.

'Hold your horses, I'm getting there,' Joe said, squinting at the writing. 'Yes, it's Frieda

— is that right? That your gramma? She — '
he read word for word from the note ' — had
a heart attack earlier this morning, is out of
danger, but will be staying in the hospital for
a couple of days.' He looked up. 'Maggie said
you'd want to know.'

Kurt stood up and walked to the window,
staring out at the thick forest and the bare
rocks rising to the top of the mountains.
'Thanks, Joe, he said quietly. 'I'll go right
back.'

'Not without something to eat, you won't.
Maggie said there's no rush.' Joe lifted the
phone receiver. 'Call to check on her. Betty
heard you were on your way and made
something special. You better stay, otherwise I
won't get any.'

The reassuring call completed, Kurt strode
through to Betty's gleaming kitchen in the
living quarters behind the official offices.
Joe's wife set steaming plates of venison stew
in front of them and they began to eat. After a
couple of mouthfuls, Kurt questioned Joe
about the investigation.

'Sorry to bring you back like that,' Joe said,
chewing slowly, 'but I was a bit anxious about
you. We lost track of the main suspect for a
while there, and we thought he might be
headed down to find you.'

'Thanks a lot.'

Betty broke in. 'I told Joe to get you back here pronto,' she said sharply. 'I knew you needed looking after, even if he was too obsessed to think about it. Cast on your arm, stab wound and all. How did he think you were going to defend yourself if they did find you?'

Kurt smiled at her fondly. Joe didn't manage to keep many secrets within the four walls of his own house. 'I took one of the rental cars from the movie site and found someone to look after me.'

Betty wasn't impressed. 'Harebrained schemes,' she snorted, 'need your heads examined, both of you. Men!'

Kurt patted her hand. 'It was worth coming back just for one of your stews.'

She swatted at him. 'Get away with you. Talk about charming the birds from the trees!' But he could see she was pleased. The few days with Maggie had shown him only too clearly how empty his life had been for the last twelve years after he'd left Oma and Maggie behind him, safely tucked away in his past. He loved Joe and Betty like the parents he never had — they were the only people he knew well or who cared about him.

He turned to Joe to bring his mind back from what awaited him in Branscombe. 'So what have you found out?'

Joe pushed his plate away and sat back, rubbing a hand over his abdomen and sighing with contentment. 'We found out lots,' he began. 'You know that little blonde starlet?' He picked a toothpick from the small earthenware pot on the table and stuck it in a corner of his mouth.

'Bambi or Babie or something?'

'Yeah, that's her name.' Joe rolled the toothpick to the other side. 'Silly name for a silly little piece. Well, Johnny Gunn was trying to cozy up to her, if you get my drift?'

Betty snorted again and rattled some plates.

'I found her hanging around the equipment a couple of times,' Kurt said, laying down his fork.

'More like hanging around you,' Joe said. 'It seems Johnny thought she was sweet on you, Doc, didn't make him like you much,' Joe said.

'It was mutual.' Kurt mopped the last of the sauce with the homemade bread. He hadn't realized how hungry he was.

Joe nodded. 'That was part of the problem. Far as we can make out, Johnny thought he'd rig the harness so it looked as if you'd been careless. Of course, it would still be safe enough — just something loose enough for him to be able to throw a tantrum. Probably thought at least Bambi-babie would give you a wide berth if she thought you had homicidal tendencies, even if they didn't fire you for incompetence.'

'Johnny decided to do that? I never thought he'd have the gumption.'

'The trouble is, when you start asking certain people for favors, you might get more than you bargain for. Seems that Johnny was in bad with a few people who make a lot of money through different — commodities.'

'Drugs,' Betty stated.

Joe nodded. 'Amongst other things. He asked the wrong person for help and put an idea in their heads. They strung him along and decided to do the job properly. He owed money, he was unreliable. They probably thought he'd be a good example to keep some others in line. You were right there in the frame.'

'But why attack me in the hospital? What did they think I knew?'

'Seems you stopped to talk to one of them when you'd checked the ropes for the last time. They thought you might remember something.'

Kurt frowned. 'Talked to — ' He stared open mouthed at Joe as light dawned. 'I talked to Freddy, the producer's assistant. I'd forgotten, I talked to him so many times about so many details. He was in on this?'

Joe nodded. 'He was indeed, with one of the camera crew. An unsavory bunch. Enough to take your appetite away. Got any dessert, Betty?'

'In a minute,' Betty said. 'There's a bed for you, Kurt, all ready. It's almost evening — you know how treacherous the canyon is at night. Stay and leave early tomorrow. You can phone the hospital again about your grand-mother.'

'She's right, you know,' Joe added, spitting out the toothpick. 'She who must be obeyed.' Joe had no idea where the expression came from, but he enjoyed applying it to his tiny wife. 'Anyway, I do need to get some details from you, double-check a couple of things.'

After a second heaping of apple cobbler, Kurt drove with Joe to his own car, parked it facing the highway, and then rolled into a comfortable bed. He set the alarm for dawn.

★   ★   ★

At noon the next day, Maggie spotted Ellen already waiting for her, seated at a window table in the small restaurant by the harbor. She slipped into the chair opposite her friend and looked around.

'Busy,' she said.

Ellen put aside the menu. 'Very popular, but no-one can hear anything except their neighbor, so we can have a good chat.'

'I'm glad you called,' Maggie said. 'I needed some down time.'

Ellen asked no questions but smiled in sympathy. They ordered from the extensive menu and settled down to their conversation.

'Do you have any pictures?' Ellen asked. She always helped pick out the best shots for selection for submission. Maggie had sold a couple of pictures and had hopes of working on a coffee table book. She trusted her friend's eye for detail and atmosphere.

Maggie shook her head. 'I tell you, Ellie, life's been one hectic scramble since I saw you last.'

'Last time I saw you at the market, you'd taken Jeff to camp. How is he?'

Maggie sat back to allow the server to place her plate of salad in front of her. 'Thank you,' she said. 'That does look good.' She picked up her fork and speared a cherry tomato.

Ellen looked dubiously at her plate. 'Don't know if I was wise to order this,' she whispered and turned it around, looking for something she recognized. 'The menu said chicken, but I don't know . . . '

'I'm sure it's delicious,' Maggie smiled, watching her. Ellen was always fun to be with.

'Well, here goes.' Ellen began to eat.

'So,' she said, chewing carefully. 'Did Roger drive you both up to the camp? Did he give you lunch? Did Jeff settle in okay?'

Maggie laughed. 'Slow down. One question at a time. Jeff's fine. I got a call from him. But wait till I tell you the rest. We dropped Jeff, and Roger had this fabulous picnic all prepared. Of course, first we had to bounce along some old logging roads until he found a secluded spot. He'd got lawn chairs and an enormous ice chest in the back. He'd brought smoked salmon, strawberries, and *champagne*.'

'Wow,' Ellen said. 'What a guy. Cliff should take lessons. That vehicle's fabulous.'

Maggie took a drink of water. 'The Land Cruiser? It's huge.'

There was a pause while they concentrated on their food.

'So,' Ellen prodded. 'Go on.' Ellen was never shy about asking questions.

'He said it was a celebration,' Maggie said. 'What of?'

'I didn't want to ask him exactly what he was celebrating.'

'Coward. I can guess,' Ellen said smugly. 'It's because you've seemed to make a decision about him.'

She had indeed made a decision. Roger

was reliable, affectionate and charming, looking out for her every need. He would pick her up at five today. The room at Golden Point was waiting for them.

'Earth to Maggie,' Ellen said. 'Anything else?'

Maggie told her how she'd wanted to relax and enjoy the pampering at the idyllic spot in the woods, how they'd walked by the stream after lunch, but she stopped short of relating how he'd taken her hand and kissed her very gently. 'I've said I'll go to Golden Point with him,' she said.

'Well,' Ellen stated. 'I think it's great. What more do you want?'

She put down her fork to count off points on her fingers. 'He's kind and patient. He gets on well with Jeff, he seems to be smitten. He's certainly not lacking in worldly goods, and you like being with him. Wait!' She held up a hand to prevent Maggie's interruption. 'There's more. He's also good looking with an interesting social life, and it looks as if he wants to share it with you. I rest my case.' She sat back in her chair.

Ellen was right. She had to stop thinking of Kurt and get her life in order once more. Any hope of a committed relationship with him was destroyed long ago. She'd demanded things he hadn't wanted to give.

'You're right,' she said. 'I need to settle for the great opportunity I have right here in front of me. I like stability, routines.'

'Tell me about it,' Ellen said with a grin.

'Spontaneity's not my strong suit, I'll admit. You give in once, and everything shifts.'

Ellen's smile faded, and she leaned forward, listening, but not interrupting.

'I'm not looking for an interesting life,' Maggie continued. 'Not in the sense of never knowing what will happen next.' She paused. 'My world exploded once, and I had to build another life for myself.'

Ellen was nothing if not intuitive. She reached out a hand and grasped Maggie's fingers. 'Tell me to shut up if you want,' she said, 'but does it have anything to do with that newspaper report? About Steve's brother?'

Maggie nodded, sudden tears spilling over onto her cheeks. She brushed them away impatiently with the back of her hand.

Ellen fished in her purse, passed her a tissue, and stood up. 'Let's get out of here,' she said. She signaled for the check, put down some money, and steered Maggie out of the crowded restaurant.

A few minutes later, they sat in Ellen's car

facing the water while Maggie sniffed and mopped her eyes.

'Better?' Ellen asked.

Maggie nodded and forced a smile. 'Yes. I don't do this often.'

'How long is it since you had a good cry?'

'Too long, I guess. I'm sorry.'

Ellen patted her hand. 'Crying never needs an apology. It's the best release.' She'd been a psychiatric nurse before her marriage and still took some counseling referrals. 'I've always known you were bottling something up. Talk if you want. If not, we'll just sit and watch the water and the windsurfers.'

They sat in silence for a long moment while Maggie kept her eyes on the moving waves and the bright sails.

'I want to tell you,' she said. 'It will help me think things through.'

'I'd be honored by the trust.' Ellen laid one hand on Maggie's, her eyes fixed on the sparkling ocean.

'Steve was my age,' Maggie began, 'but Kurt was older. Kurt's mother died and his dad remarried. He was ahead of me in school. Most of the girls were crazy about him because he looked dangerous. He'd sort of swagger around and glare at everyone. He had a terrible relationship with his father, tremendous fights, physical ones sometimes.'

She bit her lip, remembering the bruises and the hard look that appeared so frequently on Kurt's face.

'As a teenager everyone thought he was surly, bad-tempered, and aloof. My parents warned me about him. I was madly attracted to him of course. The dark, brooding looks and the angry eyes. I was into Charlotte Bronte and Heathcliff at the time.'

'Romantic.' Ellen said.

Maggie smiled thinly. 'Romantic as hell. He usually had a day or so's stubble and those eyes . . . They made my stomach shrivel and my throat go dry.'

Ellen gave a little shiver in empathy. 'What did he think of you?'

'I thought he loved me,' Maggie said simply. 'I was wild about him, defied my parents at every turn. We kept it secret, don't ask me how. But I got to know him, learned about the vulnerability under the bravado. He wasn't a simple man.' She paused in reflection.

'What happened?' Ellen asked gently.

'He worked for his dad but lived mainly with Frieda in the house I have now. He had a room at the back. When I was finishing college, we planned to go away together. Then all hell broke loose. My parents were in a bad car accident, and Kurt's father accused him of stealing. I'd never seen him so hurt, so wounded. He couldn't, wouldn't stay in Branscombe.'

She heard Ellen let out a long sigh.

She steeled herself to continue. 'Kurt took off, and I couldn't go with him because of my parents. He has no time for family ties and blamed me for putting my family before him. He obviously never forgave me for letting him down. He said that. Said I was betraying him, that everything I'd promised him was a lie. He left — and I found I was pregnant.' She drew in a long, shuddering breath.

'He's Jeff's dad?'

Maggie nodded.

'And you've been carrying all that inside you for all these years?' 'Once I started, it was hard to stop. No one knew, not even my parents. Looking back, I made some poor decisions.'

'Doing the wrong thing for the right reasons.'

'You could say that. Oh, my reasons sounded good — protect Jeff, protect my mom and dad, protect me from gossip. I should have faced up to it, been honest. We'd all have been happier . . .

'You see, Steve was always around,' she explained. 'He said he loved me and would look after me and the baby. My parents would never have gotten over the news of me having Kurt Rainer's baby. Kurt never called, never wrote, never came back.'

'But your parents were okay with Steve? Tell me about him.'

'Most people liked Steve, at least at first. Steve always wanted to be like Kurt and never made it. Looking back, he was always a self-willed rather selfish little boy.'

'How about as an adult?'

'Well, yes. He was charming, and he sweet-talked his way through most things, even when he was shrugging off his responsibilities. He was good at that. His father spoiled him, and he used it to his advantage. That left Kurt as the whipping boy.'

'Steve was killed?'

'He had a small plane. Of course, after Jeff was born he used it for — parties — up at a lodge the family owned.' She could taste the bitter memories like acid in her throat. 'One morning he was coming back and crashed. He might have been high on something, but his father's influence kept it hushed up.'

'Was he good to Jeff at least?'

'I suppose so, in many ways. But he never let me forget how he'd 'saved' me. He threatened to tell the secret many times,' she said bitterly. 'Although my parents died still believing Jeff was Steve's son, so he kept his word in keeping it from them.'

'Kurt didn't ever learn about Jeff?'

Maggie shook her head.

'What about now?' Ellen turned to her, understanding dawning in her face. 'He was at your house wasn't he? That's who the food and first aid stuff were for?'

Maggie nodded, a sob building in her throat. 'He was hurt. I thought he was on the run. I thought he'd killed someone. How could I tell him and risk letting him near Jeff?'

'You let him stay?'

'I had no choice. I even told the police he wasn't there.'

'What about the injuries?'

'He passed out on my kitchen floor. He had a cast on his arm, there was blood on his side. He was a mess. I had to help him.' Maggie turned to look at Ellen, seeking approval.

Ellen nodded in reassurance. 'Of course you did.'

'The next day he was on his feet again — looking like hell but on his feet.'

'Where is he now?'

Maggie twisted the damp tissue between her fingers. 'The police have taken him back to Wellington.'

'That where it happened?'

'Yes.'

'Is he guilty?'

Ellen looked directly at her, and Maggie stared back, firmly. 'I don't — no, he's not.'

'And now what?'

'I'll tell him about Jeff, if I ever see him again,' she said miserably. 'And I suppose he'll have the right to see him. But I can't let that interfere.'

'With Roger, you mean?'

Maggie nodded. 'With Roger.'

'You care for him?'

'I think I do,' Maggie said slowly. 'He can give me so much. I want to be a family again, Ellie. I want what my mom and dad had when Phil and I were kids. Is that wrong?'

'Of course it's not wrong,' Ellen answered. 'It's the most natural thing in the world.' Ellen shifted in the driver's seat to face her and took her hand. 'You have tremendous courage, Maggie. You were hurt in every possible way. Yet you fought your way through it. You faced up to what many people couldn't face and did what you had to do.'

'I don't feel courageous. I feel like crawling into a hole until everything goes away.'

'You won't do that. You'll make the right decision, I know. Let's go back for your car.'

Maggie stopped just inside the room at Golden Point Lodge. 'That was a wonderful dinner,' she said.

The king-sized bed loomed at her, dwarfing the other furnishings. She tore her gaze from the vast expanse of expensive silk, closed her eyes for a moment, and moved towards the window, pretending to be absorbed in the view. It was true that dinner had been elegant and delicious. Roger knew his way around wine lists and food. Waiters seemed to hover to do his bidding. It was definitely not chicken and canned vegetables with an old, dusty bottle of wine.

The drapes were open and she could hear the rumble of the surf pounding on the rocks. Every room in the Lodge had a view of the ocean, and in winter people came just for a ringside seat at the spectacular storms.

'How did you manage to get a room like this at the last minute?' Maggie threw her small black purse and her thin shawl on to an upholstered chair. She stood looking out at the silvery path of the moon on the black water. The wide band of light shimmered with the movement of the waves far out on the strait, sending molten ripples to blur the ever shifting edges.

Roger came to stand behind her. She felt his warmth on her back and his hands resting lightly on her shoulders. 'Anything is possible,' he answered. She was reluctant to probe the ambiguous remark.

She leaned back against him, watching their reflections in the glass. She saw his head bend down and then felt his lips touch her hair, moving down her neck to her shoulder. With one arm he reached out and pulled the cord of the drapes, shutting out the outside world. Now she was alone with only him, cut off from the glow of the moonlight and the restless movement of the water. Gently, he increased the pressure of his hands until she turned to him. She felt the long length of him against her as he gathered her closer to him.

She saw his look change, saw the desire in his eyes and couldn't look away. Her breath came faster, her heart pounded, her knees were shaky.

'Roger,' she said huskily.

'Don't fight it Maggie,' he said in a low whisper. 'It's what we both want. I've waited so long for this.'

He lowered his face to hers, and his lips traced her mouth and jaw with tiny butterfly kisses. She felt the strong muscles of his back under her fingers and stroked down to his waist. His hands traced the line of the top of her dress, finding the opening at the back. His warm fingers pulled down the zipper, and then his palms caressed her bare flesh.

His thigh pressed against her leg, pushing and insistent. She felt herself melting, becoming pliant in his arms. She ached so much for this kind of closeness, this kind of physical intimacy. She'd missed it so much. It felt so good to be held, touched, kissed, *wanted* . . .

As her response grew, she tightened her arms around him and heard the muffled groan in his throat. His hands hesitated for a moment, and she knew he was wanting confirmation to go further. She leaned into him and kissed him harder. He was what she longed for. She was ready to give in her turn. He desired her, and the knowledge made her tremble.

She opened her eyes and saw the emotions in his face. She saw the flush on his cheeks, the luster in his eyes. His breath was warm on her face, and his chest heaved beneath her hands.

She allowed herself to delight in the involuntary physical responses and moved with him as he brought his hands to his shirt front.

He undid each little button, and she slid it from his shoulders and over his hands to let it fall in a soft heap on the floor. His hands were on her back again, feeling for the clasp between her shoulder blades. He released the catch and pulled her dress and lacy bra forward to free her breasts. His head bent to nuzzle between them, and she arched backwards.

She dropped her hands to his waist and fumbled with his belt buckle. No, she would not think of the last time she'd done this. Now the act was cushioned with laughter and warmth instead of hostility and anger. This was what she wanted. She allowed herself to drift with the sensations Roger was arousing in her. She savored the taste of him on her lips, delighted in the stroking of his hands on her naked flesh and ruthlessly squashed deep down inside her the small, mournful, grieving voice that could not be silenced.

Her dress fell to the floor, and she no longer knew or cared what was happening. All she knew was that she was surrounded by warm desire, that she was treasured, loved, worshipped. Roger told her so as his kisses grew harder and his hands hotter and more impatient. She dropped her head back to allow him to follow the line of her throat with his lips. His mouth settled in the hollow at the base of her throat and she felt his tongue begin to explore the sensitive spot.

She was entirely lost in the sensations invading her body. 'Kurt,' she gasped.

Immediately Roger tensed, his movements stilled. Maggie froze, still hearing the name echo in her head. She dropped her arms from Roger's shoulders and stood motionless in disbelief. Suddenly she was alone, the space between their two bodies seeming to vibrate, holding them apart. After endless moments, she bent to retrieve her dress. My God, she thought, how could I do that? With shaking hands, she pulled the material up around her, covering her nakedness.

At last, she dared lift her eyes to Roger's face.

'I'm sorry,' she said. 'This was a mistake.' She only needed to reach out, grasping the wealth of emotion and caring that was offered to her at this moment. But she couldn't do it.

Roger's lips were pressed in a hard, thin line. His eyes were narrowed and his jaw tense.

'What's going on?' he said harshly.

'Please,' Maggie whispered, blinking back tears. 'I shouldn't have agreed to this. I'll leave.'

She felt Roger's hands on her upper arms, holding her tight, squeezing hard. 'Just what are you playing at?' His voice showed his anger.

'I didn't want to hurt you, Roger. I like you — '

'Like me? You've been teasing me, giving me the come-on for weeks, months. I want what you promised me.'

His arms were right round her now, holding her fast, he thrust his face down and kissed her fiercely, hurting her lips. She struggled to wriggle free. When he removed his mouth, she drew in a breath at last and pushed against his chest with both hands.

'You don't want to do this, Roger,' she said.

'The hell I don't.' He renewed his attack on her lips.

All tender feelings, warm emotions had fled, replaced by fear and apprehension. Would anyone hear her if she screamed? What would happen to Roger if she called for help? He would be humiliated, embarrassed. He didn't deserve that, although now he was behaving like an over-sexed adolescent.

She tried to think logically. Of course, there was the knee in the groin, but only as a last resort. She thought she knew enough about him to try something else. He was no rapist, nor was he the kind of man to force himself on an unwilling woman.

She stopped moving and stood stock still, tensing herself from pulling away from his plundering mouth and hunting hands. She was inert, a statue, a plastic doll with no life, no emotion.

After a moment, he hesitated and lifted his head. He gave her a searching stare and flung her away from him. She caught the back of a chair to steady herself.

'Damn it all to hell,' he growled. He turned away from her and pulled on his pants.

She repressed a wild impulse to giggle from sheer nervousness and relief. A man with his pants round his ankles can be a ridiculous sight, but she had no wish to anger him further by implying she was laughing at him. She said a small prayer of thanks at his change of heart and attended to the zipper on her dress. She slipped on her shoes and retrieved her purse and shawl. Roger was still buttoning his shirt as she paused at the door.

'I really am sorry, Roger,' she said. 'It was my fault. I hope you can forgive me.'

9

The next morning, Maggie dumped the fading roses in the composting bin in the yard and went down to the darkroom. The tiny space in the basement offered a domain that was entirely hers, cut off from the outside world. Neither Kurt nor Roger had ever set foot in it. She heard the phone ringing faintly while she was absorbed in her work but lacked the energy or the will to climb the stairs to answer. She felt drained and miserable, and all her joints ached, as if she were starting a bad case of flu.

She'd dragged herself out of bed and avoided looking in the mirror as she pulled a comb through her hair. She didn't need to see her red and swollen eyes and the droop to her mouth to know that she looked terrible. She'd wept silently all the way home in the cab, cried in humiliation and self loathing as she got ready for bed, then fallen into a deep and dreamless sleep, as if poleaxed.

She'd woken still feeling tired and lethargic. After two quick cups of coffee and a pill for her throbbing head, she'd made her way down the basement stairs and thrown herself into catching up on developing the shots she'd taken over the last few days.

It was hard to believe that it was only last Sunday night she'd heard the news about Kurt. It was now Thursday morning, and she'd spent two nights in the same house as Kurt — although, thank god, not in the same bed or even in the same room. She'd taken Jeff to camp, dealt with Dianna's blackmail, accompanied Frieda to the hospital, spilled her guts to Ellen, and decided to sleep with Roger. No wonder she felt as if she'd been through an emotional wringer.

And what was she to do about Roger? She poured the developing solution and watched it swirl in the tray. Could she face him again? Would he be willing to work with her as he had before, knowing she was remembering him aroused and hot and panting with his shirt off and his pants down around his ankles? She grimaced. Roger was a proud man. The very sight of her would be like rubbing salt in a wound.

Add to that the fact she'd seen a side of him she didn't particularly like. Yes, he'd been enraged, and yes, he'd controlled himself, but she'd seen the violent temper she'd sometimes suspected lay below the surface. How could they treat each other with respect and trust after that?

She dipped the film into the liquid and wiped her hands on an old piece of towel. Maybe she'd been wrong to stay in Branscombe. Maybe it was time to move on, distance herself from all the memories. There was only Frieda to keep her here, and there were ways of keeping in touch without being so close at hand. She would miss the house, but every time she went into the kitchen and looked at the short passageway leading to Kurt's old room she would see him there in his red shirt and his jeans. She would see the tanned skin, taut over bone and muscle. She would see the black hair curling down to the nape of his neck, she would remember his hands, long-fingered and agile on the wine bottle. She would never be rid of his ghost in that house.

So if she couldn't work at Glenhaven because of Roger, and she couldn't live in the house because of Kurt, it was time to look elsewhere.

She pinned her prints on the string that stretched above her head and ducked under them to leave the basement room. As she climbed the rough wooden stairs, she was already composing her letter of resignation. It would be fair to give Roger a month but no more. There were other jobs that had been hinted at as she'd talked to administrators in other buildings. She had the names on file. She only needed to find them and make contact. Then she would see Frieda about what to do with the house.

She brushed her hair and fixed it with a barrette, feeling as if half the burden had been lifted. She would clean up, go over to her office, and search for that letter from Ardmore Seniors Home she'd tucked away, never dreaming she would use it. And she would type up a resignation letter to Roger.

★   ★   ★

Roger's Mercedes sat gleaming in the parking lot with her own slot empty next to it. Not wanting even her car near his, she carefully pulled her old beater into a space as far away as possible. She thought of slipping in the side door, which would make a longer route to her office, but decided to go in through the main entrance as she always had. There was no need to skulk around the building like a criminal. She'd nothing to be ashamed of. She'd realized her mistake, stopped the action, and apologized.

But she couldn't help wishing she'd never talked herself into believing Roger was the answer to what she wanted. Kurt wasn't the answer either, so she'd better concentrate on making her own way as she had until now. She refused to be spun around, thrown off track by a man — two men, in fact. From now on she would return to looking after her own self. Maybe she just wasn't meant to find someone who shared all her longings and aspirations. Her choice of men — Kurt, Steve, and now Roger — should maybe be telling her something.

She was deep in thought as she walked down the main corridor, so deep that she started when Roger's door opened, and he emerged as she was passing by.

She placed a hand on her chest as if to still the thumping of her heart and swallowed hard.

'Good morning,' she said and gave a little laugh. 'You startled me.'

Roger did not return her greeting. 'I was hoping to see you,' he said coldly. 'I tried to call. Please come in.'

She followed him into his offices, noting that Carol's desk in the outer one was empty. He ushered her into the inner room and shut the door.

'Please sit down,' he said, formally.

She sat on the edge of one of the leather chairs, her hands clasped on her knees.

Roger cleared his throat and sat behind his desk.

'About the business with Dianna,' he began, 'I've been giving it some thought.'

She waited to hear what he'd decided to do about reimbursing the residents.

He leaned forward and straightened the edges of the papers on his desk. 'You, as the administrator, are responsible for everything that happens in the residence — everything non-medical, that is.' She suddenly knew what he was going to say.

'Not only is there this — ,' he paused, ' — inexcusable lack of integrity with regards to the nurse, but I have also been informed you brought a wanted criminal into the building late at night. The police were called, and fortunately our residents suffered no harm, no thanks to you. You exposed everyone here to enormous risk by such thoughtless, irresponsible acts.'

He cleared his throat and straightened some papers on his desk. Maggie kept her eyes on him, but he refused to look up to meet her gaze.

'I no longer feel that I can place my trust and confidence in a manager who has so little awareness of what is going on, so little sense of duty and responsibility,' he continued. 'I have no choice but to ask for your resignation.'

She rose to her feet, feeling as if she were

watching a slow motion scene unfold in a movie. She stood to face him, as he sat sleek and pompous behind his ostentatious oak desk. She would have thought more of him had he admitted to feeling humiliated, ill-used by her. Instead, he was hiding behind trumped-up excuses for removing her from his environment. She raged inside at not having got her letter of resignation in first. And she had been feeling guilty, even sorry for him! She opened her mouth to tell him exactly what she thought of him, but closed it again and turned on her heel.

At the door, she paused and turned towards him. 'You will have my resignation on your desk within the hour,' she said, stepped haughtily through the door, and pulled it behind her, careful not to make more than a discreet click as it closed.

* * *

The letter of resignation was easy to write. She printed it up, made a copy, signed them both and placed the original on Carol's desk before she left. The door to Roger's inner sanctum was closed. She stood for a moment looking at the solid barrier and knew she didn't care if Roger was shutting her out both literally and symbolically. Feeling the strength of the empowerment this gave her, she knew she was well out of any involvement with him.

'Enjoy,' she muttered to herself and left for the hospital.

She found Frieda sitting up in bed, looking pale but alert. Tubes still snaked under the covers and a needle led a drip into her arm.

She smiled brightly at the sight of Maggie and held out her free arm.

'I'm still here,' she said.

'So I see. I'm delighted to see you looking so well. How are you feeling?'

'Pretty antsy. They won't let me read more than one newspaper. I can't talk to Jane Wentworth, and they feed me slops. I'm ready to leave.'

Maggie laughed. 'They might be glad to be rid of you.'

'Yes, well, I figure if I make myself objectionable enough, they'll let me go. That doctor, the one that looks about eighteen, doesn't quite know how to handle me.' She chuckled and patted Maggie's arm.

'I'll talk to him,' Maggie said. 'We don't want you back until you're fit.'

Frieda let go of Maggie's arm to pick up her spectacles from the bedside table. She settled them on her nose and peered more closely at her visitor.

'You look like death warmed over,' she

announced. 'What's wrong?'

'I was worried about you — ' Maggie began.

'Pshaw!' Frieda dismissed that with an eloquent wave. 'Not enough to have cried all night.' She waited expectantly. 'I'm not too old and blind to see that.'

Maggie smiled and took back the thin hand. She stroked the back of it and leaned closer.

'I'm fine,' she said, as cheerfully as she could.

Frieda moved impatiently. 'Sit me up more,' she commanded. 'And then tell me what's going on. Is it Kurt?'

Maggie repositioned the pillows and gently pushed the old lady back until she was comfortable.

'As far as I know Kurt's fine,' she said. 'I talked to the policeman in Wellington and he'll be free to leave any time now.'

Frieda closed her eyes. 'Thank God,' she said quietly. 'I love that boy, you know Maggie. I knew he couldn't have done anything wrong. He's a good soul.'

Maggie sat down again in the chair by the bed. Frieda looked at her again.

'So, there's something wrong with you,' she stated. 'Tell me what it is.'

'Let's wait until you're better before we

talk about any problems.'

'Well, if you want me to fret and worry, send myself into a relapse, go ahead. I'll tell the doctor to give you a good talking to. He'd like to have something useful to do.'

Maggie sighed and gave in. 'Okay, you win. What would you say if I said I was thinking of leaving Branscombe?'

Frieda withdrew her hand, looked down, and carefully pleated the edge of the top sheet. Maggie waited. Frieda was the first one to whom she'd articulated her decision to leave. Saying the words aloud made it real, almost inevitable. But she needed to know Frieda would accept the idea, for the old lady had been her only family apart from Jeff for the last years.

'I'd say it was a good idea,' Frieda said at last.

'You would?' Maggie couldn't hide her surprise and relief. 'I was worried about the house . . . '

Frieda shook her head. 'Houses are just possessions,' she said. 'We can work that out.' She smoothed out the pleat she'd just made. 'There are too many bad memories for you in this town. But what about Dr. Saint George?' Her spectacles had slipped down her nose, and she peered slyly at Maggie over the top.

'He won't keep me here.'

Frieda continued to nod thoughtfully. 'I'm glad to hear that, too,' she said. 'He was never the right one for you. You need a man more like Kurt.'

'No, I don't,' Maggie said vehemently. 'I'm going to concentrate on a new job, on Jeff, and on my photography. That's all I need.'

'Hmm.' Frieda didn't sound convinced, but she dropped the topic. 'Where will you go?'

'I'm not sure. Not too far away, I hope. I've met people over the years. I'll find their names and addresses in my files in the office. I thought this weekend I'd update my résumé, do a covering letter.'

'Don't take yourself clear across the country like Kurt.'

'Kurt? Across the country?' She sat very still, listening to the sudden pounding of her heart, the rush of blood in her ears.

'He's got an offer from a college in New York. Teaching Environmental Studies. Did you know he got a degree?'

'Not just a first degree, a doctorate.'

'I always knew he was a clever boy,' Frieda said fondly. 'He's such a fine man.'

Maggie could not agree. Here she was, planning to tell him he had a son, willing to give him the opportunity to create a bond with the boy, and he was thinking of living thousands of miles away. Unreasonably, she was angry with him that he wouldn't be around, even if he didn't know yet that he had a good reason to stay close.

This might not change what she told him, but as sure as shooting it would change what she offered him. No negotiations on visiting. No way would she ever put her son on a plane to New York to see a father who didn't care enough to stay around. Being an 'uncle' was maybe all Kurt could hope for. Why hadn't he told her of his plans?

'Will he give up his business?' she asked.

'I think so.'

'He told you a lot while he was here.'

'Yes, yes, he did.' Frieda hesitated as if about to say more and seemed to change her mind. 'I'm looking forward to seeing him again. You bring him to see me as soon as he arrives.' She patted Maggie's hand again.

Before Maggie could find the words gentle enough to say tactfully that Kurt could find his own way anywhere he wanted and didn't need her help, the door opened. They both looked up. The young doctor whom Frieda loved to tease, poked his head in.

'You've won, Mrs. Haydon,' he said cheerfully. 'We're going to have to get rid of you.'

'About time.' Frieda began to sit up and push the covers back.

'Whoa,' the doctor said, coming right into the room. 'Give us a couple of hours to make the arrangements. You'll be back in your own bed tonight.'

★   ★   ★

Maggie spent the rest of Friday in her darkroom, developing and printing her latest pictures. The stark black and white brought out the subtleties of line and expression, chronicling the events of the past week, from Jeff playing touch football on Sunday, to the magnificent shots of the eagle as it dipped and soared over the water at the beach.

Halfway through the pile, her fingers hesitated and picked out the pictures of Roger. Carefully, she tore them into small pieces, then dropped the scraps into the garbage can, dusted off her hands and turned back to the important stuff — those photographs that had a good chance of acceptance for the book. She'd submit the best and then file them all away for the exhibition she secretly longed for one day.

There were plenty of shots of people and places, but the only face that was missing was the one that filled her thoughts and dreams. Kurt's sudden, secretive arrival had dominated her life for the last week, and still all she had was the blurred newspaper photograph and the old yearbook. Frieda had said she was looking forward to seeing him again. Maggie was not. She could feel him, imagine him, without him even being there. Dammit, she could feel him in the secret, hidden spots of her body she shouldn't even be thinking of.

Her face grew hot at the memory of the awful slip she'd made with Roger. What did that mean about her subconscious thoughts and desires? She would need to keep a very tight rein on her feelings until Kurt was gone from here, all temptation removed.

She went to bed early, reading a novel until her eyes drooped. Her sleep was restless, punctuated with half-waking moments where she thought she heard Kurt's voice in the kitchen, thought she felt his presence next to her. Frieda was right. It was time to leave this house with its ghosts and this town with its memories at every corner. She'd thought it best at the time to keep Jeff in an environment he knew and where he had friends. She'd taken care of them both for a long time, she could continue to do so. Kurt would say sometimes you had to cut the ties, set yourself adrift and allow the winds of fate to carry you to a new shore. He'd been a good example of that philosophy. Could she do that?

She chose Saturday morning to return to her office to search through her files for the information she needed. Although a full complement of attendants would be on duty, she knew the business areas would be deserted. She pushed the door of her office behind her, not bothering to close it completely, and opened the slats of the blinds to let in more light. Quickly she unlocked the filing cabinet, removed two or three of her personal files, and carried them to the desk. Leafing through each folder in turn, she checked that the names and addresses she needed were all there.

She laid the 'Contacts' file on her desk and then picked out the one with copies of her references and recommendations. The list of places she'd worked was not long and most of the material dealt with Glenhaven. But there were letters from appreciative families, from suppliers and a couple of attestations of courses taken. She spread the papers out and switched on her computer.

Suddenly, there was a movement in the hall, and a shadow fell across the threshold. Startled, she caught her breath and glanced up, her heart pounding. It was probably a cleaner. There was no reason for Roger or anyone else to be there. She listened, then nudged her chair back, ready to stand up and investigate.

Kurt appeared in the doorway, pushing the opening wider. He looked better, with more color in his face. His arm was no longer in a firm cast bound to his chest but wrapped in an elastic strapping. He was wearing a midnight blue shirt and clean jeans. The bruises had begun to fade, as had the lines of tiredness around his mouth.

'Sorry, didn't mean to scare you,' he said.

'You didn't,' she fibbed. 'What — what are you doing here?'

'I could ask you the same.' Kurt eased himself into the room. 'I thought you were on vacation?'

She pressed her hands onto the desktop to hide the tremble that was shuddering through her whole body. She'd known he would come back. Why should she be surprised?

'Yes, I am really.' She paused. 'Why are you here?'

'I came to see Oma. The hospital told me she was back here. I saw your car outside. What are you doing at your desk on a Saturday morning?' He came closer, bent over her. She could feel the warmth of his breath stirring her hair. The tiny hairs on her arms seemed to quiver with the nearness of his hand.

He picked up the paper on the desk and turned it to read the list. One eyebrow rose. 'References? Are you leaving Glenhaven?'

She nodded without speaking.

'Why, Maggie?' His voice was soft. 'What made you decide this?'

Suddenly, the caring tone of his voice wrenched at her heart. Her eyes burned with tears, and she blinked hard to stop them spilling over. She bit her lip and shook her head. His hand on her shoulder was warm and comforting. Dammit, here she was melting into tears twice in as many days. So much for being powerful!

'Maggie, I hate to see you like this. This isn't the feisty woman I know. Tell me about it.' He wiped away a telltale tear with gentle fingertips. He understood her, knew how she hated to lose control. The gesture over-whelmed her and the dam broke as harsh, racking sobs tore her throat. Kurt pulled up a chair and sat beside her, taking her hands, warming them between his own.

'Please, Maggie. Let me help if I can.'

'Roger,' she gulped. How could she possibly tell Kurt about Roger? She could no more relate Roger's trumped-up reasons than she could reveal what happened in the bedroom at Golden Point. 'I've quit,' she finished on a deep breath. 'A business disagreement.'

'Hmm.' It was almost a grunt. He squeezed her hands.

'I thought I could handle it.' The tears had stopped, her voice was a whisper. She took her hand from his and reached for a box of tissues on the corner of her desk. 'Sorry to give you such a spectacle. I guess I hadn't realized what I was really feeling. A very important part of my life was spent here. Glenhaven gave me the chance to work and to build my skills. There was satisfaction in the job and good friends.'

She told him about Frieda's investigation and Dianna's activities. But she still didn't mention the evening with Roger. Kurt didn't say anything about taking a job in New York.

'I'm fine now,' she said after a few minutes. 'I'll finish finding what I want.'

Kurt stood up. 'You and I need to talk,' he said. 'I'm staying at the cabin. I'll go and see Oma, then we can go for lunch. You choose the place.' With a wave he turned to the door.

She watched him leave the office, still favoring his wounded leg. He was a complicated man. One moment he was forceful, independent, and commanding as a feudal lord. The next instant he metamorphosed into a kind man who, she believed, could look after her, had depths of feelings and the empathy she longed for. Although she'd loved him once, she'd long ago told herself that believing she was in love with him was the stupidest thing she'd ever done. Except that the doomed love affair had given her Jeff. She could never feel regret for having him. But there was no future with Kurt Rainer while there were so many unresolved issues of trust.

She thought she'd rid herself of him, but now he was back with more heart-wrenching declarations. He stirred up the phantoms, recreated the emotions that she'd hoped were long buried.

She'd accused him of being untrustworthy, which she still believed to be true, but her conscience pricked her in turn for her secretiveness. He would be going away to his new position in New York. He was not interested in family ties. She would be honest with him, let him know that Jeff was his son. But there would be no on-going relationship with the boy because, judging from his remarks, Kurt just wouldn't care enough. There was no danger in letting him know the truth because he would depart and leave them to pick up the pieces of their lives. If he insisted on seeing Jeff after camp, on talking to him, she could handle that. She and Jeff had each other. None of the past could destroy her. She was a survivor. She had to make her peace, wrestle her demons, and take a chance on her destiny.

★ ★ ★

Kurt left Frieda's room with a smile on his face. The old lady had always had the knack of making him feel good, making him believe in himself. But she was loyal. She'd not really answered his questions about Maggie.

'I know nothing about Maggie's life with Steve,' she'd said, 'or with anyone else. And even if I did, I wouldn't gossip to you about it. Maggie is the only one who can answer those questions, if she chooses to do so.' She could certainly put a guy in his place.

Who was this 'anyone else?' He remembered the roses and the few times Roger Saint George's name had been mentioned. Had something been brewing there? Was that why Maggie was so upset about leaving? He tried to ignore the stab of jealousy that struck at the mere hint of the doctor's name.

With Frieda, he changed the subject to his upcoming lunch date with Maggie.

'Good,' Frieda nodded emphatically. 'Be

gentle with her. She's going through a difficult time.'

He walked quickly back down to Maggie's office, taking the stairs.

She had her back to the door, putting papers back into their folders. He took a moment to admire the line that swept down from her neck to her waist. Her head was bowed, and the sunlight from the half-open blinds turned her hair into a halo of gold. He thought about the women he'd been with over the years. He'd been no saint. But now he couldn't even remember their names. Surely there should have been at least one that stood out more than the others? But there wasn't. The only woman whose every feature, every gesture he remembered was Maggie. Maggie, his first love. His only love.

'Ready?' he asked softly.

She turned swiftly, and he caught a fleeting expression that he couldn't read. Surely she wasn't afraid of him? He recalled the scent of her hair as he bent over her at the desk, felt again the softness of her cheek as he wiped away the tear. His hands balled into fists in his pockets because he wanted to touch her again. No, who was he kidding? He wanted to hold her, push her down on the soft carpet, and do unbelievable things to her . . .

'Just about.' Her voice wrenched him out of his fantasy.

They walked side by side through the entrance foyer and out into the sunshine of the parking lot. She was wearing a long, flowered skirt in a nice blue color, and her hair was clipped low on the nape of her neck with a silver barrette. He would like to slip his hand under the mane and rub the tender, hidden spot like he used to. He'd like —

'Where to?' he asked.

'Do you remember Jake's?'

'Do I remember! The longest, coldest beers and the greasiest, juiciest burgers this side of heaven.' He stopped and looked at her with a wide grin. 'Don't tell me it's still there?'

She nodded and walked on. 'Sure is.' She hesitated and looked around. 'Which car?'

He headed to the silver BMW and heard her muffled exclamation from close behind him. The car embarrassed him in a way, and he should have known better than to buy it. But the purchase had been made at a time when he thought expensive toys would make up for all of the other things he'd been unable to come to terms with. Later, he'd realized that symbols and accessories of any kind can't define a man's value, but it had seemed easier to keep the machine than to pass it along to someone else.

The top was down, and the vehicle purred easily when he started it up.

'It's beautiful,' Maggie said.

'It's ostentatious. A big boy's toy, a symbol of conspicuous consumption,' he replied. 'Then why do you have it?'

'For the same reason I have a lot of things,' he said. 'Because I thought I needed it.' Maggie turned to look at him. 'Just a minute,' she said. 'Joe said you're not still wanted by the police. Is that true?'

'A totally free man,' he grinned. 'No shackles, no chain gang. Honest.'

'So what did he find out?'

He settled the seat belt around him. 'Joe says it's always the same,' he answered. 'Business or pleasure.'

'What does that mean?'

'Money or sex.' He started the motor.

She frowned. 'Who did it? Who attacked you?'

'It started as a trick, then got more complicated. All tied up with drugs, money, sparring over a girl — '

She felt a stab of jealousy at the thought that the contest over the girl might have included Kurt. 'I still don't really understand — '

'Don't worry about it. It's Joe's baby now. By the way, he said he liked talking to you.'

He turned right at the junction towards the old part of town. 'Said your voice told him a lot.'

He left her to ponder that remark. In fact, besides calling her cute, Joe had said her voice was sexy as hell and gave him cold shivers. Kurt couldn't argue with that.

Jake's was just as he remembered it — a ramshackle, wooden building with a huge deck and chairs that were cobbled together from driftwood. He climbed the steps holding Maggie's arm and looked around at the assembled crowd, hoping there'd be no one there he recognized or who recognized him. He wanted this time alone with Maggie. At least he didn't have to worry anymore about them calling the police. They found a table in the shade and looked at the handwritten menu.

'I don't think this has changed in twelve years,' he said. 'There's still the same spelling mistakes. And I think I remember this mustard stain.'

'Some things don't change,' Maggie said cryptically, her eyes lowered as she read the items listed.

He ordered two beers and the burger specials and then sat back sideways to the table, stretching out his legs. The tatty old umbrella that had once been blue and white still cast enough shade so that Maggie's eyes were difficult to read. She'd loved him once. Told him she would do anything for him. Where had that love gone? Why had she shut him out so completely from her life?

He wanted to know about the boy, wanted to hear her say that he was Jeff's father. He wanted to know what had happened to her, why she'd married Steve, what her life had been like. Surely, she couldn't have loved Steve? His stomach muscles tightened at the mere thought. It was becoming more and more important to him to reestablish the relationship they once had. He ached to touch her again, to see her smile in that sweet, shy way of hers, and for her to tell him she cared for him. He wanted her to care about who he was, what he was, how he felt inside.

'Tell me about yourself,' Maggie said, as if on cue, sipping the foam from her beer. 'When did you get your degrees?'

'You know about that?' He took a long gulp from his own glass, feeling the cool liquid flow comfortingly down his throat. He was pleased she knew, glad that she seemed interested. It had been a damned hard struggle, needing planning and organization. No one could say now he couldn't set his priorities and stick to them. If the truth were known, he was damned proud of what he'd done.

'I know that, and I know you have a condo and a business,' she said.

'That's right.'

The food arrived, great heaping plates of overflowing buns and French fried potatoes. 'This looks great,' he said, cutting through the juicy hamburger. 'Cheeseburger in Paradise, something, something, an onion slice,' he sang under his breath. The Jimmy Buffet tune had been a signal to meet up at Jake's, and now he couldn't even remember all the words.

'Shush. They'll think you're choking on it,' Maggie whispered.

He nodded, his mouth full. They ate in silence for a few minutes, then he wiped his lips. He wanted to share some details with her.

'I started studying soon after I left Branscombe,' he began. 'It seemed a good way to occupy my mind and to prove I could do it. My father,' he hesitated on the words, 'never believed I would amount to anything, so I was determined to prove him wrong, even if he never knew.' He speared a couple of fries and chewed them thoughtfully, then took another draft of beer.

'I wanted to be the opposite of everything the old man stood for.' He could still taste the bitterness and hatred in the back of his throat. The years had dulled but not eliminated the legacy of mistrust and humiliation he'd suffered. 'I wanted to be educated because he despised what he called book learning. Said it was unnatural. I wanted to be responsible for as much of the world as I could because he grabbed what he wanted and never gave a thought to anything but himself. I wanted to be strong, physically and mentally. I wanted to be successful in my own way, despite all his predictions.'

'And are you? Successful?'

He met her eyes unflinchingly. 'Yes, I am. I have a thriving business, money in the bank.'

'Is that the only way you measure success?' she asked.

He had accomplished too much to suffer scorn. His hands itched to seize her, to hold her, to make her understand what he'd struggled to achieve. Suddenly, he discovered that the most important thing was her approval of him. He wanted her to smile at him, to tell him how well he'd done. All his work, his studying, the buying of expensive

trappings had been to lay at her feet as
booty. Maybe he hadn't understood it at the
time, but he'd wanted to say: 'Here, I did
amount to something after all. Take all this,
it's yours.'

10

'I have a nice condo in Seattle,' Kurt said tightly. 'I have all the money I'll ever need. I have some friends I enjoy and a business I'm proud of. What's more, I've made a difference in the world. I teach people how to take care of the earth, how to look after the wilderness that's left to us. I haven't done too badly.' He waited for her words of approbation.

'Never married?'

God, she probed every nerve. Portia coldly apportioning the pound of flesh.

'Never.' He looked up into her inquiring eyes. 'You know what my family was like. My dad had kids. He did his best to ruin both of them. Steve, by indulging his every whim, and me, by breaking my spirit. With me, he didn't succeed. So, no, in answer to your question. I never found anyone I wanted that much, and families were never top of my priority list.'

He saw the shadow pass over her face. 'So you've accomplished your goals,' she said. 'You're a reliable, ethical person?'

'I think so.'

'People can trust your word now?'

'What do you mean, 'now'?' This conversation wasn't going at all the way he planned.

'Well, I was just thinking.' She pushed her plate away. 'When you left Branscombe, I expected to hear from you again.'

He felt as if she'd delivered a blow to his gut. 'Expected? I phoned, I wrote — '

She threw her napkin on top of the plate of untouched food in front of her. 'Don't make it worse,' she snapped. 'You forgot about me, the same as you forgot about your family. You put us all behind you. Out of sight, out of mind, if you'll forgive the cliché.'

He pushed his chair away from the table. 'I can forgive you a lot, Maggie, but I can't forgive you not believing me, not trusting me. There are things — '

'Can't you?' she interrupted 'I don't know what trust means to you, Kurt, but to me it means keeping your word, standing by people, not leaving your old grandmother who loves you to wonder if you're dead or alive for twelve years.' Her eyes blazed with anger. He could feel the heat of her as he stepped closer to take her arm.

She thrust him away. 'Don't touch me!' She picked up her purse from the back of the chair.

'Wait,' he said throwing a few bills on the table. 'I'll take you back.' He caught up with her in a few strides. Who did she think she was to talk about trust and openness when she was keeping the biggest secret of all from him?

'Regardless of what you think of me,' he said, sliding behind the wheel of the car, 'I've made my peace with Oma. I'm going to make it up to her. But we still have some things to talk about.'

'I think we've said it all.'

'No,' he insisted, 'I have some questions for you. And I have to collect my rental car and my clothes. I'll be by this evening.'

They rode back in strained silence to Glenhaven to pick up her car. Kurt drove off with a curt, 'See you later.'

He could see her in his mirror, standing by her old car, watching him slam through the gears and down the driveway. She was right, of course. He'd been wrong to leave Oma without a word. Pressure of work, isolation on back country treks, never wanting to set foot in Branscombe again, all these had served as excuses. But none of them was true. He'd been wrong. It didn't help his present mood to admit that Maggie had him dead to rights on that one.

But he'd tried to reach Maggie many times in those first weeks after he left. Her silence, her refusal to come to the phone, to answer his letters had driven him further away. His anger at his father had seeped through him like a creeping pool of dirty, stinking water until it covered his feelings for Maggie and replaced them with a seething resentment. Except that the small spark of memory and love had stayed alive, flickering almost into oblivion at times, but always there.

He pounded his fist on the steering wheel. He knew what his reputation had been all those years ago. He knew that girls were excited by his looks as well as by his antics, by his defiance of all kinds of authority, by his brushes with the law. He'd thought Maggie was different. But he could have been wrong there too. Had she been using him for thrills as well, just as his father had used him for cheap labor? Had both just thrown a crust from time to time, wanting to keep him amenable and dependent?

He'd tried to answer her questions honestly, and he'd seen the look on her face when he'd said he'd never found anyone he wanted.

Resisting the sexual pull she still had over him would be no worse than the months of celibacy, no harder than spending weeks at a time isolated from civilization, existing on dried rations and mountain water.

If he went to her house tonight to collect

his belongings and the rental car, he'd be able to challenge her about the boy. He'd tried charm, he'd tried candor. Now he would try forcefulness. But he wouldn't lose his temper.

★ ★ ★

'Hey, let's call a truce!' Kurt looked quizzically at the old pair of garden shears in Maggie's hand as he emerged from the silver BMW. He held up his hands in mock surrender. A young man emerged from the passenger seat, wearing the uniform of a car rental company.

She glanced down at the rusty old shears and shrugged, smiling despite herself. 'They're not much use,' she said. 'They need sharpening. Come in.'

She kicked the broken twigs and branches scattered from the bushes under the windows into an untidy heap. The fresh evening air smelled good, and she inhaled with pleasure the scents released by the clippings.

'I had another visit from the police,' she said. 'They're concerned for my security. I figured they're right about cutting down some of these shrubs.' The mindless physical activity of hacking and slashing at the excess growth had also helped her prepare mentally for Kurt's visit.

'Good idea,' Kurt said. 'Thanks for getting the rental car out.' The vehicle stood ready on the driveway.

'No problem.' She said nothing about cleaning off the smudges of blood on the upholstery, the reminders of Kurt's need for her a few short days ago.

She watched as he turned to the boy from the rental company, directing him to the car. Kurt was wearing freshly laundered jeans and a white polo shirt that seemed to glow in the fading light. She saw the movement of muscles under the thin material, noted the firm line of his knew only too well what it felt like to push her fingers through the crisp curls to trace the form of his ear, to kiss the spot where his neck met his chest . . .

He waved to the boy in the rental car and turned towards her. She caught her breath. The moment echoed her long ago dreams, Kurt returning home, walking towards her, love and tenderness in his eyes. They'd go in their house and draw the drapes. He'd kiss her until they couldn't keep their hands off each other . . .

Kurt was beside her, overwhelmingly male, overwhelmingly sensual. Carefully, he took the shears from her hand and laid them on the steps. He cupped her elbow in his hand and a shiver rippled through her. She let him lead her up the to the screened porch.

She'd laid out glasses and a bottle of white wine in front of the two rattan chairs with their faded floral cushions. She supposed it was a subconscious gesture of reconciliation after the conversation over lunch. At Jake's the beers had been left unfinished, the food uneaten, symbols perhaps of this limping relationship.

Beside the corkscrew and the ice bucket sat the photo album. One standing lamp with a weak bulb shed a honey-colored pool of light where they were to sit, and the far corners of the porch were already in deeper shadow. She wished she'd thought to bring out an extra lamp. The present atmosphere was too reminiscent of candlelight. The perfume from the cedar clippings under the window was mingling with the night-scented stock and honeysuckle.

With an effort of will, she tried to pull herself together. This evening was not one for self-indulgent make-believe. This was the moment she'd been dreading, the moment when she would tell him about Jeff.

She watched Kurt settle into one of the chairs, moving to find a comfortable spot. God, she'd loved this man. With her body she still loved him, still knew she would melt into his arms and count the world well lost for love. Except she was older now, wiser, more aware of the traps of the heart. And she had Jeff to think of. Caring for him through his infancy and childhood had been all-absorbing, with emotional rewards that had surprised her with their intensity.

She might understand with her head she should share her child, allow this man to be close to her as the acknowledged father of her son, but her heart screamed a warning.

They sat side by side in silence on the comfortable old chairs, looking out as dusk blurred the edges of the trees and shrubs. Even the birds were silent, giving only a muted chirp from time to time as they settled for the night. The whole universe seemed to be holding its breath.

At last Kurt moved and took hold of the neck of the bottle. 'Shall I?' he asked, quietly.

She nodded and watched his hands deal with the wine. He delicately stripped off the foil seal, unwinding it with his long, supple fingers. He thrust the tip of the corkscrew into the cork and twisted. The muscles on his forearms bunched and relaxed as he worked the stopper free. Still without a word, he poured wine into her glass and set it before her.

'Don't you want any?'

He shook his head. 'Not yet. I've a feeling I might need a clear head for this evening.'

That didn't say much for what he thought she would need. Defiantly, she took a sip of the cold wine, letting it slide down her throat like a frosty rivulet. She swallowed and shivered again. The night was magical, fraught with tension, with earthy aromas, with words hanging in the air as yet unspoken, with movements anticipated but not yet chosen.

Very deliberately, Kurt laid the tips of his fingers on the photo album. 'You want to tell me about this?' he asked.

'Not yet. We need to talk first.'

He sat back and linked his hands around a raised knee. 'Go ahead.'

'You told me a lot yesterday,' she began.

'I wanted you to approve of me,' he said. 'But I couldn't please you, even now.'

'Oh no.' Touched, she reached for his hand and clasped the fingers tight. 'I'm so sorry, Kurt. I don't know what got into me. Of course I approve. You should be proud of what you've done. You're an academic, a businessman, a scientist . . . '

'And alone.'

'Yes.' She squeezed the fingers again. 'I was upset yesterday. My nerves were on edge.

Can we try again?'

She let go of his fingers to take more wine. She grimaced. 'Dutch courage,' she said.

'Maybe I need some too.' He poured a finger of wine into his glass.

Maggie sat back, nursing the glass, turning the stem in her fingers. 'I want you to understand how devastated I was when you walked out of my life. How I waited and watched for a letter, a phone call — ' She raised her hand as he opened his mouth to interrupt. 'It doesn't really matter if you did or you didn't. The point is I was abandoned. I waited, but you never came. It was worse than if we'd agreed to part.' Kurt said nothing, his eyes fixed on the swirling insects on the other side of the porch screens. Maggie licked her lips, acutely conscious of his stillness, the containment of passion that she sensed beneath the surface. His fingers were still now, his shoulders squared as he sat with one foot propped on the other knee. He was like a panther biding his time, waiting to see which way the prey would jump.

She cleared her throat. 'You see, when you came back, I thought you might be a murderer.' He gave an involuntary movement and then subsided again. 'And of course, I didn't want to bring a criminal into my — into our — lives.' His eyes flicked towards her, but still he remained mute.

This was getting harder and harder. Why didn't he say something? She gathered her forces.

'When I realized that wasn't true, I was still afraid. I was afraid of what was between us in the past, and I was afraid of what you might do to me — to us — in the future.' She was not looking at him now, keeping her eyes cast down.

'You see, I know about the job you're considering,' she continued. 'You've probably accepted it by now. And you'll be gone again. You said, no ties. That's the way you like it, and I accept that. You have your life and I — we — have ours. I don't expect anything from you.'

'I've already declined.'

'You what?'

'I declined with thanks. It's one of the reasons I never mentioned it. I didn't think it important.'

He had turned now, was looking at her with those deep blue eyes. He was challenging her to accept him, to trust him. It was her turn to be lost for words.

'You see, Maggie, trust means sharing, but it also means not assuming the worst.'

He moistened his lips with some wine, and she watched his tongue lick a stray drop. She was suddenly hot, her breath came faster, her heart throbbed in her chest.

'I'd like to think we still have a chance to make something work between us,' he said. 'Words aren't my strong point. I'm better at doing than talking. I want to show you what I feel, not talk about it.'

Without warning, he reached for her, took her hands, and drew her to him. She rose effortlessly and seemed to float to him and settled on his lap, snuggling her head under his chin with a small cry of pleasure. She slipped her arms around his neck. His thighs were hard and she slipped her arms around his neck. His thighs were hard and supporting under her. Through her thin skirt, she could feel the other hardness swelling beneath her.

'God, Maggie,' she heard him whisper.

The many past moments spent in his arms assailed her, claimed her, reached deep inside her. This was a mercurial, baffling moment with conflicting thoughts and emotions, but she didn't pull away. The scent of his skin, of his hair, the utter rightness of his arms around her, all of it blazed with half-forgotten images. She lifted her head. His mouth was as soothing and well-known to her as her own body. Perhaps it had been too long since she had felt intimacy, perhaps it was just the wonderful familiarity of him against her, but she melted into the kiss and briefly lost herself in it.

His words echoed in her mind: 'To make something work between us,' he'd said. She hadn't answered him, knowing it would have been so simple to stay there, letting him hold her, feeling safe. Simple wasn't always right or smart. She pulled back gently. He'd refused New York, but how many other tempting offers would there be? He still had made no real commitment, and his bitterness still showed. She didn't want this, didn't want any more empty nights waiting for the phone to ring, like the first time he'd gone away. Waiting for Kurt to pick up the pieces, fill the hollows spaces of her life.

'This isn't a good idea,' she said.

'Maggie — '

She touched her finger to his mouth, stopping the words. 'Let's just leave it at that.'

She forced herself to leave his lap, trailing her fingers along his shoulder as she stood. Letting him go was one of the hardest things she'd ever done. She forced herself to smile brightly at him and sat again in her old chair. He was looking at her intently. She dropped her eyes again and picked up her glass.

She lifted it in a toast. 'Here's to whatever you decide to do,' she said.

She saw the muscles tighten in his jaw.

'Maybe you'd better tell me what the 'I — we' stuff is about,' he said curtly.

She looked at him blankly.

'When you were telling me how untrustworthy I was, you kept correcting yourself, using 'I' then 'we'.'

'I meant Jeff and I.'

'Jeff being the boy in the photo album. I looked at it the other day,' he said, by way of explanation. 'I did some calculations,' he added.

He stood and loomed over her, his hands thrust in his pockets. 'Is he mine?' he asked bluntly.

'What if he isn't?'

'Dammit, Maggie, stop it with these games. I know he's mine. Does *he* know?'

'He thinks Steve was his father.' She saw him close his eyes briefly, his mouth twist in pain or anger, she couldn't tell which.

'God, that hurts,' he said softly. 'When will you tell him the truth?' She looked up at him. 'I don't know that I will. Yet. Until now, both his fathers have failed him. I don't see giving him back a father who doesn't want him.'

She stood in turn and faced him across the half empty bottle of wine and the soiled glasses. 'You must realize that when you have the responsibility of a child, you don't place your trust blindly.'

'But I'm his father!'

'Yes, you are his biological father. But there's more to parenting than biology as you well know. I have a son who needs a real father. A father nurtures, sacrifices, comforts. He's strong and wise and, above all, he's present.'

'Dammit all, Maggie,' he barked. 'Why do you think I turned the job down?'.

She moved to the screen door and opened it. 'I'm willing to make arrangements for you to see him,' she said, 'when he gets back from camp. But the fact remains that you left me when I needed you, you stayed away twelve whole years without a single word to let us know you were at least still alive, and you freely admit you never wanted a family. It scares me to think what could happen. Unless and until you can be all I want for him, that's as far as it goes.'

He spun on his heel, opened his mouth as if to say something, then closed it quickly. She saw the deep intake of breath, the quiver as his whole body vibrated with suppressed emotions.

The screen door swung closed with a dull slapping sound behind him. She stood motionless, listening to his quick footsteps and then the sound of the car engine. She caught a shimmer of silver in the darkness as the BMW paused before pulling onto the roadway. Gradually the hum of the motor faded into the distance.

★ ★ ★

The scene replayed continuously in his mind for the next few days. At least he'd kept his word about not losing his temper, Kurt told himself, but it'd been damned hard. He'd driven up to the cabin and taken his frustrations out on anything he could find to hammer, remove or clean. But after a couple of days, there wasn't much left in the way of chores or repairs that he could do on his own and virtually one handed.

A couple of days had been more than enough to fix one or two of the rails that were hanging loose, sweep out the dust of years and reacquaint himself with the shorter trails snaking up into the dense conifers on the mountain ridge. He'd drunk too many cups of coffee, tried to read three yellowed, tattered copies of Louis Lamour cowboy tales that he'd once loved, and flung them all back onto the shelves after twenty pages. The tumult of doubts, hopes, and fears about Maggie and Jeff still whirled in his head like the dust devils in those westerns he could no longer read. His mood had swung from tightly controlled, self-righteous anger at being mistrusted and misunderstood, then simmered through a soul-destroying sense of injustice. Some people would talk it out with someone else, get another perspective. One of the women he'd known had been a great one for that. 'Tell me what you feel,' she'd say at every opportunity. She'd been disappointed more often than not.

He hated this kind of wondering and negotiating. It was like walking through a mine-field. In his experience, men usually liked straightforward things. Put a tool or a toy in a man's hand and point him in the right direction, and he was happy. Women were better at this. They had insights, instincts. They liked talking things over, liked listening to people explain things. They had different ways of solving problems. At least, that's what he'd seen mostly in his limited contacts with women. Of course, with his track record, he could be wrong about that too.

Anyway, who could he talk to? The only person he'd seen around was Dave Hirsch that night of his arrest at the clinic, and god knows he wouldn't take him up on the offer of a beer. That wouldn't do. Dave was a virtual stranger, besides being linked to a woman who should probably be in court facing legal consequences for what she did. He had no desire to share his problems with an old football player, whom he hadn't liked much anyway when they were kids. And if he wasn't going to share his problems, what was the point of talking to anyone? He took himself for a punishing hike instead.

As he tramped up the steep path, his thoughts returned to the chance meeting with Dave Hirsch and the nurse, Dianna. Nasty little creature she'd turned out to be, according to what Maggie had told him. He wondered what Roger Saint George was going to do about it. He'd never met Roger, but he had his suspicions about him in relation to Maggie. Roger was likely the guy who'd sent the roses. Maggie'd also hadn't made Kurt's day either. Maybe he should let good old Roger know he wasn't an incipient ax murderer.

Why had Roger sent those flowers? Had Maggie been about to give Jeff another father? The thought brought back all the boiling anger. How could she have believed Kurt was a murderer? How could she have married Steve? How could she have not wanted to tell Jeff who his father was?

He came back from the climb and stomped into the cabin, his mood no lighter than when he'd left. The problems were still sitting there like mice in an open backpack. Try to shoo them away, or pretend they didn't exist, and back they came, with friends, taking over everything. He'd had enough of licking his wounds and brooding. He needed some action. If nothing else, the long hike had given him an idea.

Invigorated by the sense of decisive action, Kurt showered and dressed in chinos and a white shirt. He even put on a tie.

There was a Mercedes in the Director's parking slot at the clinic, and Kurt figured the doctor was 'in.'

It was after four p.m. and the secretary's desk in Roger's outer office was cleaned and bare. Kurt took a quick look at the miniature switchboard. No lines were lit. He trusted Doctor Saint George was alone.

He tapped on the door and opened it without waiting for an answer. The clinic director looked up from some papers on his desk in surprise. He was a smooth-looking guy. Blond and groomed. All teeth and hair.

He was obviously annoyed at the unannounced interruption but was too good a diplomat to let it show for more than a flicker.

'Can I help you?' he said.

'Dr. Rainer,' Kurt said, advancing with a hand out and putting on a friendly grin. 'Kurt

Rainer. I'm Maggie's brother in law. Frieda Haydon's my grandmother.'

'Of course, of course. Sit down.' Roger's hand brushed his in a perfunctory shake.

Kurt took a leather chair and watched him working on the dilemma. Was this a client, he was wondering, a relative of a resident, or an advocate for Maggie? Or both? Kurt was beginning to enjoy this.

'I'm glad to see Mrs. Haydon is doing well,' Roger said as he sat in the other chair of the grouping.

'Yes, she is. Physically.'

'Oh?' He was too smart to give Kurt an opening.

'Emotionally, she's very fragile. Recent events haven't helped,' Kurt continued.

'Of course we'll monitor her heart problem.'

'I don't mean that.'

Roger cleared his throat. 'I don't quite follow.'

Kurt sat back, steepled the fingers of his two hands and put one foot on the opposite knee. 'She's very attached to Maggie,' he said.

Roger nodded. Kurt smiled. This was like stalking a bear for a photo shoot.

'So she was distressed to learn that Maggie will be leaving,' Kurt added.

Roger matched Kurt's posture and added an encouraging smile. The guy had done mediation training. Damn, he thought he was taking over the whole thing! Slimy bastard!

Kurt sat forward. 'I understand you were concerned about the police visit the other night,' he said.

Roger didn't like direct talk. 'I must admit . . . ' he hesitated, searching for the right response.

'Just so you know,' Kurt continued, ' — in case there's a problem with references or anything for Maggie — I was helping the police in their investigations. They needed me urgently at a murder scene.' Well, not strictly true, but close enough. 'So Maggie wasn't bringing a criminal into the building — I think those were your words?'

Roger put out a well-manicured hand.

'An honest mistake, Dr. Rainer,' he said. 'I just had the best interests of my residents at heart. I'm sure you understand.'

'I do indeed,' Kurt said, ignoring the hand and standing up. 'And as that's the case, I'm sure you'll deal adequately with the other issue.'

Roger had to stand up to face Kurt or else remain below his eye level. 'Other issue?' He was reduced to repeating words for fear of stepping into a quagmire.

'Yes, the issue of the nurse who was blackmailing patients.'

Kurt saw him flinch, but he was good. The mask came down again pretty fast.

'That is under advisement with my lawyers,' he said stiffly.

'Good,' Kurt answered cheerfully, 'because as the relative of a resident here, I wouldn't like to think anything would be hushed up, swept under the rug.' He deliberately repeated Maggie's words to him, knowing she must have said the same thing to Roger.

'Of course not.' Roger managed to sound hurt, unjustly accused.

'Good, because I'll be returning to live in the area, to take up some of the threads of my old life. You'll be able to keep my grandmother and me informed of developments. She did a nice job, didn't she, of ferreting out what was going on?'

Roger smiled weakly, as if it hurt him to move his lips. 'She did indeed. We're very grateful to her,' he said.

'Great. Glad to hear it.' Kurt slapped him on the shoulder, knowing it would annoy him even more. 'Look forward to another chat about this, Roger. I'll let you get back to your paper work.'

Without allowing time for a reply, Kurt left

him standing in the middle of his elegant office.

★ ★ ★

The trouble with that kind of action is that it gets the adrenaline pumping for a while, Kurt told himself. You feel good, able to conquer demons. But the original problem is still there when you come down from the high. He'd done it often enough, accepting long and demanding assignments to try to forget his inner loneliness and desolation. But the ghosts were still there in his apartment when he returned.

It was the same now. He whistled under his breath in the car all the way back to the cabin. He was still pretty cheerful as he cooked himself a steak on the outside barbecue and went for a swim in the lake. But the darkness and the empty bed brought back the thoughts of Maggie and Jeff.

He punched up the pillows and lay back, his hands behind his head.

There'd been no word from Maggie. She'd not phoned, and he'd not caught sight of her during his infrequent forays into town. He told himself it was for the best, since they no longer cared for each other as they once had. He'd tried, shown her a piece of his heart and she'd rejected him. He'd got the message loud and clear. She wanted a distant, business-like arrangement. He could handle that.

So, he'd resign himself to doing what Maggie wanted in order to see the boy. At least he now knew the truth. Jeff was his! His mind galloped joyfully ahead, planning trips, overnight camps, how to teach Jeff about the back country — when he wasn't shaking in his shoes at the thought of the responsibility.

A small voice of optimism persisted in encouraging him to believe he could still win Maggie round, still convince her of his feelings. She'd been severely hurt twelve years ago and it was obviously still too easy to tear the fragile skin from the wound. If he'd learned anything out in the wilderness, he'd learned patience. He'd think of her like a frightened deer, needing a gentle touch.

The next morning, still feeling down after the high of the minor victory in the confrontation with Roger Saint George, he made a list of his options and sat for a long time staring at the one around which he'd doodled a wavy line, tiny trees and stars. His subconscious might be trying to tell him something. Deep inside, he knew he had to go back to Maggie, salvage what he could. He threw down his pencil and swung his legs onto the wooden chair opposite.

He was getting as stir crazy as a mountain lion in a cage. He couldn't keep repeating the foray out into the world, snagging a victim as he'd done with Roger, and retreat snarling to his lair. Time to get out of the cabin, reconnect properly with people and try to make some sense of what to do next. He'd called Frieda every morning and evening and gone to see her once. She was doing well and loved to chat with him. Another pull on his heart, a good reason to want to stay near Branscombe. He could make up some of that lost time with Oma. As he had done countless times from his mother's death to his departure from Branscombe, he went to see his grandmother.

11

In the peaceful elegance of Glenhaven, Frieda was settled in her living room with a view over the ocean and the distant mountains. She sat by the window, looking frail and brittle as old porcelain, so she could see the grounds of the residence with the smooth lawns sloping down to the water. The flowers in the well-tended beds were a riot of color. A few residents were making use of the shady benches or were wheeled by family or attendants along the stone paths. Some walked, in pairs or alone, with the careful steps of age.

Frieda turned as he came in and held out her hands in the familiar gesture of greeting.

'A breath of fresh air at last,' she said kissing him on the cheek as he bent over her. She moved her hands over his shoulders and upper arms. 'So good to feel you, so full of life.' She tugged gently on his hand until he sat beside her on an embroidered footstool. It was too low and too hard, but he didn't want to let go of her hand to fetch a chair. He sat with his knees almost up to his ears and tried to ignore the lack of padding.

Frieda's eyes were on the people outside again. 'These places are all very fine,' she said suddenly, 'but I can't help agreeing with the person who called them the antechambers of death. We're all waiting,' she continued, 'all waiting out our time.'

'Don't — '

She took a deep breath and patted his hand. 'You're right. No morbid thoughts,' she said in a more cheerful voice before he could say anything more. 'Life has its stages. They all have their good and bad sides.' She looked at him more closely. 'What are you sitting on that thing for?' she asked. 'Your backside must be numb. Get yourself a proper chair.'

Thankfully, he rose to his feet, stretched, and repositioned himself beside her.

'That's better. Now, tell me what the problem is.'

'No problem, I'm doing well. Hardly feel my leg at all now, and I can take a deep breath without it hitting me like another stab wound.'

'That's good. But not what I meant. Tell me about your real problems.'

He shook his head, searching for a way to answer her.

'Well, I don't have all the time in the world for you to make up your mind,' Frieda said sharply. 'Why don't I start?'

He looked at her in surprise.

⋆ ⋆ ⋆

'One of the symptoms of old age,' Frieda began, 'is getting maudlin about family and posterity. It starts off by wanting to know about your past. Just bear with me.' She raised a thin hand. 'I've the right to be long-winded if I want. I did all that, traced the family back for nearly two hundred years. The papers are in my bureau.' She pointed to a walnut roll-top desk on the other side of the room. 'You can take them when you want.

'After that,' she said, patting the rug over her knees, 'you start to think about those that are going to carry on. Children and grandchildren and so forth.' She looked at him searchingly over the top of her spectacles.

Kurt shifted in discomfort. He was beginning to have an idea of what she was going to say.

'For a number of years, I thought I could treat Steve's child as my great grandchild, since you'd dropped out of sight. We'll deal with *that* part later,' she finished sternly.

'Yes, Oma,' he replied meekly.

'Steve was not my flesh and blood, but I loved him when he was little and tried to understand him when he was a man. We can talk about all that later too. So, I loved Jeff and considered him my great grandchild. Just pass me that glass of water will you?'

She took a sip and handed back the glass. 'That was all very well until Jeff started to grow up. He's just about twelve now, you know. That's significant, isn't it? I began to see the shape of his face, the set of his jaw. I looked at that dratted piece of hair that kept falling over his face. It didn't take a genius. He's yours.'

He sat forward in the chair, leaning his elbows on his knees, and rubbed his hands over his face. 'Yes.'

'So what are you going to do about it?'

'Do?'

'Don't be obtuse, my boy. You're a father. Fathers have responsibilities, obligations.'

'That's apparently the problem.'

'Tell me.'

'Maggie thinks I abandoned her . . . '

'It looked that way.'

'Well, I did try to reach her but never mind that now.' He thrust a fist into his open hand. 'I didn't know about the child.'

'No, of course you didn't. But why wait twelve years?'

He grimaced. 'I was angry. I was hurt. Time passed, and I told myself it didn't matter. I'd wanted her to go away with me, and she wouldn't. She wouldn't leave her parents. I couldn't imagine anyone choosing to stay with their parents.'

'No, of course you couldn't. Not with a father like yours. Poor boy.'

He stood up and paced to the window and back, hands thrust in his pockets, fists in a ball. 'I had to get away. I wanted her with me. She wouldn't put me first. I would have looked after her. I would have cared for the boy. Instead, she gave him to Steve. She let Steve see him grow up.'

'Steve wasn't an ideal father either,' Frieda remarked. 'Neither of you had a good role model.'

'She's still doing it,' he steamrollered on, ignoring Frieda's remark, letting out all the resentments he didn't even know he was harboring. 'She's paying off her brother Phil's debts, driving an old wreck of a car. All because of family. I find that — ,' he paused, searching for words, ' — damned hard to understand I can tell you. She doesn't seem to have much cash.'

He whirled to face her. 'What happened to all dad's money?'

'Oh, that went pretty fast. Steve got it all. I always had a feeling your dad suspected about Jeff. He wouldn't leave anything to him

260

in trust, although I tried to convince him. What power did his first wife's mother have when he rarely listened to any advice? Steve liked airplanes and cars and entertaining, if you know what I mean.'

He looked at her, understanding dawning. 'He was unfaithful?'

'Oh, yes. Steve couldn't have been faithful to anyone or anything for long. He got what he wanted — your girl and then he lost interest, just like he used to at Christmas. We always found his discarded presents around the house. Plus those of yours he'd taken over.'

'He never grew up.' Kurt was still on his feet, moving in the narrow space.

'But you did. Just mind where you're walking,' she said as he turned again. 'You're liable to whisk everything off my bureau.'

Kurt pulled in his elbows and slowed his pacing.

'That's better,' Frieda said soothingly. 'Now, where was I? You grew up and you know what you have to do.'

He sat down again. 'I have to stop feeling sorry for myself. I have to break the pattern. I can't be a man if I behave like a spoiled child.'

'You were never spoiled as Steve was spoiled. But you were damaged. You need to let those wounds heal once and for all. Maggie's right. Loving someone means putting them first when they need you. Can you do that?'

'I love her, Oma. I love her till I think it will choke me. I don't think she loves me anymore. I think I've hurt her too much to expect that.'

'Maybe.'

'I'll go see her.' He thrust his hands in his pockets and hunched his shoulders.

'Good boy.' Frieda patted his arm. 'I knew you would do the right thing. Be humble. Do you want the boy?'

'I think I want him as much as I want Maggie.'

'Go on with you then and let me have my nap.'

He bent down to her embrace, and she rubbed his back, resting her cheek against his shoulder. With a final kiss, Kurt left his grandmother's room and made his way back to his car. Well, he'd wanted advice from a woman and that's what he'd got. It was up to him to go through with what he'd promised.

The sun reflected off the parked cars in the main street and gleamed on the colorful umbrellas of outdoor cafes. Things had changed a bit over the years. On an impulse, he pulled into a free spot near a row of stores and restaurants. A coffee and something to eat would fortify the inner man.

Three or four crows were pecking at some discarded food near the entrance to a screened patio. A few sparrows hopped hopefully nearby. Carefully, he kicked a piece of discarded bread roll towards them, hoping they'd seize a mouthful before the big guys caught on.

He took a seat in the shade and ordered a light lunch. The terrace was busy with business people obviously on their lunch break, moms and dads out with their kids.

He watched a young family at a nearby table. Each parent held a young child on their lap while an older boy and girl played a game in a magazine and sipped drinks through long straws. Four kids! How did people manage it? Here he was worrying about taking on one nearly adolescent boy.

He looked around beyond the family group and settled his gaze on a trio of teens, giggling and snorting over a plate of French fries. Each one had something that stood out. One with green hair, one with a nose ring, one with a tattoo on a bare shoulder. Yet beside them was a pile of school texts. How much latitude did parents have to give? What did the expressions of teenage rebellion mean? At the age of those kids at the other table he'd have done the same, maybe worse. Jeff looked like him. Was he as much of a rebel as he'd been himself? As a father, could he handle that?

For a moment he let his mind drift, allowing himself to imagine himself and Maggie in the place of the family across the stone patio. The mom was constantly watching the children, moving things out of the way, responding to her husband's remarks with short answers. Was she the kind of woman whose life revolved around the offspring? Supposing he and Maggie got back together again? Supposing she was totally devoted to Jeff? Supposing he felt left out again, unwilling to share her love with a child? Supposing he blew every decision, failed to understand Jeff's needs?

He signaled for the check, suddenly needing to move, to think through these new insecurities. How could he tell what she was like without seeing her with the boy? The first objective, as Oma had said, was to talk to her, listen to her, get to know her again. His grandmother had only confirmed the option he'd settled on himself when he made his list. He strode with purpose to his car. Heck, he would eat humble pie if he needed to. Let her think what she liked about his past actions and motives. A surge of exhilaration swept through him.

★ ★ ★

Maggie patted the camera on the seat beside her. Today, she'd climbed high above the town, starting soon after dawn, capturing some panoramic views while the air was still clear and the light pure.

She was looking forward to a quiet evening, a quick dinner, a book on the porch in the fading light. Slowly, she was beginning to regain her equanimity, putting things back in perspective. The idea of moving away, starting a new job, was looking more and more attractive now she'd taken the first steps. She'd talked to the people at Ardmore and they were interested in her.

There'd been no word from Kurt. He'd probably left town. But she knew he would be back, to see Frieda and to arrange a visit with Jeff after camp. Kurt had always been self-willed. A few angry words from her were not likely to dissuade him from making contact with his new-found son.

The silver BMW was sitting outside her house under the shade of the elm, its black leather top folded back. She lifted her foot

265

from the gas in surprise, and the engine stuttered.

'Damn,' she whispered under her breath and allowed the vehicle to coast to a stop.

The door of the sports car opened, and Kurt stepped out.

'Want me to take it?' he asked.

'No, thank you, I can manage. I've had enough practice.' She concentrated on turning the key smoothly and working the accelerator just so. He had no right to come here without warning, startling her and her poor old wreck. The engine coughed and died again. Kurt stood to one side, watching her efforts. He would think she was totally incompetent. She turned the key again, silently willing the motor to turn over, and to her relief it did. She grinned triumphantly and eased into the driveway, turning the car so she wouldn't have to back out. No point in making things more difficult than they were.

She slid out from behind the wheel and carefully closed the door. The latch could be as temperamental as the motor.

'Hallo, Kurt,' she said. 'I wasn't sure you were still around.'

'I've been at the cabin.'

She led the way up the steps onto the porch. All traces of the other evening were gone. The sunlight poured in through the screens, and dust motes hung heavy in the air.

'May I sit down?'

'Of course. I'll take my camera in.'

Inside the house, she did a quick repair job on her hair and tucked her shirt more neatly into her skirt.

He was sitting in one of the rattan chairs, leafing through an old photography magazine. He looked up as she perched on the edge of the other chair.

'Can we start again?' he said, throwing the magazine back on the table.

She narrowed her eyes. He had no business looking like he did. With his back to the light, the years faded and he was the old Kurt, asking her the impossible. 'In what way?'

'I've been thinking about Jeff,' he began. 'Hell, I've thought about nothing else since I left here.' He ran a hand through his hair. 'Look, Maggie, would you show me the pictures in the album? I'd like to see what he looked like growing up.' His smile was uncertain, as if expecting rejection, and it tore at her heart.

'Of course. I'll get them.'

She got to her feet, her knees suddenly weak and moved into the house. For a moment, she leaned against the jamb of the living room door, out of sight from the porch before picking up the album and cradling it in her arms. She stood poised on the edge of a deep, dark pool, readying herself to jump in. The bottom was invisible, with hidden things waiting in the depths. She only knew she had to take this step. There was no turning back.

Maggie laid the book on the little rattan porch table and pushed away the magazines and newspapers. With tender fingers, she opened the first page.

'Tell me what it is,' he said quietly.

In a low hesitant voice she began to point out the photographs, adding a detail here and there until she grew more confidant and absorbed in the story of Jeff's life.

She leaned closer to him until their heads were almost touching. She could feel the warmth from his bare arm, so close that it almost brushed hers as they turned and smoothed the pages. The skin on her forearms shivered as if in a force field.

They arrived at a shot of Jeff holding a baseball bat and grinning widely, showing the gap where his two front teeth should have been. Kurt gave a hoot of laughter.

'How old was he here?'

'Six.'

He sobered. 'Was that when Steve died?'

She nodded. 'It was a bad time.'

She felt his hand on hers and clutched at his fingers.

'You've been a wonderful mother, Maggie,' he said. 'Jeff looks like a happy boy.'

She turned another page in the album with her free hand. Before she could withdraw her fingers, he took them prisoner too. She sat motionless, both her hands imprisoned between his warm palms, her eyes still on the last picture of their son. His hands were strong and hard, the fingers tanned and nimble, obviously used to hard work.

'Look at me, Maggie.'

She raised her eyes, terrified of what she would see in his. He was looking at her with tenderness, but she could see pain and distress too in his expression.

'I want to be a good father,' he stated simply. 'I want to do the honorable thing. But I can tell you, I'm scared half to death at the responsibility. Hell, I'm terrified of the decisions I'll have to make, worse than any encounter with any animal in the mountains. My heart's going a mile a minute.' He placed the palm of her hand on his chest. 'Can you feel it?' The pounding vibrated under her fingers, traveling to her own heart and setting it to racing.

'Will you let me in enough for that?' he said softly. 'I'm not asking any more.'

'Where will you be living?'

'Not far away. Can we talk about that some other time? You decide first where you're going. I'll look for something.'

She could still feel the heat of him seeping into her through her fingertips as he still held her hand fast. 'What about your business?'

'Already negotiating with my partner for him to take over. It was half done anyway. I'll be around Maggie, just as much as you want. No more, no less. You can trust me on this.'

She felt a tremor at the dreaded 'trust' word but pushed it away. Was she going to trust him? It was time to do what was right for Jeff and for Kurt. She prayed she was doing the right thing.

'Yes,' she said. 'Jeff should know his father.'

The words hung between them, vibrating in the air. Maggie knew she'd taken a giant step forward, as if stepping over a chasm. Now she was on the other side, facing a whole new landscape. She was in uncharted territory. Kurt's fingers tightened on hers, drawing her slowly towards him. She let her body move closer, sensing the heat, the tension that pulsed through him. An answering throb began in her, low down, insistent, all-consuming, not to be ignored.

She moved as if in a dream. Everything soft and blurred, just a notch out of focus. His hands were in her hair, buried in it, loosening the fastener at the nape of her neck. His lips were soft and hard at the same time and warm, beautifully warm. Her arms rose around his neck as if they had been waiting just for this. Slowly her eyes drifted shut, a delightful heaviness stole through her limbs while her mind seemed to float. As if from a long distance, she heard his long, deep sigh. The sweetest of aches stole through her as he covered her parted lips with his mouth.

Her thoughts drifted back to the past, to a more light-hearted time. She felt young again and in love. She'd had so many longings and desires that had never been fulfilled. The images of her past faded into the blackness, wiping out the memories of all that had happened — the love, deaths, joys, and pain. But this was not what she intended. How was this happening?

'I shouldn't be doing this,' she whispered.

He held her closer and rained tiny kisses on her face, her eyelids, her eager mouth. His tongue gently parted her lips once more and she rose to meet him. One hand dropped to her breast and cupped it through the light material of her shirt. She felt the nipple pucker and the ache spread deeper through her.

'I love the feel of you,' he whispered back.

'It's been so long.'

'I'm trying to be honest with you.' She struggled to sit up, but his arms held her firmly.

'Lie to me instead,' he said. 'Soothe me. Let's keep it simple for today, tonight. Save the complications. Let me dream. This kind — ' He kissed her again, and his hand stole under the hem of her shirt, lifting it from her body, creeping smoothly up to her naked breast. His thumbs caressed her rib cage, moving to the softness of her belly.

'I'm not one of your dreams,' she gasped.

'Oh, but you are, you are.'

She was not foolish enough to deny her reaction to him. She was dizzy with pleasure, longing for the void in her innermost being to be filled. She ran her hand down his chest and hesitated over the buckle of his belt. He made a noise of encouragement deep in his throat and she tugged uncertainly at his shirt.

He stood up, pulling her up with him. He wrapped his arms around her and drew her bottom lip into his mouth, sucking gently until she moaned in pleasure.

'There's never been anyone in my life like you, Maggie. Come.'

'What are you doing?'

'I'm taking you to bed.'

He passed an arm round her waist in a

reversal of their roles only a few days before and, closely joined at hip and shoulder, walked her into the house. Maggie did not try to resist. His desire overwhelmed her. Now he'd announced his intention to take her, she found herself powerless to resist him. She no longer wished to resist.

In the bedroom where they had both slept separately and dreamed of the other, they joined without reservation and moved together in the mysterious, leisurely cadence of men and women, totally in tune, totally in accord. Hip and thigh, breast and belly, lips and hands touched and flowed in delightful unison as they lost themselves in their pleasure.

Kurt's eyes were on her face as his hands and then his lips moved over, around, under, and in her as they loved each other with their eyes open in the warm summer sunlight, watching one another in silent delight. She saw him waiting for the changing expression in her eyes, the languorous smile that curved her lips and guided him to build the mounting storm within her. She came alive under his ministering fingers, moving and arching and twisting beneath him. When he entered her, she felt complete at last.

The storm of their passion abated slowly, leaving an aftermath of sweet lethargy,

Maggie pulled the comforter over them. She lay inside the curve of Kurt's powerful arm, her own arm draped like a protective shield across his hip. Her pounding heart began to slow as she watched him. His eyes were closed, his dark lashes curved against the barely visible bruises. This was, and yet was not, the same man she'd known years ago. The added years had also brought out his maturity, integrity, and sense of honor.

She'd thought him irresponsible and unreliable when he'd left her, never sending word for so long. But he'd built a career that demanded stability and integrity. He'd refused to back down in the police investigation, even if there was a threat to his life. He had courage, a need to fight for justice.

'You've changed,' she murmured, stroking a bare shoulder with the tips of her fingers.

He opened one eye. 'Have I? Not in every way.'

He took her hand and moved it down under the comforter to touch his hardness.

'My, and I thought you were asleep.'

'Just something I dreamed up for you.'

'I like the way you dream.'

She gave herself to him again, totally trusting. Once more, in blending with him, she found a wholeness that had long eluded her.

The birdsong woke her first, and she lay on her back, one hand on Kurt's naked thigh. She offered a silent prayer of thanks that she'd had the good sense to draw back from making love with Roger at the Golden Point Lodge. Nothing Roger could give her could match this priceless treasure of total union, of perfect meshing of bodies and minds.

Kurt muttered and stirred in his sleep, and she sat up to cover him again. The dressing on his side had slipped, exposing the wound. The gash was healing well as was the slash in his leg. The ribs had to be less painful — at least the exertions of last night had not seemed to cause a problem. She smiled to herself, remembering the tangle of limbs, the moist explorations, the haze of desire. She stretched and turned to lie spoon like against his back. The long warmth of him fitted perfectly against her.

Lazily she traced the curl of his chest hair with the hand that lay across him. He murmured again and pushed a little against her. She felt the delicious ache start again, spreading like an opening bud from her abdomen to her breasts, to her parted lips.

The telephone by the bed rang with a shrill

summons. She started and reached out, leaning across Kurt's body.

'Hi, mom.' Jeff yelled.

She pulled up the coverlet over her breasts as if her son could see her nakedness in bed with a man.

'Jeff,' she said. 'What's up?'

Beside her Kurt rolled over and sat up. She tilted the receiver so he could hear.

'I need your permission,' Jeff said. 'We can go on this special trek. Only six of us — the best in the group,' he added proudly.

She was suddenly cold and shivered, leaning against Kurt for support and warmth. 'Where to? How long?'

'Three days. Up to the top of Black Bear Ridge,' Jeff explained excitedly. 'It's a proper climb, with ropes and pitons and everything. It'll be awesome.'

'It sounds — ' she searched for a word.

'Don't get all wimpy, mom,' Jeff interjected. 'We've done lots of practice. It's perfectly safe. But it's not on the list of activities or something stupid, so I've got to call you.'

'Let me talk to the leader,' she said.

'Oh, *mom!*' All Jeff's potential disappointment and frustration was in the single word.

'Is he there?'

'Yes, just a minute,' he said resignedly. 'Hold on.'

She could hear the phone clunk against the wall as Jeff let it drop. Then she heard him yelling for Alan, his voice receding against the background of boys' shouts and clomping boots. She remembered the phone was in the hallway to the equipment store.

She put her hand over the mouthpiece and turned to Kurt. 'It's about a climb. I don't know if it's dangerous. Will you talk to him?'

Kurt nodded and put out his hand for the phone. She swung her legs over the edge of the bed and reached for her T-shirt. 'Hello,' she heard Kurt say. 'This is a friend of Mrs. Rainer's. I know a bit about climbing. What do you plan to do?'

The questions and answers went on for several minutes while she pulled on the rest of her clothes. Fully dressed, she turned back to Kurt, still sitting bare-chested in the bed. She waited anxiously. At last, Kurt looked up, lowering the receiver to the bedclothes to muffle their discussion.

'I think it sounds okay,' he said. 'They seem to know what they're doing.' He reached for her and kissed her.

'Isn't it risky?'

'Not really, if the boys follow directions. You have to let a kid take some risks.'

Of course that was true. Wasn't this why she wanted a male influence in her son's life? To allow him to do some of the things that scared her to death?

Kurt held out the phone and she took it, her eyes still on him. He nodded encouragingly and gave a half smile.

She took a deep breath. 'Alan? This is Mrs. Rainer. Of course Jeff can go with you. Just make sure he listens to you. Thank you. You'll call when you get back? Goodbye.'

She handed the phone back to Kurt to replace on the bedside table and gave him a tentative smile. 'Thanks for your advice,' she said.

'Don't worry,' he said again. 'It will be a great experience for him.'

His warm arms encircled her, reassuring, strong. She moved with him, pulling him to her. She couldn't get enough of the feel of him.

★   ★   ★

They showered together, unable to let go of each other, moving hungry hands over every inch of sensitive skin. It felt right to have him in her world. They'd never spent all day and all night together. The stolen moments of passion had been heady stuff, but now the

278

pleasure of seeing him in her house, hearing him move from room to room, dealing with the mundane tasks of finding clean towels, deciding on breakfast, and setting up the table, brought a surge of joy to her heart. This was her dream. Love and a complete family. She could hardly wait for Jeff to come home to be part of this and to complete the circle.

Kurt looked at her over his second cup of coffee. 'Know what I'd like to do?'

'Surely not?' she teased him. 'You're insatiable.'

His lips twitched in an answering smile. She knew just how they would feel under hers.

He reached across the table and drew her to him. Willingly, she stood and slid on to his lap.

'You feel so good,' she said. 'I don't deserve this.'

'That's your Puritan upbringing,' he said. 'Your family did a good job.'

Families still meant pain to him. He caught her as she pulled away. 'No, forgive me,' he said quickly. 'I didn't mean that. I'll watch my mouth.'

She relaxed and kissed him. 'Me too,' she said.

'The best way of muzzling a man yet invented. Now, stop distracting me, woman.

You're still on vacation?'

'Uh-huh,' she agreed, nuzzling his neck. 'Until next Monday, officially. Then I work out my notice.'

'It's only eight o'clock. I'd like to pack some baloney sandwiches and some beer and go back up to Outlook Ridge. We can start from the cabin.'

She sat back in the circle of his arms and stared at him. Outlook Ridge was where they had first made love. He recalled all the details down to the sandwiches and beer and he surely wouldn't have forgotten anything else. She moistened her lips. The memory of that first time made her stomach clench.

'Wouldn't it be wonderful to go up there again, knowing nobody can tell us to stop? Nobody to yell at us, be disappointed in us?' Kurt whispered in her ear. 'We might even reach the refuge hut this time.'

The hut had been their goal, but the lovemaking on the warm grass of the Alpine meadow had delayed them. She could smell again the sweet perfume of the crushed plants beneath their bodies, the feel of his skin, the reckless abandonment that had swept through her, taking with it all sense of shame, of reticence, of guilt. Deep in her abdomen, she felt the ache that only Kurt could quench.

'A re-enactment?' she whispered.

'Well, not necessarily of everything.' The desire in his eyes gave the lie to his words.

'If you're not up to it, so to speak,' she teased.

'Oh Maggie,' he said, hugging her close. 'Maggie, I'll do whatever has to be done.'

★　★　★

Maggie hoisted her pack on to her back and looked across at Kurt. The deck of the cabin was bathed in sunlight despite the early hour and the distant peaks shimmered already in the haze. She'd wanted to change the sandwich filling but Kurt insisted on the same thing. She'd never realized how much that first time had meant to him, how he'd treasured the memory of it.

They'd made love more than once already, but she still felt a hollow sensation of anticipation in the pit of her abdomen.

Kurt seemed unaware of her gaze as he busied himself packing his rucksack. He'd found some abbreviated corduroy shorts that allowed free movement of his thighs and molded the taut muscles of his buttocks. The plaid shirt was open at the throat, revealing the beginning of the tangle of dark hair, and the long sleeves were rolled up above the elbows. Her eyes followed the line down from the base of his throat, over the flat stomach . . .

They finished the check of supplies, verifying that each was carrying a warm track suit and rain gear as well as extra socks. They both wore stout shoes and thick hose. Although they were clad in shorts and shirts for the start, they knew that mountain weather was treacherous and that they must be prepared for sudden changes that could catch the unprepared hiker unawares.

'I'll take the food,' he called. 'Do you have the ground-sheet?'

'It's rolled up and tied to my pack.'

Kurt swung his pack up onto his shoulders. He grinned at her, the crinkles around his eyes apparent in the strong sunlight. 'Fine, let's go!'

12

Obediently, Maggie followed Kurt off the deck and across the flat expanse of grass leading to the beginning of the trail. The walk began with a stiff climb, allowing neither of them breath or thought for extra conversation. Their communication was limited to Kurt's warnings: 'Watch your footing here' and 'Let me go first' on a particularly narrow spot.

Gradually, they fell into an easy rhythm, anticipating where each would need a helping hand or a warning. They became companions, drinking in the beauty of the surroundings, delighting in the exertion of muscle and sinew as they climbed higher.

After a good hour of steady walking, the path opened out onto a ledge overlooking a spectacular view. Of one accord, they stopped and slipped their packs to the ground. Maggie chose a flat rock, warmed by the sun and, without speaking, sat to gaze out over the panorama of peaks before them. Kurt sank down beside her. She could hear him breathing harder from the exertions. She took deep breaths of the mountain air to slow the rate of her own heart.

Kurt took out the water bottle, ignoring the cups that were in his pack, and unscrewed the top. He passed it to her without a word. She put it to her lips, drank deep and offered it back. Without wiping the neck where her lips had rested, he placed his mouth to the same spot and drank, his eyes fastened on hers. She saw his throat quiver as he swallowed the cool water.

A heat rose in her from the pit of her stomach, leaving her weak and breathless, unable to wrench her eyes from his. Still without a word, he replaced the cap, stowed the bottle, and put out his hand to pull her to her feet. His hand burned in hers, and she felt the tremor go up her arm. Eyes down, she picked up her pack and led the way along the trail.

Her throat was dry despite the drink, her pulse racing from more than the exertion of the walk, and her whole body tingled with anticipation. She'd never succeeded in subduing the longing that invaded her whenever he was near, and now the delight of knowing she could love him without dissimulation, knowing he loved her, made her long for the magical joining of their bodies.

She'd been running scared ever since he'd appeared, not only because of the anger she still harbored but also because he threatened her in the innermost part of her being. He'd put at risk all her careful plans. And now those plans were gone, she saw they were worthless and could never have brought her happiness. From head to toe, her body was yearning for his touch, for the consummation of their love. A bird rose up in front of her with a clatter of wings. She checked, startled at the sudden noise and movement. A rock spun away from her careless foot.

'What is it?' Kurt called from behind her.

'Nothing. No problem.'

It was nearly noon when they came to the most difficult part of the climb. Kurt went first, scrambling on all fours at the steepest section.

He'd removed his shirt, leaving only the shorts to cover his slim hips. She found that the view from behind did nothing for her peace of mind. He reached the top and turned to her, breathing hard and flushed from his exertions. A thin film of sweat oiled his muscles. He stood like a hero from mythology, outlined against the sky, intensely male and dominating.

'Come up the same way,' he called. 'I'll come down a bit.'

She started up the narrow cleft, grabbing small bushes for a handhold. Near the top, she saw Kurt's foot braced against an outcrop of rock and his hand reaching down for her. She took hold of the outstretched arm and allowed him to haul her up. He was ready for her at the top as she came up with a rush and cannoned into him. Without hesitation, his arms came around her and before she could protest, his mouth was hard on hers.

'This is it,' she thought, before her mind ceased to function, and she was conscious only of the sun warm on her back, the steely arms around her, and the voracious mouth feeding on hers. At last he lifted his head.

'My God,' he said. 'I don't know how I've kept my hands off you this morning. I've longed to do this ever since we set off.' His voice was thick and muted as he bent his head closer again, and his lips came down to hers, the tip of his tongue flickering and teasing, forcing her lips to open to him like a flower to a bee.

The tongue slid into her mouth, probing, taking possession. Her hands rose to his upper arms and began a slow circle around his back. The muscles were smooth and hard, slightly slippery with his sweat. The male scent of soap and exertion filled her nostrils as she traced the groove of his spine with fluttering fingertips.

Still linked, they moved forward onto the wide, grassy ledge that was the beginning of the alpine meadow. The grass was short and thick, spread like a blanket dotted with small flowers. Together, they sank down into the sun-warmed ground, into the scents of earth and vegetation.

His hand was on her breast, caressing and stroking through the thin fabric of her shirt. She felt the nipple swell and harden under the heat of his hand and the moistness begin, signaling her readiness for what was happening. His fingers moved to the buttons and wandered inside the loosened fabric. With a small groan, he knelt beside her and slid his hands behind her back, lifting her effortlessly to allow him access to the fastenings of her bra. Under his touch, the garments slipped from her shoulders and she lay exposed, her breasts free to his gaze. His eyes were dark and hungry as he drank in the sight.

'You're so beautiful,' he whispered and put out one gentle finger to trace the swell of her breast down to the peak. She quivered as he touched the sensitive spot.

'Do you remember?' His voice was husky with desire.

Wide-eyed, she lay back before him. Slowly her tongue came out to lick her swollen lips and she whispered, 'Yes.'

His hands trembled as he continued to undress her with the same gentleness and reverence. At last, she lay completely naked on the soft, sweet smelling grass, drugged by the warm sensuality of his caress. He lay down to embrace her, still wearing his hiking shorts. The erotic feel of the harsh cloth against her sensitive flesh served to arouse her more. She ran her fingers down the sleek skin of his chest, scratching slightly at his side. She heard him suck in his breath.

'I'm going to have to take off these shorts,' he whispered. 'Or I'll never be any use to a woman again.'

'What woman might that be?' she asked.

'You, Maggie, only you.' He stood over her against the sun, his legs apart as he unbuckled his belt and unzipped the shorts. They slid down his legs, revealing the depth of his need and desire for her. The lovely shaft stood already firm and quivering. He watched her looking at him and gave a small, understanding smile. Stepping out of his boots, he tossed aside his remaining clothes and settled by her again. He plunged his hand into a pocket of his pack and turned away for a moment while her fingers played along his back. Soon he was looming over her again, blotting out the sun and the sky.

'Put it on for me,' he whispered.

Hesitating at first, she put out a trembling hand and took the small package from him. She loved him for insisting each time on protecting her, from allowing their blossoming love to be complicated until they knew for sure it was the right thing to do.

'Leaves my hands free if you do it.' As if to emphasize the truth of what he said, his fingers stroked up her thigh, higher and inward. She heard his grunt of appreciation as he encountered the warm moistness hidden there.

She looked down to guide her own hand and slipped the shield gently over the strong hardness waiting her attention. Lovingly, she stroked him and saw the pulsing response.

'That's very sexy,' she whispered.

He leaned on one arm, looming over her again, blotting out the sun and the sky.

Once more his probing fingers wandered over her, tracing the line of her hip bones, finding again the moistness hiding below the thatch of blonde curls at their base. She moaned in pleasure, and he nipped her lips, muffling the sound. When she could bear it no longer, she grasped the silken shaft and guided him to her. For a moment he balanced, poised above her, and then slid slowly, gently towards her. All sensation was concentrated in the pulsing of their two bodies as they rose together into the infinite blue of the sky and exploded into a thousand suns.

'History repeats itself,' Maggie said, her head resting comfortably on Kurt's chest. He lay with one arm over his eyes and the other stroking her back. 'We'll never get to the hut now,' she added. Lazily, she traced the pattern of hairs on Kurt's chest and brushed off an adventurous ant about to lose itself in the jungle. He stirred.

'Are you hungry?' he muttered.

'How can you think of food now?' she scolded with mock seriousness.

'Easily. I have to keep up my strength.' He rolled onto his side, removing his arm from where it had come to rest in the curve of her waist. The spot where it had lain felt suddenly cold. Maggie shivered. The sun had moved on, leaving their grassy hollow in shadow. Some clouds were building in the distance.

Quickly, she sat up, reaching for her clothes. 'Let's eat.'

★ ★ ★

Some time later, they prepared for the descent. As they picked up the packs, Maggie pointed farther up the mountain.

'There's the hut,' she said. 'You can just see it behind that outcrop.'

Kurt shaded his eyes as he looked up.

'It's a stiff climb up there,' she said.

'It's pretty steep in parts, but it's not dangerous if you're careful. We'll get there one day.' He glanced up anxiously at the sky. 'We might only just make it down before the rain.'

'I saw the clouds earlier — is it worse?' She stopped to look behind them. The resplendent mountain top that had called to them in the sunshine was now obscured by a layer of dark cloud, building visibly as they watched. The air had grown colder, and a stiff breeze ruffled their hair.

'Let's get the rain gear out now, Maggie. We're going to need it.'

Quickly, they extracted pants and sweaters from their packs and slipped their waterproof ponchos over the top. Better clad against the threatening storm, they resumed the descent, picking their way carefully as the light faded fast.

'Tell me about Jeff,' he said as they hurried.

Maggie launched into an account of some of Jeff's escapades.

Kurt listened, laughing out loud at some of the situations Maggie had had to deal with. He admired the strength and patience she'd shown to handle a boy with Jeff's energy, intelligence and adventurous temperament. He knew just how difficult such a temperament could be. All he had to do was look in the mirror.

He hitched his pack more comfortably and strode on, listening to the stories, preceding her down the path in silence. But his amusement gradually turned to darker feelings. The memories flashed in his head like segments of a bad movie. His father's ravings echoed in his mind, almost as real as when he was a boy. That was when he had decided to make no commitment in his life, refusing to run the risk of turning into a harsh, unloving man — like his father. He'd thought it better never to expose a child to the possibility he would repeat his father's pattern.

Would he have the same understanding as Maggie if he had to deal with some teenage prank? Would the role model he'd been served come back to haunt him?

So he was being irrational, inconsistent — wanting to be part of the boy's life one minute, intrigued by the challenge, longing to be part of his growing up — and then withdrawing as if burned when Maggie touched the secret places, making him remember his childhood.

His brooding cast a pall, matching the chilling wind and scudding clouds. Rain was in the wind now, sending unpleasant, cold darts into his face. Unreasonably, he wanted to withdraw, hide his wounds as he'd done in the past, refuse human warmth and contact.

Maggie caught up with him. 'Jeff must be out in this,' she said. 'It's probably worse where they are.' She had to raise her voice over the soughing of the branches.

He raised the hood of his poncho and turned to her. 'They're well equipped, they know what they're doing,' he said.

Without a word, he turned and trudged on, not looking back. Stones slithered behind him on the steep path, followed by a small cry.

He spun round at the sound and hurried back.

Maggie was sitting on the wet earth, hunched over, grasping her leg.

'I slid on the stones, twisted my knee.' Gingerly, she stood up and tested her weight on the leg. She winced. At the same moment, the scattered drops turned into a heavy, cold downpour.

'Oh, no!' she exclaimed, pulling her hood tighter around her face. 'That's all we need!'

'Put an arm round my waist, and I'll support you. We have to get down.'

They struggled down through the rain

which now was falling even more heavily, shutting out the surroundings with a curtain of water. The cold and wet penetrated everywhere. It trickled off their ponchos and down the back of their necks, soaked the bottom of their pants, and chilled the exposed skin of their faces and hands.

Maggie's knee throbbed with pain and heat as she tried to place as little weight as possible on Kurt's supporting arm. She tried not to think of Jeff out in this, sitting somewhere on an exposed ridge, trying to keep warm and dry. Darkness would fall early with the low, black clouds that now entirely blocked the sky.

Kurt didn't speak except to give her directions, in a great hurry to get back to the cottage. She'd never seen him like this in his own domain, totally focused on the problem at hand.

At last they came to the flat stretch of the path, leading to the cottage. Maggie limped across the open ground and sank thankfully on to the deck while Kurt fished out the key. Once inside, she hobbled to a chair and lay back. Such relief to be out of the driving rain and to take the strain from her knee! It felt like the size of a football, and small stabs of pain shot down her calf as her muscles relaxed.

'Let's look at the problem and see if we can find a support for that knee. Take off your poncho and roll up the leg of your pants while I hunt for the first aid kit.' He disappeared into another room only to come back quickly with a length of elasticized bandage.

Swiftly, he knelt before her and placed probing fingers on her leg. 'Still very painful?'

She shook her head. 'Not bad now that I'm sitting.'

'You'll have to use ice once we get you home. Let's try this bandage for now.'

His fingers were quick and sure as he wrapped the knee.

She watched his bowed head as he worked. She shivered, from his touch, from apprehension, from doubt. He'd assured her again and again that Jeff would be fine. She had to believe that.

'Cold?' Kurt looked up from where he was fastening the pin in the bandage.

'A little. Tired too. It's after supper time. I just want to get home.

Kurt's expression was inscrutable. 'You're upset with me aren't you?'

'I'm anxious about Jeff. I'm wondering if we did the right thing in allowing him to do that climb. Maybe we weren't thinking clearly.'

He sighed and stood up. 'I'll start the car.' He left without another word and she heard the engine fire.

They drove without a word to the house, and Maggie laid her head on the padded rest and closed her eyes.

In her own kitchen, Maggie sat with her leg propped up on a cushion on an chair and watched Kurt prepare some supper. They chatted about nothing in particular until he rose to clear everything away.

'You can't keep your eyes open,' he said. 'Let's get you to bed.'

When she was settled, he reappeared in the doorway, pulling on his coat.

'Where are you going?'

He came to kneel by the edge of the bed, took her hands in his and kissed her. 'Just back to the cabin. I have to make sure everything's okay in the storm. Besides, we both need some time alone. You should rest tonight. Let's digest what's happening to us.'

She'd been the one not wanting to push things too fast. Now she was disappointed at his rational approach. He put his arms round her and held her tenderly.

'I want you to love me, Maggie,' he said. 'I wouldn't do anything to hurt you. You know I've loved you from the first moment I saw you.' He kissed her forehead. 'Since I came back, I've told myself you couldn't feel the same way, no matter how much I wanted it. So I'm holding this new relationship very carefully, like a wild bird's egg, because I don't want to smash it. We both need some space, some time to think things through. I'm a wild man of the woods, you know, I need time to adjust and so do you.' He kissed her again, gently. 'These are big changes in our lives,' he whispered. 'I'll see you tomorrow.'

★ ★ ★

The small, nagging pain in her knee persisted the next morning despite the application of ice and a compression bandage. She found that she could get around without too much trouble, and she sat whenever she could. The rain persisted, casting a dank, gray cast over the house and the garden. She could hear the wind in the treetops, sighing and whining as it whipped the leaves and small branches.

At noon, Kurt reappeared. She rose and limped toward him, holding him as he stood in the doorway. He hugged her tight and rubbed his cheek on her hair.

'Maybe it wasn't such a good idea to leave you last night,' he said. 'I couldn't sleep for wishing you were next to me.'

She poured him a cup of coffee, and he

shrugged out of his waterproof jacket.

'I had to repair a couple of shutters,' he said, taking a long sip of the hot liquid. 'That's what I needed. As well as a sight of you.' He gathered her close to his side.

'I drove on the road near the water,' he said. 'It's pretty wild.'

She pushed away from him a little but stayed in the circle of his arms. 'Do you suppose Jeff's okay? He must be wet and cold. Did they have enough food? What about blankets, flashlights?'

'Hush,' he said, squeezing her closer. 'If you can think of all that, the young guys with them can too. If Jeff's anything like me, he'll be having the time of his life. They had shelter and extra clothing.'

'Maybe I should call.'

Kurt sighed but let her go, dropping his arms to his side. She knew she was over-reacting and gave him a half-smile and a shrug in apology for her protectiveness. Then she picked up the phone and dialed the number of the camp. She asked a few questions and listened at length while Kurt drank his coffee and removed his boots.

'Thank you,' she said. 'Yes, I'll call again later.'

She put down the phone and turned to face Kurt.

'What is it?' he said. 'Maggie, are you all right?'

Her throat was so tight it was difficult to get out the words.

'They haven't heard from Jeff's group since yesterday afternoon.'

The world around her started to move, sideways at first and then farther away as if being sucked into a vacuum. She heard Kurt's voice as if from a distance and felt his hands on her arms and round her shoulders, steadying her and supporting her back to the chair.

He knelt before her and rubbed her hands. 'Put your head down.' His hands were on the back of her head, forcing it down between her knees. 'Stay there.'

He rose to his feet and returned quickly with a glass of water. 'Drink this.' She obeyed his commands and sat back, her eyes closed.

'Sorry,' she said. 'I don't usually do this.'

'You've been brooding about all this all night, haven't you?'

She nodded. She'd hardly slept, fretting and worrying, trying to forget the ache in her knee, trying to find a comfortable position in the bed without Kurt to snuggle against. In only a few days he'd become an indispensable part of her life. But she'd still worried about the wisdom of having accepted Kurt's advice, all the time telling herself that all would be well.

She wasn't used to happiness and couldn't help a superstitious reaction that things were going too well with Kurt. A primitive, irrational voice even whispered in her subconscious that she'd pay for having Kurt back by losing Jeff. She had a sick feeling of premonition of disaster.

'Now, tell me what they said.' Kurt was still by her side, holding her hand.

'They said,' she began slowly, 'that the group reported in on a mobile unit every morning and evening and gave their position. They heard from them yesterday morning but not last night. They haven't been able to reach them this morning. They'll keep trying.'

Her mouth felt stiff, as if she'd been out in a winter cold.

'Did they say they thought something had happened?'

She shook her head. 'No. They're assuming there's something wrong with the mobile phone. They said the same as you. They have shelter and clothes and food. The leaders are experienced.'

'They're quite right.'

'Why don't they go looking for them?'

'There's no reason at the moment.

Everything says equipment failure or interference from the storm. When it clears, they'll call in and tell us what a great time they had.'

She looked at him in silence a long moment. 'I shouldn't have let him go,' she said.

'Of course you should have. Jeff will be fine.'

Kurt rubbed her hands, trying to convey reassurance and certainty, but inwardly he battled the same panic that was so close to the surface in Maggie. This was what it meant to be a parent. Fears that could be dismissed after objective assessment suddenly became more real, more gut-wrenching when it was your own child.

The professional guide in him knew the small group was quite safe somewhere, warm and dry, waiting out the summer storm. The new dad fumed and fretted, second guessing the leaders, worrying at his own decision in convincing Maggie to let Jeff participate.

Supposing something had happened to them? A fall? A meeting with a bear or a cougar? A sudden fever? A broken limb? Was Jeff out there, wondering why no one was coming to help them? Was he injured, lying wet and cold and in pain? Kurt knew only too well all the possibilities for disaster in the wilderness. Had he discovered his son only to lose him again without ever knowing him?

Despite all his experience, despite knowing that the odds were all in favor of the group of kids and their leaders, despite the probability that Bob Miller was right and they would straggle back into the camp, cold and wet and hungry, he was still afraid. The fear crept up through him like a thief, stealing his rational thinking, replacing it with wild imaginings.

If Jeff were lost or injured, how could he face Maggie? This relationship, this love that was blossoming, would wither and die like a flower in an alpine meadow that blooms too soon. How could she forgive him if her son was injured or dead? How could he forgive himself?

He let go of Maggie and rubbed his hands over his face, searching desperately for calm and logic. He made himself list mentally the equipment he had with him. He calculated how long it would take to reach the camp and then the site where the boys were last heard from. He'd participated in enough Search and Rescue missions to know the procedure.

A team would be called in when there were grounds to believe the small group was in trouble. That would probably mean tomorrow when they didn't return as expected. The camp authorities would allow a few extra hours before sounding the alarm. Then a crew would be assembled, flown in. He could be on the spot, ready to set off as soon as the word was given, or even before.

In the meantime, he must not panic. He must be reassuring for Maggie. They must find something else to think about without brooding about frightening possibilities that hadn't happened and likely never would. He went out in the rain to the car and brought in some maps.

'Let's talk about us,' he said. 'Show me where you'd like to move to. We'll look at schools, places where I could settle.' Of course, he'd want to be right there with her, but he'd not dared broach the subject of marriage yet. He needed Jeff back safe and sound, needed to establish a relationship with the boy. One step at a time.

They pored over the maps, and he coaxed her into conversation about her job prospects, the kind of school she'd like for Jeff. He ringed the colleges in the area and made a list of phone numbers.

'I'll call for the names of the heads of the Environmental Studies department,' he said.

He spent a half hour on the phone, collecting information and returned to the kitchen. Maggie had made sandwiches and was glancing at her watch every few minutes. She nibbled at one sandwich and left it half eaten. A cup of tea was untouched by her plate.

At three o'clock she stood up. 'I'm going to call again.' she said.

'They won't know any more,' he warned her. 'Not until the rain stops.'

She glanced out of the window. 'It's easing here.'

In fact, it was no longer falling rain misting the windows but a steady drip, drip from the eaves and the surrounding trees. A watery sunlight was breaking through the gray, and already the stones were beginning to steam.

She flicked the 'speaker' setting on the phone, and Kurt sat close to her and listened.

Bob Miller, the camp organizer, was still cheerful. 'No need to worry, Mr. and Mrs. Rainer,' he said. Kurt looked at Maggie. Her face was impassive. What was she feeling about this linking of their names? Miller obviously thought they were a couple. Maggie didn't offer to correct him.

The disembodied voice on the telephone continued. 'The two leaders are great. They wouldn't let anything happen to the group. Don't worry about the phone, it's just a glitch. I sometimes think it's more trouble than it's worth to carry the darn thing. They're not very reliable, but it's a reassurance for anxious parents. Of course, they're great when they're working.'

'But do you think the boys are safe?' Maggie asked.

'I think so. They're not due back until tomorrow. They're likely on Hurricane Ridge, and there's plenty of shelter there for them. They'll come walking back in tomorrow with silly grins on their faces.'

When the conversation was ended, Kurt disconnected the phone. He looked at Maggie's pale face, at the tender spot on her lip where she'd pressed her teeth in her anxiety. He could stand the inaction no longer. What was the point of waiting here? If they went up to the camp, he would be on hand if he was needed, or he'd wait to meet Jeff for the first time and share in the hoped-for silly grin as the bedraggled group trudged back into camp.

He folded the maps and stood up. 'Let's go,' he said. 'There's still some daylight left.'

★ ★ ★

The sleek silver sports car purred effortlessly up the ascent towards the main camp on Mount Vardon. Despite its incongruous looks in this setting, it was handling the road just as well as Roger's four by four. Kurt drove fast but carefully, concentrating on the twists and turns. The rain was over, but the foliage was still sodden and dark with water. The evening was closing in early because of the cloud cover, and the few glimpses of the sun through the tattered breaks were pale and weak-looking, like watery custard.

Maggie had watched Kurt at the cabin assembling his equipment, muttering about what he didn't have with him. He hadn't expected to set off on Search and Rescue, but he had thought of hiking and climbing and so had some basic gear.

She didn't know for sure what she was feeling right now. One moment, she couldn't believe Jeff and the other boys were missing, and a few seconds later, the sick fear clutched at her stomach, and she fought the waves of panic that kept washing over her. Kurt had called again to the camp to give his car phone number and to let them know they were on their way.

After an hour's silent drive through the forest, the phone shrilled, making her jump.

Kurt took it from the holder between them.

She heard a man's voice, a long speech, the cadence rising and falling in emphasis. Kurt listened in silence.

'Where?' he said at last.

The voice answered with three or four words. 'When?' he countered.

He put the phone back carefully and squared his shoulders.

'What is it? What's happened?' She swallowed the nausea threatening to rise in her throat. 'Is it Jeff?'

Kurt cleared his throat. 'They've heard from the group leaders,' he began. 'They were right, there was a glitch with the phone.'

Maggie closed her eyes in relief. 'Thank goodness.' She turned to look at him. 'So they're all okay?'

Kurt hesitated. 'Well . . . '

She sat up straighter. 'Tell me about Jeff.'

'The report's still a bit vague. They don't have much detail and they can't assess the extent — '

'Dammit it all to hell, Kurt, this is not a legal inquiry. Tell me what's happened to my son!'

He licked his lips. Maggie saw the tense jaw muscles under the tanned skin. 'Jeff fell, late yesterday afternoon,' he said in a low voice. 'It was getting dark, the storm was pretty bad. He must have slipped.'

'He's dead,' she whispered.

'No, he's not dead. But he is hurt. They don't know how badly. They think he might have a broken arm or leg, so he can't pull himself up. Someone has to go down to him.'

She gave a low moan and hugged her arms around her body.

'They managed to lower some equipment to him. A thermal blanket, a waterproof sheet, and some water. They can see him but aren't sure how to reach him.'

'Does he have any food?'

'No. They can't let him have anything, in case — '

'What?' She spoke through stiff lips.

Kurt shifted uncomfortable in the leather seat. 'It's standard procedure. No solid food until they know the extent of the injuries.'

She looked at him in silence for a long moment, digesting the implications of what he'd said. 'We should never — '

'Hell, Maggie. Don't you think I'm saying the same thing over and over in my head? Don't you think I'm worried sick too? I keep asking myself how I could have said yes to the idea. Why didn't I make sure I could meet him, talk to him before I sent him off into something he couldn't handle? Why did I convince you to let him go?' He broke off, unable to say any more.

She saw his knuckles white on the steering wheel. He took a deep breath. 'I know you won't want to see me again,' he said, his eyes firmly on the road ahead. 'But I'm hoping that you'll let me see Jeff. I'll get him out and bring him back to you. But I'll understand you won't want me participating in any more decisions about him.'

She felt his pain and guilt like a stab wound to her own heart. He'd given his honest opinion that was all. No one had held a gun to her head to give permission.

'We made the decision together,' she said quietly. 'Now's not the time to blame anyone. I'm not blaming you.' She placed a hand lightly over his on the wheel. 'I won't deny we have a lot to talk about, but our first priority has to be Jeff.'

Neither of them spoke again, each lost in their own thoughts, until they came in sight of the wooden buildings. The compound was quiet when they arrived. Kurt pulled the car in next to a couple of Jeeps marked with the logo of the camp. Bob Miller hurried out to greet them. He took Maggie's hand and shook it.

'We've heard from them again,' he said. 'We're calling out Search and Rescue. They should be with us tomorrow morning.'

'Tomorrow morning? Why not now?'

He grimaced in sympathy, leading them into the main building. 'They need time to bring out the team, fly them up. It's nearly dark now. They should be organized by the morning. I'm sorry.' He gestured helplessly.

Maggie glanced out of the window, at the still threatening clouds, and shivered. 'Another night . . . '

'I'm afraid so. I'm as anxious as you are to bring him out. But we just don't have the equipment or the expertise.'

'I do.' Kurt spoke for the first time. Bob Miller turned to him in surprise.

'There's three hours of fairly good light left,' Kurt continued. 'I can be almost there and set off again at dawn.'

'Kurt!' Maggie grabbed his arm. 'Don't go alone. Your arm, your leg — '

'I can manage.' His mouth was set in a grim line, his eyes focused on his inward preparation. This man, wounded or not, was ready to rush swiftly to the rescue of a boy he didn't yet know. He'd revealed his own torment in the car, but now he was transformed again into the Viking warrior, intent, single-minded, fearless. She'd been right when she'd dubbed him a complicated man. In his mind, he owed both her and Jeff a debt and was willing to go to any extreme to make good the wrong he considered he'd done them.

'I'm going with you,' she said.

13

The climb towards the ridge was long and slow. They trudged in silence except for Kurt's brief warnings to 'watch this patch' or 'give me your hand' from time to time. All Maggie could hear was the scrape of their boots on rock, the occasional slither of small stones from under their feet, and her own heavy breathing. The air was cloying and damp, trees dripping moisture as they trudged on underneath.

The fading light and the closeness of the trees made certain patches of the trail hard to see. She hated every minute of it. She hated the encroaching darkness, the air that grew colder by the minute. She hated knowing that the hillside dropped off steeply just beyond her range of vision. She hated not knowing what awaited them, hated the thought of Kurt endangering himself. But she could not ask him to wait, could not bear the thought of Jeff lying chilled and alone in the wet darkness any longer than necessary. If Kurt could put an end to that ordeal, she would help him with every ounce of her courage and strength.

At last Kurt called a halt. 'It's too

dangerous to continue,' he said, easing the straps on his shoulders. 'We'll make camp here while we can still see.'

He slipped the pack from his back and began to unload the sleeping bags. They had sacrificed bringing a tent in favor of medical supplies and provisions. They would spend the short hours before dawn fully clothed in hooded sleeping bags after a supper of cold food and water.

An hour or so later, they were lying side by side like two mummies in a tomb. Total blackness was around them, the only sounds their own breathing and the rustle of the wind in the trees. Supposing she fell asleep and rolled over, over the edge of the cliff, and went bouncing down the side of the mountain? She shivered.

'Are you cold?' Kurt tucked the hood more closely around her face, his fingers lingering for a moment on her cheek.

'No,' she answered. 'Just thinking about Jeff. I'm terrified here with you. What must it be like for him?'

She sensed movement next to her. Kurt was heaving himself towards her in his sleeping bag to narrow the already slim gap between them. The solid, dark shape settled next to her, and an arm came out and around her, gathering her in. He snuggled his face next to her ear and kissed her cheek.

'Try to sleep,' he whispered. 'We'll need everything we've got tomorrow.'

He woke her at dawn as the first fingers of light crept between the trees. She was stiff and cold, but she had dozed, fitfully. She was immediately awake and alert at the pressure of his fingers on her shoulder. He moved away from where he'd lain against her all night, and she was suddenly chilled as the warmth of his body left her.

'Let's go,' he said quietly. She wriggled out of the bag and rolled it up into a tight cylinder. After a mouthful of water and a handful of dried nuts and fruit, they were ready to resume the climb.

Around seven in the morning, they came within sight of the ridge. Fifteen minutes later they saw the tents of the climbing group. Maggie scrambled over the last few yards, running to keep up with Kurt and hear the first words of the group leader, Tim Jones.

'Jeff's doing okay,' Tim was saying. 'He's sort of wedged into a space between a rock and a tree, a hundred or so feet down. He's safe enough but can't move much. He's got thermal blankets and water. But we know he's in pain. We just don't know how bad it is, so we haven't been able to give him anything for it. He's a plucky kid. He's doing great.'

They moved off towards the edge of the cliff as he continued talking. 'We've posted someone close by to keep talking to him, mainly to keep him awake. He knows it won't be too long now.'

They reached the edge, and Maggie slid down onto her stomach and inched forward to peer over. Her head began to swim at the height and the sheer drop and she drew back slightly as someone handed her a pair of binoculars. She fumbled to adjust the lenses and moved back closer to the edge, longing to grip the solid tufts of grass for an illusion of security but needing both hands for the glasses. She wedged her elbows firmly into the ground and lifted the binoculars.

A tree loomed into her sight, huge and intricately detailed. She panned up and then down again, looking for the outcrop where Jeff lay. Suddenly, she was looking right into Jeff's face, every feature so clear, she believed she could have reached out and touched him. She caught her breath and scanned the silver of the thermal blanket and then Jeff's black hair, sticking up around his white face. He was lying in the only spot where the terrain and the vegetation could have broken his fall. All around him, the ground fell away in a sheer plunge down to the valley.

Maggie closed her eyes, took a deep breath

and opened them again. 'Jeff,' she called.

He looked up at once. 'Hi, mom,' he answered. His voice was small and far away. 'You should sell tickets.' She saw him wince and her heart lurched. How could he joke when he was hurt and weary and cold?

'Are you okay?' Dumb question.

'I'm okay,' he called back with a brave smile. 'But my arm hurts. I've had enough of this game. Can you get me out of here?'

'We're sure going to try.' She moved aside to make room for Kurt. 'I've got someone with me who'll help you.'

'Who is it?'

'It's — ' she hesitated, ' — your uncle Kurt. He does this kind of thing for a living.'

'He the one we read about?'

'Yes.'

Kurt leaned further out and called down. 'I'm going to rig up a harness, Jeff,' he said.

'I hope it's better than the one for Johnny Gunn!'

Maggie saw Kurt hesitate for a moment, and a shadow flitted over his face. She knew he must be hurt by the fact that Jeff linked him to the murder. She reached out and placed a reassuring hand on his arm.

Kurt acknowledged the gesture with a quick glance and then turned his attention back to Jeff. 'This one will work fine,' he said firmly. 'Now, tell me where you have pain.'

Kurt and Jeff talked for a few minutes while Maggie strained to see Jeff's face and movements to try to judge how badly he was hurt. He looked tired but seemed in good spirits.

Kurt swung to his feet and took her aside. 'I'm going to send someone down to him,' he said.

Immediately her knees went weak as she visualized the rescuer swinging in space over the tree tops far below.

'I'll pick one of the group here.' He nodded to the cluster of boys. 'He'll have to attach himself and put the harness on Jeff. I'd go myself,' he continued, bending over the equipment spilling from his backpack, 'but I'm too heavy for these guys to hold, and I'd be distracted by the harness round my ribs.'

She licked her lips. 'I'll go,' she said.

He paused in what he was doing and looked up at her. 'You'd be terrified,' he said. 'I know how you feel about heights.'

'I can do it. I'm his mother. Don't you think it would be worse to see someone else go down, wondering if they would do it right or even get hurt themselves? I can't send one of them.' He resumed readying the ropes and shackles, his fingers quick and sure. After a moment's thought, he nodded his understanding. 'I'll explain what you have to do,' he said calmly.

Maggie willed herself to keep all the instructions in her head. Kurt had been calm, reassuring, totally competent. There was no question that she trusted him with her son's life and her own.

In a mercifully brief time after their arrival, she swung into space, closing her eyes as the rope lurched. She concentrated on keeping her body as still as she could. Kurt had explained the danger of arcing out too far and bouncing off the rock walls, like a pendulum. She was to stay still and relaxed, allowing the crew at the top to lower her gently and steadily.

She could hear the shouts of the group Kurt had detailed to dismantle the tents to make space for the incoming helicopter. The sounds seemed far away. A minute later, she cautiously opened her eyes and watched the stones and bushes move past her. She'd be fine as long as she didn't look down!

After an eternity of descent, her feet touched the ledge where Jeff was lying and she grabbed a branch to stop and anchor herself. His dear face appeared next to her, trying a brave grin.

'Hi, mom,' he said in a small voice. 'Nice of you to drop in.'

On closer inspection, he was even paler, with lines of strain and fatigue around his mouth and eyes. She patted his face carefully, wary of unbalancing him from his precarious perch. The tricky part was going to be keeping him safe, not letting her momentum push him away from the safety of the ledge. Swiftly, she anchored him to her ropes and then unpacked the harness sent with her and helped him into it, slow movement by slow movement. His left arm hung uselessly by his side, and she used a strap to hold it to his body.

All the time she worked on the straps and clips, she talked to him, telling him how brave he was, how proud she was of him, how he only had to hold on for a few more minutes. In the concentration on the task, she forgot the sick feeling in her stomach, her breathing slowed, and she felt calm and competent. When she was sure the harness was properly attached, she smoothed Jeff's hair back from his face, gave him a kiss, and tugged on the ropes to give the signal to haul them up. Jeff went up first, rising in slow motion, like a rag doll in a cocoon.

She followed minutes later, her eyes on Kurt above her, as he reached out with strong arms to grasp his son. At the top, she rolled over, fingers scrabbling at the buckles and fastenings to release the climbing ropes. She scrambled over to where Jeff was lying on a pile of blankets. His eyes were closed, his face deathly white.

She knelt by him. 'Jeff,' she said and looked up at Kurt. 'Is he — ?'

Jeff's eyes opened, and he stared up at them. 'That was awesome,' he breathed. 'Can we do that again when my arm's okay?'

Before she could answer, a faint drone that had hardly registered on her consciousness turned into an ear-splitting clatter. Kurt was immediately on his feet, running towards the helicopter settling like a drunken bee on the cleared space.

The Search and Rescue team made quick work of checking out Jeff. One of them tipped his helmet to the back of his head and tapped Kurt on the shoulder.

'No harm done this time, pal,' he said, 'but your wife and kid could have been in real trouble. Wait for us next time, it'll be safer for all of us. Wouldn't have wanted to have to get the two of them if they'd fallen further. Think about it.' He nodded brusquely and moved to rejoin the group that was busy with the preparations for loading them all into the waiting machine.

Maggie crouched by the stretcher in the noisy interior, unable to make herself heard, but clutching Jeff's hand for reassurance.

In the ambulance on the ground she was at last able to speak. 'You did wonderfully,' she said to Kurt, 'despite what those guys said.'

He was sitting hunched onto a small space between some equipment and the back door. He looked at her. 'They were probably right,' he said quietly. 'I could have waited.'

'No — '

'I could have made things worse,' he interrupted. 'I could have endangered you and Jeff.'

Maggie looked at him in distress. Suddenly, his self-confidence was gone. 'I believe in you,' she said firmly. 'I'm glad you took the initiative. No one knew when the rescue team would arrive. You saved Jeff from an extra hour of misery, and it could have been more.'

'Maybe.' He lapsed into a somber silence until they reached the open doors of the Emergency Unit.

⋆　⋆　⋆

Maggie watched Kurt and Jeff from the porch, remembering the game at Ellen's house with Cliff and Jennifer only three weeks before. The two had devised a way of playing

320

one-handed football where their special rules took account of the broken arm, the scrapes, and bruises each had suffered.

When they'd returned from the mountains, Cliff had been waiting at the hospital, checked Jeff out, set his arm, and pronounced him fit and in need only of rest and good food. Kurt had returned to the cabin but appeared at breakfast time every morning. She'd never seen Jeff happier. He and Kurt spent hours in conversation and incomprehensible male tasks they found to do. Last night she'd overheard Jeff asking about a camping trip to a wilderness park.

Trust took a while to build, but they were taking it slowly. She wasn't ready to have Kurt in her bed with Jeff at home and sometimes the longing for him made her weak and dizzy. Kurt had been strangely reticent with her since the mountain trip, but she figured he was getting used to being around her and Jeff. It was a big change in his life.

She sat back, day-dreaming. Maybe they could go away for a couple of days. Her lips twitched in a smile as she mentally rejected the thought of Golden Point Lodge. It would be a long time before she went there again. In fact, they didn't have to go far. The cabin would do fine.

Kurt and Jeff pounded up the steps, flushed and sweating. Kurt smiled at her. No man should make her stomach do flip-flops that way just because he smiled at her.

'Don't overdo it,' she admonished.

'Don't fuss,' Kurt said.

'Yeah, mom,' Jeff said. 'Don't sweat it.' He stood before them, still bouncing the ball.

Kurt flopped down next to her, took a drink of water, and wiped his mouth with the back of his hand. 'Gotta be going soon, buddy,' he said to Jeff.

'Okay,' Jeff answered. He turned to Maggie. 'Can I go over to Tim's house?' he asked.

'Sure, if you're not too tired.'

'I'm fine. Thanks mom,' he called back over his shoulder as he galloped back down the steps, then stopped and looked back at the two adults on the porch. 'Why don't you two get married?' he said. 'Then he could stay here all the time.'

Kurt blew out a big breath. 'The energy of youth,' he said.

'Not to mention precociousness.'

'That too,' he answered.

She sat back and crossed her legs. 'You get on well together.'

'Yes, we do. He's a fine boy.' His face had grown suddenly serious, and a frown settled between his brows. He leaned forward, clasping his hands between his knees.

'We have to talk, Maggie,' he said.

She smiled at him, loving the gravity of his face, the expression of concentration making lines around his mouth. She longed to reach out and touch the lines, smooth them away with her fingertips until they were gone and the old smile was back.

'There's too much between us to be coy,' he said.

This is it, Maggie thought, he's going to talk about marriage. She closed her eyes to savor the moment.

'I think about you,' he continued. 'I think about you a lot. When we're apart, I think about what you're doing, what you're thinking. I try to picture you, your face. I have such feelings for you.'

'I know,' she whispered. 'I want — '

'Let me finish.' His voice was abrupt, and she hesitated in surprise.

'After what happened with Jeff, I think they're feelings I can't afford to have. I don't think I'm good for him.' He ignored her movement of protest. His eyes were fixed on the floor, and he was doggedly determined to finish what he had to say. 'I can't take the risk.'

She struggled to make sense of what he was

telling her, to help him out. 'I already figured out you're feeling your way in this relationship. It's not surprising. But Jeff thinks the world of you, admires you. I don't understand.'

Kurt lifted his eyes to hers, and she flinched at the pain she saw in their depths.

'I'm not going to pussyfoot around,' he said. 'You know how I feel about you. I'm sexual. When I think about you, I get sexual feelings. And to follow through on that would mean bringing me completely into Jeff's life.'

Maggie nodded in agreement. Kurt took a deep breath and looked away. 'I've come to see I can't do that,' he said.

Maggie stared at him, her eyes searching his face, trying to take in what he was saying. Was he going away again? Was he going to abandon her and Jeff once more?

'I'm going to walk away, Maggie,' he said, confirming her worst fears. 'I'm not going to pretend it will be easy. I'm going to go on thinking about you every moment of the rest of my life, and I hope you'll think about me sometimes and let me know how Jeff's doing. I'll help financially of course.' His voice cracked, and he stood up, turning his back to gaze out over the grass and bushes. He waited a moment and then faced her again.

'These last few days have been hell for me,

Maggie.' he said. 'I can't get what the Search and Rescue guys said out of my head. I see you dangling there, I see Jeff on that ledge . . . if I'd waited . . . if I'd not told you to let him go . . . ' He ran his hands over his face as if trying to wash away the thoughts and the memories.

'I only knew I had a son for a few goddamned days,' he said bitterly, 'and I let it go to my head. In my arrogance, my sureness of knowing what was right, I persuaded you to let him go on the climb. Then I took over, I didn't wait for the experts with their equipment, I went ahead and did it myself. I put you and Jeff in danger. All because I wanted to do it myself, wanted to show how good I was!'

'Kurt, that's nonsense, and you know it!'

'You can't change my mind, Maggie. If I do something, I want to do it right and I screwed up. I've looked at this every way I can for the last few days. I can't honestly say I can trust myself to be in Jeff's life, and that's what would happen if I were in yours. I think about my dad and how he rode roughshod over everyone. Maybe I'm the same. I couldn't live with Jeff knowing I should hold my tongue, never participating in decisions about him. It's best for you and him for me to be out of the picture.' He picked up his pack and his car keys. 'I'll let you know where I am.'

He stepped towards her and folded her into his arms and kissed her gently on the lips. She stood close against him as if frozen, her brain desperately trying to process this shattering news, then pushed away from him. 'You're reacting to the stress — ' she began.

He closed her mouth with a kiss. 'It's for the best,' he whispered. 'Believe me. Try to understand. I'll write to you, just as I did last time. Please don't hate me.'

With a final wave he was gone. 'Understand,' he'd said. All she could understand was that she was alone, as she'd been alone for years. There was no family, there was no one to love her and Jeff, no one to hold her in the dark. There would be no whispers in the dark, no help, no sharing of pain and joy. She sat down in the rattan chair and put her head in her hands.

★ ★ ★

The attic was still as warm and musty as the last time she'd climbed the stairs to find clothes for Kurt. This time she was going to pack everything belonging to Steve into boxes for the Goodwill, and she was anxious to relegate that part of her life to another time, another dimension, anxious to complete the final sorting of her things before saying her good-byes and moving to Ardmore and her new job. Frieda was going to sell the house but keep the cabin. She had no idea what Kurt would do.

She picked up the blue cashmere jacket on the top layer of clothing and heard the rustle of paper. Last time her mind had been full of Kurt and his presence in her house. She'd not wanted to check old bills or anything else Steve might have left around. Now she would have to clean out all the pockets. Steve's long ago expenses and business plans meant nothing to her now.

She thrust a hand into the side pocket and took out the packet of folded sheets she'd pushed back unread a month ago. With a small shock, she recognized Kurt's handwriting, a heading and a date of twelve years ago. Sitting back on her heels, she carefully smoothed out the pages. Slowly she read them through.

All those years ago, Kurt had written wild sentences of hope, love, and despair. He talked of trying to reach her, told her how much he loved her, how many messages he'd left with Steve. What was going on? he asked. Why was she always unable to come to the phone? Why did she never call him back? He wanted her with him. He had some plans and ideas he wanted to share with her.

At the end of the last page, she lowered the papers to her lap and stayed lost in thought. The last, small barrier to her complete trust in Kurt was gone. She loved him anyway, it was no longer important if he'd tried to reach her or not all those years ago. She trusted and she loved the man he was today. She understood his integrity, the rock solidness, the unselfishness, the love of justice that now were integral parts of him. But it was good to know that he was honest all through, that he'd been honest with her from the beginning.

If she didn't already know only too well the extent of his sense of honor and the misguided things it sometimes drove him to do, she'd found the proof of his integrity when she no longer needed it. What path might her life have taken if she'd received these messages? How would she and Jeff and Kurt be different if they'd been together for the past twelve years?

Steve had manipulated them both, kept them apart and secretly rejoiced at his triumph. All those years and he knew the truth, knew the power he had over her, knew he was taking revenge on the brother who was bigger, smarter, more popular than he.

Suddenly, she knew she would not let Kurt

go. She had no idea how, when or where she would do it, but she would win him back, show him how much she loved and trusted him, how his son needed him.

Somehow, she would show him how misguided he was in his thinking, how senseless was the decision to protect Jeff from his own father. Of course she could understand the pain and the insecurity that drove him to it, but she would not accept it. The foundation of the pattern of withdrawing from hurt might have been laid in his childhood, but together they could break it. She could be patient, bide her time, wait for the perfect opportunity. She knew he could not be pushed, could be stubborn and hotheaded. She would pick her moment.

★   ★   ★

Maggie turned as Ellen came out of the house and sank into the wicker chair. The porch furniture from the old house looked out of place on the patio of the smart townhouse, but new purchases would have to wait. Her friend nodded approvingly at the kids on the pocket handkerchief square of grass. Jeff was settling into his new school and had already made friends. At least there were lots of neighbors around, mostly young families.

'They're doing okay,' Ellen said. She now knew the whole story.

'How about you?' she asked, her eyes fixed on Maggie's face.

'I'm doing okay too.'

'The new job working out?'

Maggie nodded and stretched. 'So far, so good,' she said. 'How're Jennifer and Cliff?'

'They're fine. Cliff was sorry he couldn't come. Some potential emergency as usual.'

Maggie murmured her understanding and they lapsed into companionable silence.

'Have you heard from Kurt?' Ellen asked at last.

'A few times,' Maggie nodded. 'He's still living at the cabin, but he's sold his company and doing some consulting. He's been traveling a bit.'

'What will happen?'

Maggie knew what her friend meant. 'I've had time to think,' she said. 'I made one bad mistake with Steve and almost made another with Roger. So some people might say my track record's not that good. But this time I'm sure. I'll marry him for all the right reasons.'

'When's the wedding?'

'Sometime soon,' Maggie said airily. 'He doesn't know about it yet, so I've got to pick the right time to let him in on it.'

Ellen looked at her quizzically. 'Boy, have you changed,' she said. 'Where's the old careful Maggie who didn't like surprises?'

'She's gone,' Maggie said cheerfully. 'She's changed jobs, ditched a boyfriend, moved house, and fallen in love. Next, I have some tall buildings lined up.'

Silence again while Ellen took this in.

'I like the car,' Ellen remarked.

The shiny sports utility vehicle sat on the driveway next to Ellen's sedan.

'Only new to me,' Maggie said, 'but better than anything I've had before. Everything worked out fine, Ellie. My brother Phil's debts are all paid off, and he's working again. I'm free to follow my heart.'

After Ellen left, Maggie sat for a while watching Jeff play ball with his new friends. He seemed happy enough and had adapted surprisingly well to the new town and school. She should be glad he was so resilient. She liked her neighbors, liked her new colleagues, but she was still waiting for the time to be right to bring Kurt back into their lives.

Kurt had written to her a couple of times, letting her know where he was, asking about Jeff. She was glad he'd not phoned, for the sound of his voice might have upset her equanimity, forced her to rush into confronting him. It had only been two months after all. What were two months when they'd waited twelve years?

She'd slipped the notes under her pillow, imagining she could catch the scent of him from where his fingers had folded and smoothed the paper. Each night she dreamed a little of him, sometimes soft, hazy dreams and sometimes hot, passionate episodes that awoke her drained and covered in perspiration.

The days were slipping by, settling into a reassuring routine. One evening after work she found a message on her answering machine from Jeff's home room teacher. He was an older man, calm and experienced, but he ran a tight ship. She'd been glad that Jeff was to have a good male model. She felt a stab of apprehension at the prospect of some infraction grave enough to warrant a call home.

After supper, she sent Jeff to his room for homework and returned the call.

'Mrs. Rainer,' Bill Maynard said cheerfully, 'Thanks for calling back.'

'Is there a problem?' she asked anxiously.

'None at all. Sorry if I worried you.'

Maggie let out a sigh of relief.

'I wanted to talk to you about an assignment Jeff wrote.'

'Yes? Was there something wrong with it? I know he was late with a couple of math sheets . . . '

'No, Mrs. Rainer, I said there was no problem. The fact is, Jeff wrote an excellent essay entitled '*A hero*'.'

Now Maggie was completely lost.

'It was well written, thoughtful and very engaging,' the teacher went on. 'It seems he has an uncle who's an expert mountain climber and got him out of some difficulty.'

'Yes, this last summer . . . '

'He obviously admires this man very much and wrote very convincingly about when it's right to take risks and what makes a deed heroic. I understand there was some discussion about whether his uncle should have waited for Search and Rescue?'

'Some discussion, yes.'

'Well, the way Jeff tells it there was no doubt. He says he didn't know if he could have held on any longer and — well, Mrs. Rainer, I'm getting carried away here. The point is, Jeff has won first prize in our Creative Writing contest and will be reading his work at an assembly next week.'

'That's wonderful.'

'You'll get a letter of invitation from the principal of course, but we wanted to ask you something else. Would Jeff's uncle be free to attend? If you could tell us how to get in touch with him, we'd like to invite him.'

Maggie drew in a deep breath. She didn't need a sound and light show to grasp that this was the opportunity she'd been waiting for. 'I'll pick up the invitation, Mr. Maynard, and take it to him myself. Thank you very much. I'll certainly see Jeff's uncle is there.'

With bells on, she thought to herself as she replaced the phone and then did a little dance around the kitchen.

★　★　★

Kids poured noisily out of the gymnasium, exuberant at their release after sitting for an hour in the assembly. Kurt stood next to her, solid and reassuring, waiting for Jeff. Their son appeared suddenly beside them, grinning and carrying the plaque he'd received.

'Well done,' Maggie said, careful not to display open affection, although she longed to hug him. 'Shall I take that home for you?'

'Sure,' Jeff handed over the award and turned shyly to Kurt. 'I didn't know it would all be public,' he said. 'I didn't want to embarrass you.'

Maggie could see how Kurt was trying to contain his emotions. The testimonial to his courage and resourcefulness had been heart-felt and very moving. There was no doubt in anyone's mind in that school gymnasium that Kurt had done the right thing, the only thing.

Kurt obviously had no qualms about losing his macho image and clasped Jeff to him in a bear hug. 'It meant a lot to me, what you said.'

'I meant it,' Jeff replied. 'You're the best!'

Someone yelled from the other side of the basketball court. 'Gotta go,' Jeff said, giving Kurt a slap on the arm. 'Will you be at home later?'

Kurt looked at Maggie over Jeff's head. 'I'd like to be,' he answered.

Maggie nodded. 'We'll both be there,' she said. 'Kurt might even make supper. I think there's some chicken in the freezer.' She held his eyes for a moment as they both remembered.

They watched Jeff race off to join his classmates as the outdoor area slowly emptied of kids and parents and staff. At last they were alone in the autumn sunshine. A few leaves had started to fall and crunched under their feet as they made their way to the parking lot.

Without a word, they reached Maggie's car and got in. Still in silence, she drove to the new townhouse and parked carefully. She led him from her car, into her house, upstairs to her bedroom.

He followed her into the room, suddenly filling the whole space with his male presence. She turned to him and began to unbutton her blouse. Her eyes on his face, she slipped out of her skirt and stood, waiting. She saw him moisten his lips. He took a deep breath and moved one pace towards her. She stepped back, and he followed until her knees were touching the edge of the bed.

He kept his eyes on her as they both removed the rest of their clothes, piece by piece. The sunlight warmed the room through the translucent blinds and sent a pattern of light and shadow over the cornflower blue spread on the bed.

Gently, Kurt took her into his arms, and they sank together onto the warm softness.

'I want you,' he whispered, 'just as I've always wanted you. If you take me back, I swear you won't regret loving me.'

The hair on his chest grazed the sensitive skin on her breasts as he gathered her to him, and she felt the pressure of him against her belly. She reached up and smoothed his hair with her hand and touched his cheek. It was wet.

An almost physical dart stabbed her heart at the thought of all the pain he'd endured all his life, at the mistaken sense of honor that had almost deprived him of the love that was waiting for him.

'I love you,' she said simply.

She felt his body convulse against her as he took in a deep breath and felt moisture on his face. She allowed him to lie with his face buried in her shoulder, cradling him in her arms, hushing him like a child.

As he grew calm, she caressed him gently; his back, his shoulders, his chest, and his thighs passed under her exploring fingers. Soon she felt his hands on her, cradling her bottom, lifting her on top of him. She looked down into his dear face and kissed his eyes, his lips, his cheek.

Still his fingers wandered over her back and thighs and settled at last on her side. She lifted herself slightly so he could feel her breasts. When she could wait no longer, she lowered herself gently and easily until he was firm and anchored inside her, and she began to ride, slowly at first and then more quickly until she heard her own shout of pleasure and felt Kurt quiver and buck beneath her.

Afterwards, they lay spent and contented on the rumpled sheets. Someone started a lawn mower on the next block, and a child was calling from a neighboring house. All the common, everyday sounds of family life.

'Afternoon delight,' she murmured.

Kurt turned his head. 'I want to be with you forever,' he said.

'You will be. You don't get a choice.'

'Will we be good at it, this family business?'

'We'll be good at being there for each other,' she answered, 'and at being there for Jeff. In fact, we'll be great at it.'

'I never thought I'd marry,' he said.

'You'll have to work at it. But I think I could tame you.' She ran her hand up his side.

'You could tame the wild man of the woods.' He caught the wandering hand and brought it to his lips.

'I want our son to have you in his life. I want you to guide him, take care of him . . . '

'I was so angry at myself for screwing up. I knew how it was important for him to have the right father,' Kurt said.

'You wanted to give the unhappy child in you a good life. The child you used to be.'

He looked at her, obviously struggling with what she'd said. He sighed. 'I'm not into all that psychology stuff.'

'It's true if you think about it. But I'm tired of talking about the past. When shall we tell him?'

'We'll do it together,' he said.

'He'll be happy, he loves you already.' Suddenly, she sat up and swung her legs over the edge of the bed.

'Where are you going?' Kurt sat up on one elbow.

'I've got something for you.'

'More of the same?' He raised an eyebrow. 'You'll need to come back here.'

'Not right now.' She padded naked to the closet and took down a box from the upper shelf.

Kurt watched her. 'What is it?' he asked.

She retrieved the bundle of old letters, covered in his handwriting, and held them out to him. 'Everything is fine,' she answered. 'All the ghosts of the past are gone.'

'What are these?'

She climbed back onto the bed, turned to him, and put her arms round him, lifting her face for his kiss. 'All your letters you wrote from god knows where,' she said. 'Steve hid them from me. I've no idea why he kept them all those years, unless it was to gloat about how clever he'd been.'

Kurt raised himself on one elbow and pitched the bundle to the waste paper basket. They fell into the bin with a satisfying 'plop'.

'What time does Jeff come back from school?' he murmured.

'We've lots of time. What did you have in mind?'

THE END

MY FATHER'S HOUSE

Kathleen Conlon

'Your father has another woman'. Nine-year-old Anna Blake is only mildly surprised when a schoolfriend lets drop this piece of information. And when her father finally leaves home to live with Olivia in Hampstead, that place becomes, for Anna, the epitome of sinful glamour. But Hampstead, though welcoming, is not home. So Anna, now in her teens, sets out to find a place where she can really belong. At first she thinks love may be the answer, and certainly Jonathon — and Raymond — and Jake, have a devastating effect on her life. But can anyone really supply what she needs?

GHOSTLY MURDERS

P. C. Doherty

When Chaucer's Canterbury pilgrims pass
a deserted village, the sight of its decaying
church provokes the poor Priest to tears.
When they take shelter, he tells a tale of
ancient evil, greed, devilish murder and
chilling hauntings . . . There was once a
young man, Philip Trumpington, who was
appointed parish priest of a pleasant
village with an old church, built many
centuries earlier. However, Philip soon
discovers that the church and presbytery
are haunted. A great and ancient evil
pervades, which must be brought into the
light, resolved and reparation made. But
the price is great . . .

BLOODTIDE

Bill Knox

When the Fishery Protection cruiser
MARLIN was ordered to the Port Ard
area off the north-west Scottish coast,
Chief Officer Webb Carrick soon discovered that an old shipmate of Captain
Shannon had been killed in a strange
accident before they arrived. A drowned
frogman, a reticent Russian officer and a
dare-devil young fisherman were only a
few of the ingredients to come together as
Carrick tried to discover the truth. The
key to it all was as deadly as it was
unexpected.

WISE VIRGIN

Manda Mcgrath

Sisters Jean and Ailsa Leslie live on a small farm in the Scottish Grampians. Andrew Esplin, the local blacksmith, keeps a brotherly eye on the girls, loving Ailsa, the younger sister, from afar. Ailsa is in love with Stewart Morrison, who is working in Greenock. Jean is engaged to Alan Drummond, who has gone to Australia, intending to send for her when his prospects are good. But Jean shocks everyone when she elopes with Dunton from the big house . . .